PRAISE FOR *LOVING GONE*

"*Loving the Dead and Gone* is an absorbing account of two generations of women, living in North Carolina, who struggle to put love at the centre of their lives. How well Turner-Yamamoto understands the complexities of passion, the necessity of work, and the limits of small towns. This beautifully written novel, with its complicated, stubborn characters, will haunt you long after the last page."

—Margot Livesey, author of *The Boy in The Field*, the *New York Times Book Review* 100 Notable Books 2019, and the *New York Times* bestseller *The Flight of Gemma Hardy*

"There has been an accident in tiny Gold Ridge, a place where most lives revolve around farming the earth or working the hosiery mill, and everyone is changed by it. In a voice that rings with the colloquial timbre of William Faulkner melded with the rural realism of Carolyn Chute's *The Beans of Egypt, Maine*, Judith Turner-Yamamoto brilliantly uses a tragedy to draw us into a place so real you can smell it, where her tapestry of narrator voices captivates us with empathy and love. I was fortunate to be on the panel of the Ohio Artistic Awards in Literature that chose to award *Loving the Dead and Gone*, recognizing its lyric strength and deep and empathic understanding of rural America.

—Elizabeth Cohen, author of *The Hypothetical Girl*

"Turner-Yamamoto's multigenerational saga reminds me of Bobbie Gentry's great *Patchwork* album, with a touch of William Goyen, Lee Smith, and *Our Town*. This bittersweet paean to a NC Piedmont hosiery mill town is a mid-twentieth-century time capsule of car wrecks, nerve medicine, open caskets, ghosts, and gossip. Bad luck and trouble ricochet between families until desire and memories are swept away. And yet, the female lens and circular narrative make *Loving the Dead and Gone* a sensory delight."

—Richard Peabody, editor, Gargoyle Magazine

"Judith Turner-Yamamoto's *Loving the Dead and Gone* is a love story that begins with a tragedy, proceeds through loss and suffering, and winds up in a place of deeply earned redemption. Though there are several characters who guide us through this unstoppable narrative, none is more breathtakingly rendered than Aurilla Cutter. Women like Aurilla, we say in the South, will live forever because they're too mean to die. Ah, but Aurilla has a past that will touch your heart and explain her present. She's an unforgettable character among a cast of unforgettables, from her put-upon daughter Berta Mae, to the heartbroken and fiery seventeen-year-old widow, Darlene, to Berta Mae's haunted husband, Clayton. Actually, everything about *Loving the Dead and Gone*, to Judith Turner-Yamamoto's great credit, is unforgettable."

—Ed Falco, author of the New York Times best seller,
The Family Corleone

"Judith Turner-Yamamoto has written a brilliantly lyrical novel born of her native Southern heritage. Steeped in love and generational conflicts, this North Carolina family faces their romantic disappointments and difficult times with courage tempered by a tough country spirit. In lyrical, tightly-knit prose Turner-Yamamoto has created a gem reminiscent of Eudora Welty's classic stories."

—Kay Sloan, author of The Patron Saint of Red Cherrys, a Barnes
& Noble "Discover Great New Writers" selection.

LOVING THE
DEAD AND GONE

Judith Turner-Yamamoto

Regal House Publishing

Published by
Regal House Publishing, LLC
Raleigh, NC 27587
All rights reserved

ISBN -13 (paperback): 9781646032587
ISBN -13 (epub): 9781646032594
Library of Congress Control Number: 2021949148

Interior by Lafayette & Greene
Cover design © by C. B. Royal

Regal House Publishing, LLC
https://regalhousepublishing.com

The poem, "After Parting," appears in: Teasdale, Sara. *Love Poems*. New York: MacMillan Company, 1917.

Printed in the United States of America

For my son, Nicholas,
without whom there would be no writing,

for my father, Laven,
for better, for worse, my most inspiring character,

and

for my cousin, Dan, and all the blue hats, here's one.

The past is the only dead thing that smells sweet.

—Edward Thomas, 1878-1917

1

1963

CLAYTON

The day Donald Ray Spencer was killed he caught four catfish. I found them, right there beside him on the floorboard, wrapped in yesterday's paper. They looked as surprised to be dead as the boy did. He lay there all slumped over the passenger seat, his left eye staring right back at the fish.

I'd come out fishing myself that Friday. A man couldn't work on a spring afternoon like that. Hot, like the first day of summer, the sun made everything green come up looking brighter than you ever remembered. You wanted to sleep the earth was working so hard, and I didn't know a better place to do that than at the end of a fishing pole. Days like that, Gold Ridge almost deserved its name. The smell of the earth rose up sweet and clean from acres and acres of plowed furrows like something precious forgotten. In a place where farming is everything, it was easy to go blind to the rolling green hills and piney woods that made up this plateau between the Carolina coast and the Appalachian Mountains, to curse the red clay for what's missing instead of praising it for what it's got.

I'd been putting in corn all that morning for my daddy. Berta Mae says I'm a fool to work for him like I do since I don't get a red cent from what he grows in the fields he still calls his own. And I say, Look how cheap he rents me the land I do use. Berta Mae never looks at what she has, just at what she thinks she ought to have, and that's a big part of what makes her so miserable.

It must have been three o'clock by the time I got my

equipment put up and my dinner ate back at the house. Driving the gravel road snaking down to Ramsey Lake, the dirt rose behind me in big clouds that showed yellow against the blue sky. The ditches on both sides looked like orange ribbons rolled out in welcome.

When I first came around the bend everything looked fine. I saw Buford's car and Donald Ray's old Chevy parked in front. I remember thinking, I'm not the only man that can't think straight in weather like this. Donald Ray was working third shift, he had his days to kill, and Buford Jones was a little bit of a mental case and didn't do a thing but lay drunk, and he could do that at the lake as well as anywhere else.

Then I saw Buford's car had smashed into the back of Donald Ray's, the twisted grill resting in what had been the back seat. Here's two dead men, I thought, and that crackerjack day took some kind of turn. I got out, not wanting to look, but knowing I had to, being the one to find them and all.

Buford's radiator was still hissing. His car was empty, and he was nowhere around. Probably down in the woods without a scratch on him, hugging a pint, waiting for the whole thing to clear out. There was a complete quiet over things. A fish jumped and then hit the lake with a hollow slap. I watched the circles on the water's surface grow and grow until they didn't count as circles anymore.

I opened Donald Ray's passenger door, reached for the boy's right wrist where it hung limp over the seat. The flesh was warm but lifeless and the strange contradiction made my heart pound. Either the boy had just died, or the sun was playing tricks. I didn't know enough about such things to be able to tell the difference.

The boy was nineteen maybe, not a day more. I took Donald Ray's wrist again to be sure. I got back nothing but an emptiness I felt deep inside. Donald Ray didn't look like he'd suffered. More like he just slipped away, as if the going was all right by him.

The light from the lake bounced off the polished chrome

of the dashboard. Young boys made these '56 Chevys special, changing them into something faster and louder that made them feel powerful. I had last been inside one the year they came out. That innocent moment and this terrible one came together, paralyzing me. I watched the second hand of the clock travel from twelve to the fifteen-minute mark, thinking what a mess this was.

I went on back up the road to Little Beane's store to call the highway patrol. Drove right past my own house to get there. If Berta Mae was back from the beauty parlor, I'd end up having to tell her the whole thing and I couldn't take her mouth right then.

The tiny store was dark, cool, and empty. Light from the narrow windows behind the counter lit up the dust that trailed in from the road. There was a clean smell about the place, like hay that had been put up to dry.

"Mighty quick trip, Clayton." Elvin padded over to greet me. It hadn't been a half hour since I was in here buying worms. I felt so different, I might as well of been somebody else. My throat felt rusted shut, that's how hard it was to get the words out about Donald Ray. But Elvin took it in stride the way he did everything else. He put the phone on the counter and went on about his business while I got hold of the patrol.

I had to bend my knees to see to dial the number. Elvin was a midget. His wife, Ethel, was a midget too. When Elvin retired as conductor of the miniature train at a park in Winston-Salem, he bought the store and made everything over to fit him. The counters and refrigerator cases were half as tall as the ones at the grocery store in town. Sliding ladders along the shelves let him put stock away up high. On slow days he did his bookwork at a desk behind the checkout counter that was no bigger than a school child's. He and Ethel lived in the back in tiny rooms full of tiny furniture. She taught the neighborhood children music on her piano. In the early evening, Elvin milked his goats, standing below the platform he had built for them. On warm nights, they sat side by side on the porch swing he had hung low, their feet just brushing the floor.

I took the RC Cola Elvin handed me and went out on the porch, looking for a place to breathe right. I just stood there letting some time pass. I couldn't see waiting down there with Donald Ray; only thing he was waiting on now was judgment day.

Instead I thought about Elvin. This man, who wasn't even big enough to reach the pedals in a car, knew everybody's business. He saw the men sitting on his porch in the summer or around his wood-burning stove in the winter, knowing every last one would rather be there than at home. He saw the women too, the ones working at the mills in town same as the men. They stopped by on their way home to pick up saltines, Vienna sausages, or sardines—a can they could open up for supper and not have to think any more about. And now Elvin saw me, hanging here, putting off a thing that couldn't be put aside.

"You get that corn put in the ground?" Elvin asked in his small high voice.

The ordinary question felt like a stick offered to a drowning man. "Quit before I got done. Good weather got the best of me."

Elvin took a plug of tobacco out of the bib pocket of his overalls, bit off a piece, stuck it inside his right cheek. I followed his every movement like I was seeing a man chew tobacco for the first time.

"How much you reckon you lack?"

My breath came a little easier. "Fields over by the old place."

Elvin nodded, his tongue caught up working the tobacco. I watched him cross the store on feet no bigger than an eight-year-old's. Except for the rustle of the stiff denim of his overalls he moved quiet as a cat. I never got over Elvin, not even knowing him all my life. Elvin opened the screen door, sent a brown arc of tobacco juice into Ethel's little red flowers. "Think the law's got down there yet?" he asked.

I set my bottle in the crate of empties, glad Elvin was doing the thinking for me. "Guess I best go see."

When I got back to the lake, the highway patrol was measuring skid marks. It'd take the ambulance a while yet. They'd be in no hurry coming out for a dead man.

The officer adjusted his pants at his hips with the sides of his hands like a man whose hands had known fixing cars or some other dirty work. "Ain't this some sad business?" he asked. He jerked his head in the direction of the patrol car. Buford sat in the back seat, rocking back and forth fast the way he did when he was nervous. "Claims his brakes give out on him."

"You know he's not right," I said. "This is the only place his daddy lets him drive to."

The officer shook his head. "That's one place too many." He peered into the open driver's window of Donald Ray's car. "Poor boy probably never knew what hit him. Buford took that curve pretty fast to make this kind of impact. Close as I can tell without moving him, I'd say his neck broke. Anyway, that's what I'll tell the widow."

They hadn't been married a year. And there Darlene was, not ten miles up the road at her parents' house, thinking she was having catfish for supper. The patrol car would pull up at the house about the same time she'd be looking for Donald Ray to be home. At least he didn't have any disfiguring marks on him. Bad enough to bury a husband at seventeen, but to see him all tore up would be more than a young girl like that could take.

BERTA MAE

Berta Mae rubbed the washcloth over her forehead once more before dropping it in the bowl of ice water on the nightstand and heading for the bathroom. Maybe she hadn't done a thing all day but let her mama, Aurilla, off at the beauty parlor, but the rest of the world didn't have to know that. What could she have done anyway, what with her day chopped into itty-bitty pieces?

She tugged at the brush, working it through her unruly black hair. She put her lipstick on thick to last through the hot drive into town. Her eyes looked even more deep-set than usual in the harsh light thrown by the fluorescent bulbs on either side of the medicine chest. Thumb and index finger spread wide, she pushed her eyebrows up, thinking gravity was pulling at her eyes like it had her breasts. Moving her hands to her temples she stretched the skin back, testing to see if the skin was slackening. Through it all, her eyes stayed stubbornly back in her head.

Your face or your figure, she remembered reading that in one of her women's magazines. After thirty you had to choose. They gave famous examples to help you figure it out—Elizabeth Taylor chose her face, Audrey Hepburn her figure. Berta Mae didn't remember choosing anything. She had started out slim. Everybody she knew ran to fat after having a baby, but carrying Emogene had left her leaner, and over the years she'd fallen off even more.

After reading that article she decided the padding in her face had wasted away. For a while she tried to eat more, forcing seconds and desserts. All she got for her efforts was a bloated stomach. It didn't pay to fight your natural tendencies. Look at Aurilla, taking it into her head at almost sixty that she wanted to be fat. All the restaurant eating and sitting she'd done since Berta Mae's father died had given her a belly. The fat stayed right there, refusing to move to the arms and legs that were still thin as pipe cleaners.

"The closer to the bone, the sweeter the meat." That was what Clayton used to say when Berta Mae complained about being thin. It had been a long time now since he said anything about her looks.

In the kitchen she saw to Clayton's dinner. She pulled out the green beans they'd had at supper last night, poked a spoon through the congealed fat, and stirred them to break it up. Hot as it was in this kitchen the fat would melt before long. No sense making things hotter by heating up the stove. If Emogene were here she'd be carrying on about the fat and refusing to eat the beans. But she'd be at Chrissie's, the Caveness girl, until supper, so she didn't have to think about pleasing her. Not that there was any pleasing her twelve-year-old about anything anymore.

Berta Mae used to be the only one who could tell what Emogene wanted. Year after year, pearls of love fell from Emogene's mouth, unlocking something deep and untouched in Berta Mae that let her love right back with a joy she had never known. She had doted on her, giving her the mothering she herself had longed for. Clayton said she let Emogene get her way too much, but lately Berta Mae's efforts to please only deepened her daughter's adolescent sulk. Their new distance made her feel cast off. Berta Mae longed to pull her daughter close, but the way Emogene's narrow shoulders tensed when she came near told her she was no longer allowed such liberties.

She took leftover biscuits from the breadbox and put some on a plate with the beans. Clayton would be so hungry by the time he got back to the house he wouldn't notice what he was eating, not that he ever did.

Last week Berta Mae had gone to the trouble to make him a strawberry pie. Half the morning: hulling and slicing, making the crust. She put the pie in front of him, he ate it, and that was that. It was the same when she lay under him on those rare nights when he moved to her side of the bed. Nothing she did made a difference. Slow and sure as salt poured on snails, the feelings between them had shriveled up. Somewhere he'd stopped responding and she'd grown afraid to keep trying.

She put the rest of the biscuits in Fifi's bowl. Emogene had thrown a fit for that dog, promising how she'd do the extra work. Now look who was feeding it every day and thinking about bringing it in out of the hot sun. She held the screen door open, called the dog's name.

Fifi took her time coming in the heat. Part beagle, part Chihuahua, she laid her pointed ears back; her dropped tail wagged in slow greeting. Her lips pulled back from her teeth in a wide grin.

Berta Mae dropped to her knees, rubbed the dog's damp black head. "Been swimming, have you, girl?" She inhaled the smell of the creek that was like the earthy air at the start of a big rain. Her easy attachment to Fifi had surprised her. The dog's patient presence never failed to steady her tattered nerves. She pulled Fifi closer. The warmth of the sun radiated from the smooth tan fur along her back. Her delicate snuffling stirred Berta Mae's hair and tickled her neck. With a quick lick Fifi disengaged herself and wandered off to inspect the contents of her bowl.

Berta Mae rinsed a tomato, sliced it onto Clayton's plate, and covered the whole thing with waxed paper. Stretches of blacktop and gravel whizzed through her head. She saw herself driving this morning from Gold Ridge to Clear Creek to pick up her mother, taking her into Potter, coming back home, and now going back to Potter to pick her up and carry her home to Clear Creek. Sixty hot miles she'd drive before she was done riding Aurilla around today. Berta Mae wiped impatiently at an unexpected spout of tears. All this, week after week since Aurilla's stroke, and not so much as a thank you.

She grabbed her pocketbook off the dining room mantel and headed for the carport. It'd been two hours since she'd dropped Mama off, but she knew she'd have to wait. Ruby would be running around fetching and carrying for Mama like she was a helpless invalid when it was only her right hand that was a little limp. The two of them would keep right on talking after she came in as if she didn't have anything better to do on a Friday afternoon than thumb through Ruby's dog-eared magazines.

As she drove, red dust roiled up behind the car. She was nowhere near the blacktop, but already waves of heat danced back and forth and up against each other. There was only one piece of shade in the parking lot at the beauty parlor and she didn't have to think twice about whose car would be parked sideways, taking up the whole thing.

"That's some way to treat her customers," Berta Mae had said to Aurilla last Friday as she spread a beach towel across the front seat to keep their legs from melting right into the plastic covers.

"What's that?" Aurilla asked.

"Ruby's parking habits." Berta Mae jerked her head toward Ruby's car tucked in along the north side of the building.

"Car's black and sits out in the heat all day long. Ruby's stout and used to the air-conditioning." With that Aurilla had looked off, busying herself with rearranging the towel beneath her.

Berta Mae turned in at the beauty parlor and double-parked out front. She pulled her dress away from her legs and blew down her front to cool off some so she wouldn't get a chill inside. She opened the frosted glass door wide, disturbing the womb of air-conditioned air. Aurilla was in Ruby's chair, the one over by the cash register. She raised her bad hand a little ways off her lap in greeting.

Aurilla looked high and mighty, even in curlers. Age had only emphasized what Berta Mae thought of as the haughty drama of her face—sharply angled cheekbones and a narrow long nose with nostrils that flared at the slightest provocation.

Berta Mae forced a big smile. Each encounter brings the chance to start fresh, that's what they said on her radio home-maker program. "Mama, I thought you'd be ready to go. It's been two hours and I'm double-parked out front."

"Better move the car before somebody runs into it," Aurilla said. "We still got a ways to go here."

"I just made Aurilla some ice tea," Ruby said. "I'll have her done before you can turn around." Ruby waved her hand at the magazines on the coffee table.

"Berta Mae, come on over here and squeeze this lemon for me," Aurilla said. "I just can't do a thing with these fingers any-more. Not good for a damned thing but holding rings."

"Looks like you could use some help with that too," Ruby said in a loud voice that turned every head in the place. "That's some load of rocks you're carrying around." Ruby and Aurilla cackled like a couple of laying hens.

Berta Mae winced. The liberties Ruby took ran over her like nails on a chalkboard. On Aurilla's limp hand were the diamonds that once belonged to Aurilla's mother and grand-mother. Just this morning Berta Mae had thought how vulgar it looked wearing the leftovers from everybody else's marriages and here Ruby was pointing it out for all the world to see.

The two of them were carrying on like Berta Mae was invisible. She felt the stirrings of an old jealousy. Why was it everybody got along with her mother better than she did? "Mama," she said, raising her voice to match the volume of their laughter, "I've got things to do at home." The only people listening to her were Mrs. Sanders, the preacher's wife, and Phyllis, who was combing out Mrs. Sanders's hair and looking right at Berta Mae in the mirror. Florence Jenkins, the biggest talker in the county, was under the dryer, lost in her beauty magazine.

"Mama!" Berta Mae raised her voice. "I got things to do."

Aurilla took off her glasses with her left hand and wiped the tears out of her eyes before looking up at Berta Mae. "Am I keeping you from your TV stories? Ruby, I told you, you got to get a TV in here so Berta Mae won't be in such a rush to get back home." This started Aurilla howling again.

Berta Mae pulled herself up straight. She held her head up high even though she could feel the red creeping up from her chest, spreading over her neck and face. Her lips pursed tight, she said, "You can just meet me at the car, Mama." She fixed her eyes on Ruby. "It's parked in the sun, of course."

She heard Ruby talking low and then Aurilla's voice, louder. "Must be some bug…" And then the laughter again.

Berta Mae felt every eye in the place burning holes through her back. Outside she gulped down mouthfuls of hot air to calm herself. Fire and dry grass, that was her and Aurilla, no matter how she tried to make things different. What was it Clayton said? That Berta Mae never knew when to leave well enough alone. She thought back to her first moments in the beauty parlor. She'd smiled at Aurilla. She remembered that. She just said she needed Aurilla to be ready. What had she done to set Mama off?

Letting Aurilla down was a long, twisted thread that wound all the way back to when she was four. After Sunday dinner at Grandmother McMath's, Berta Mae had escaped to the garden before Aurilla could notice her underfoot and send her off for an afternoon nap. She cut a wide path around the prickly leaves of the squash and tomato plants, climbed up the mound of dirt to the butterbean tent. She parted the vines, careful not to disturb the silvery tracks her grandmother said the fairies made each night racing snails.

Here were her secret things: a blue robin's egg, the shards of a yellow plate, a mason jar filled with red dogwood berries picked the fall before, pearl buttons from Grandmother's sewing room. Overhead, fat bean pods curved like new moons and hung in heavy dark green clusters. She stood on tiptoe, picking beans for the fairies. No sooner had she divided out the beans on her yellow plates than Aurilla appeared at the opening and leaned inside, her careless hands smearing the fairy tracks. Berta Mae screamed and kicked to keep Aurilla out of her safe place, and Aurilla yelled back, calling her hateful, a hateful selfish girl.

The bitter memory joined with the uncommon heat, making her feel sick to her stomach. The weather, she told herself, just think about the weather. Summer seemed to come earlier every year; it was hardly May but the sun felt like July. She shaded her eyes against the glare and looked across the road at the All-Star Market. In her head she saw that big cool drink box that took up almost the whole front of the store. She thought about Aurilla coming out of the beauty parlor and standing in this heat, waiting for her. But Aurilla had said Ruby had a ways to go before she would be done.

Berta Mae was careful not to look straight on at the men standing around the rusted-out pickup at the end of Vinnie's parking lot. She watched out of the corner of her eye to see if they noticed her. They looked to see who was stirring up the gravel and then went right back to their sandwiches. Maybe Aurilla and Ruby were right. Maybe she was invisible.

The smell of ripe bananas met Berta Mae at the screen door. They were piled high on a table at the end of the checkout counter, a swarm of gnats blowing them. Vinnie sat behind the counter opening boxes of cigarette cartons, her rounded back to Berta Mae. At the sight of her Berta Mae felt a comforting rush of affection and the tightness in her chest relaxed. "What in the world makes you think you can keep bananas in this heat?" she asked.

"You stop in just to give advice or did you need something?" Vinnie said without turning around.

"I just might, if that drink box of yours is chilling things off like it should be."

"Only thing that is." Vinnie walked around the counter, her arms full of empty boxes. She dropped them in the trash barrel beside the table where the bitter smell of over-brewed coffee rose from the half-empty urn.

"Why don't you just unplug that thing? Who'd want coffee in this heat?" Berta Mae threw open the lid to the drink box. She rubbed the goose flesh the frosted air brought up on her arms.

"Some people would be fool enough to drink that stuff in hell if they could get it." Vinnie pulled back her faded blond hair, let the cold bite her face. "Me, I'd rather stay in this drink box."

Her friend's soft beauty still fascinated Berta Mae. Vinnie had sat right in front of her at school, gold hair falling in deep curls down her back. Her hair was like something live hanging over Berta Mae's desk, bouncing and shimmering with her every move. Berta Mae wanted more than anything to run her fingers through the yellow whorls, to make Vinnie her best friend so she could envelope herself in that accepting, soft sweetness. Vinnie was what Aurilla called plump, with dimpled hands like a baby and dimples in her cheeks that showed when something pleased her. Whenever Daddy had brought Berta Mae candy, she'd saved half for Vinnie, just to watch those delicate hollows come up in her flushed cheeks.

"Some people got it made," Vinnie said, nodding her head toward the windows specked with dead bugs that looked out on the air-conditioned beauty parlor.

"Her and Mama both," Berta Mae said, sharply closing the lid. "Lord knows Mama's there almost as much as Ruby."

"Poor thing. Aurilla's just making up for all those years with your daddy. Hard for you to see, him favoring you like he did."

Berta Mae nodded, her fingers tightening around her drink bottle. Vinnie had something good to say about everybody. Was that how she really saw things?

She watched Vinnie amble across the store to greet a new customer, the easy slope of her shoulders revealing the same unruffled air that had first drawn Berta Mae to her so long ago. She had never seen her friend upset or even excited. Vinnie was her same level, steady self with everyone.

Thoughts of Vinnie's temperament brought her to her own. I'm a grown woman, Berta Mae thought. Why can't I act like one around Aurilla? The question was too big and tiring to take on in this heat. She ran the bottle over her temples, its sweat mixing with her own, until the cold was all she could think about.

Vinnie waved her hand away when she tried to pay. "I don't want your money, just come 'round to see me more often."

"Since Mama's stroke I don't hardly have the time to pee, let alone socialize."

"You're some kind of saint is all."

She could count on one hand the people she could depend on, and Vinnie had been one of them for as long as she could remember. Back in grade school Vinnie threw gravel at the boys who walked along behind them calling Berta Mae names like bag of bones and scarecrow.

Berta Mae turned up the bottle. The syrupy liquid was no sooner down her throat than she felt it freeze the backs of her eyes. She put the bottom of the bottle in the palm of her hand, the way the nurse in Aurilla's doctor's office told her to do whenever the cold went to her head, and started back across the road.

Aurilla sat on the rear bumper of Ruby's car, her head in her hands. Berta Mae started to run. What had she been thinking, leaving an old woman to wait in this heat?

"No need to give yourself a heat stroke," Aurilla called out. "I'm fine here."

Aurilla's offhand kindness flooded her with relief. She longed to throw her arms around her mother. Instead, she handed Aurilla her drink. "Put the bottle on your forehead, it'll cool you right down." She pulled the beach towel from the back seat, gave it a serious shaking out. If Ruby cared so much about Aurilla, why had she let her out in this heat?

"Still mad at Ruby, are you?" said Aurilla. "We were just having ourselves a good time. But you never knew anything about that even when you were nothing but a little child. Just like your daddy. Colliding with everyone and everything you meet."

The unexpected swipe sent Berta Mae reeling. She forced a breath, told herself to think a different way. What if Aurilla had only meant to ask her if she was still mad at Ruby? What if she hadn't gone on with the avalanche of hurtful words that followed? What would Berta Mae have replied then—that she had felt ignored, that she hadn't meant for things to get so out of hand? The words were impossible to say. What horrible thing would Aurilla utter if she admitted such weakness? Berta Mae felt herself yield to the undertow of impulse and habit and said, "Don't talk about Daddy like that and him hardly in the ground."

"I'll talk about him any way I please. It was me had to put up with him for thirty-six years." Once in the car, Aurilla wrapped her arms around her pocketbook and dismissed her with a look out the passenger window.

On the silent drive to Mama's house, Berta Mae thought about the long string of days that had followed Daddy's death. She sat with Emogene and Mama in the funeral director's office, looking at pictures of coffins and vaults and discussing burial outfits.

"I think brown's best, don't you, Mama?" Berta Mae looked at Mr. Frazier, the funeral director, to solicit his agreement. "Blue's just so cold and he always had so much color from working outdoors."

Mama waved her hand like she was shooing a fly. "Suit

yourself," she said. "The man only had two suits. One blue and the other brown. That limits the possibilities, now doesn't it?"

"When will you be needing the suit, Mr. Frazier?" Berta Mae asked, as if Mama hadn't said anything.

"This afternoon, if you can manage it, Mrs. Bishop."

Mama began to laugh in that hooting way she had of making whatever had just been said sound ridiculous. "It'll take the rest of the day just to get the dust shook out of it. It's done nothing but hang in the closet gathering cobwebs since his brother's funeral three years ago."

Berta Mae felt bested, worse than she did when Emogene sassed her in public. She pulled herself up straight in her chair. "My mother is beside herself with grief. I'll take her home to rest and then I'll come back and settle this thing myself."

She rose without waiting to hear Mr. Frazier's "yes, of course," and pulled on her black gloves.

She handed the car keys to Emogene. "Run on out to the car and get the heat on so we don't all freeze to death." Emogene hesitated, holding her grandmother's hand tight. "Well, go on," she said, shaking the keys at her, "you don't need her permission to do like I say."

Berta Mae watched Emogene run toward the stained-glass doors at the end of the hall. "I know what you were up to in there, Mama. If you want to drag yourself down in public that's fine with me, but leave me and my dead daddy out of it. People will be coming by to pay their respects this afternoon. Try to keep a civil tongue in your head. They'll be expecting to see a grief-stricken woman."

"Then I'm sure they won't be disappointed." Mama stared straight ahead. "You've always been so good at being miserable. I've had my fill of it, thank you, and I'm ready for a change. Why don't you show some concern for the living and go get that car so I won't have to run around in this cold wind?" With that Mama dropped on the velvet settee by the front door. "Send the child for me when you're out front."

Given Mama's behavior in the days that followed, Berta Mae

felt compelled to take on the widow's role. She sobbed with the guests who came by to pay their respects and drop off food. Thanking them, she refused to eat while Mama sat in the dining room helping herself to Mrs. Sanders's baked ham and Florence Jenkins's lemon chiffon cake. During the viewings, Berta Mae stood by the casket to receive condolences. Mama sat on the love seat outside the viewing room, Emogene at her side. She claimed the perfume from all the flowers made her head ache and that Emogene was too young to see the carryings on death brought out in people.

"Come on in here and say goodbye to your granddaddy," Berta Mae said to Emogene their last night at the funeral home.

Emogene had moved closer to her grandmother, planting her patent leather shoes on the floor. She shook her head, her eyes locked on the knotted lace handkerchief she held in her lap. Berta Mae saw it was Mama's and went back inside alone.

Aurilla broke their silence near the turnoff for the Cutter house. "You haven't said a word about Emogene."

The chance alignment of their thoughts had long since lost the power to surprise Berta Mae. When she was a child, she had clung to it as evidence of a bond for which she saw little other proof. Lately she'd come to think she just spent too much time with Aurilla. "She's over at the Caveness girl's house. You remember, her brother burned up in that car wreck on Troglin Hill last spring and then the older sister, Darlene, turned right around and married in the very same church where they buried him."

"What about later?" Aurilla asked, leaning toward Berta Mae.

Aurilla hadn't heard a thing past what she said about Emogene. Aurilla's not listening to her after she got what she needed usually made Berta Mae feel two feet tall, but she could see she had Aurilla going. "Hmm?" She bit the inside of her lip to keep from smiling at the unfamiliar pleasure of baiting her mother.

"She's still coming tonight for the weekend?"

"I don't know, Mama. You'll have to find out for yourself.

She probably won't be home until after supper. That is, if she doesn't go ahead and spend the night with her little girlfriend."

Aurilla sat back against the seat, her mouth set in a fixed line.

"Well, here we are." Berta Mae reached across Aurilla and opened the door for her. "Do you need some help getting to the house?"

"I don't want to put you out any more than I already have. You just tell that girl of yours to call me soon as she gets home."

"You don't want the telephone waking you up, do you, not for a silly little thing like that?" The minute Berta Mae spoke in that sweet put-on voice Aurilla hated in everyone from waitresses to nurses, she knew she'd pushed too far.

Aurilla banged the door shut with her hip and leaned down to look in the window. "You watch yourself, Berta Mae. You're still not too big for me to slap."

Berta Mae stared after Aurilla, watching her pass the dogwoods, the goldenrod, the rhododendron hell. Aurilla had planted every last plant herself when Berta Mae was still in diapers. The branches of the bushes and trees had grown gnarled and tough and taller than the head of any man she knew. What had made her think she could best Aurilla?

The last time Aurilla had hit her she was twenty-one and a newlywed. She and Clayton had just come back from running off to South Carolina to the justice of the peace. There had been no point in trying to do anything besides elope. After a life of tearing Berta Mae in opposite directions, her parents were united in their opposition to Clayton. Each Saturday night she heard how she was marrying beneath her. Tobacco farmers were gentlemen farmers; the rest were subsistence farmers, common as field hands. Hadn't the Bishops had Clayton working full time since he was twelve, and before that they pulled him out of school for the harvest each year? The Bishops would have her hooked to a plow. Hooked to a plow and stuck in Gold Ridge.

They sat around the dining room table, finishing the last of the peach pie. Clayton and Daddy were at one end talking hogs and tobacco; Aurilla and Grandmother Cutter discussed the pickles they would be canning the next day. The meal was nearly over and there had been no unfavorable comments on their elopement. Armed with her new marital status, Berta Mae felt bold and careless, the way she imagined men did when they were liquored up.

Aurilla lunged across the table, her hand coming down hard on the side of Berta Mae's face. She sat back, picked up the rolls she had knocked out of the breadbasket. She selected one for herself, reached for the butter dish. "Don't ever let me hear you click your fork against your teeth at my table again."

Berta Mae had been a fool, a fool to think she could cross Aurilla and remain unscathed. Through smarting tears she glanced at Daddy. He carried right on with his pie like nothing had happened. Clayton was as taken aback as Berta Mae. Except for the red creeping over her face it would have been hard to tell which one of them had been hit.

"Just like a rattler," he had said later. "Just like the way you come across one of them all curled up asleep on some warm rock somewhere. Only they're not asleep. They're waiting for you to make a move that sets them off."

Berta Mae watched Aurilla stride up the walk, stop to snap a wayward rhododendron runner clean in half with her good hand. Yes, she thought, just like.

CLAYTON

I didn't understand any of it, not Berta Mae's bad feelings for her mother or Emogene's attraction to her. Like two cats in a bag—that was how these two got along, and lately all their fights were about Aurilla. Since her husband died, Aurilla had given up cooking and staying home. The relatives she'd waited on for forty years were finally dead and she had taken to pleasuring herself with a vengeance, dragging Emogene right along with her. Even her stroke hadn't slowed her down. Berta Mae had to do the driving now, that was all.

"I'd be ashamed, staying away from home the way you do," Berta Mae said.

She had been on Emogene since she came through the door. "I already told you," Emogene said. "Donald Ray's dead. Chrissie didn't want me to leave." She dropped onto Fifi's bed by the stove, her long tanned legs spilling onto the floor. When had she got so tall? Three months ago, her nose took over her face, but now it seemed to set off a new fullness in her mouth. She was changing so fast I had trouble remembering the child I'd known for so long. Then I would see some familiar gesture, like now, Emogene pulling the dog into her lap, holding its head and kissing its snout, and I'd feel less like the world was running away with me.

"What'd you want me to do?" Emogene said. "Leave Chrissie by herself while they went off to see about Donald Ray?"

Berta Mae kept right on, going for what she was really after. "Other people's troubles don't excuse how you carry on. If you weren't hanging round the Cavenesses', you'd be at Mama's. You'd think Mama was your girlfriend the way you go on about her."

"Least she leaves me alone."

"Get on up the road and stay there, you think you like it so good. Then you might find out what I know about living with her."

Berta Mae's real fuss was about losing her daughter and how bad she hurt, but I never heard her say a word about any of that. Once Berta Mae had hold of something she wouldn't let go, no matter how far off center she was. She would go on repeating things over and over until Emogene began to scream or cry from hearing it twenty times.

They were just about at the point where Emogene would come running to me, her hands over her ears, expecting me to jump in and take her side. I wasn't up to it, not tonight, not after finding Donald Ray. I slipped out the side door.

Leaving the fluorescent lights and stepping outside was like falling off the end of the earth. The lay of the land and the shaded outlines of the trees led me past the dog lot. The two pointers paced, muzzles snorting the dirt worn bare with their worrying. I crossed the cow pasture to where the earth nosed down to meet the little creek that crossed the far corner of my land.

The creek bed was filled with rocks tossed there from clearing the pasture. The water that tripped across them made a pretty sound. Listening to the water travel over rocks I'd put in its path made me feel a part of things. From the dark, other things came clear. The willow at the bend in the creek, its branches draped over the water, new leaves just touching the surface. And further down the bank, the dogwoods, their petals like scattered lights in the blackness.

How dark was it where Donald Ray was? The unbidden thought made me jump. You learn to live with ghosts if you hold on to land long enough. The chain of kin that tended it before you speak in the stumps of rotted trees, in cleared fields, and pastures flooded into ponds. But this was different. Coming home, I'd thrown myself into evening chores, caring more than I had about anything for a long time. At supper I tasted each bite, resisting my usual way of tossing back Berta Mae's cooking like it was water. The evening paper and the fight between Berta Mae and Emogene took up the rest. Now here I was, busy tearing up handfuls of grass, hoping to shake Donald Ray again.

I never did really know Donald Ray, just by sight is all. Just enough to throw my hand up when I passed him on the road. The best look I ever had at him was today, down by the lake. He was one of Dallas Spencer's boys. Dallas had so many of them, I forget now if it was six or seven. But Donald Ray was the baby and had more looks than the rest of them put together. Everybody said he should of been spoilt being the youngest and looking like he did, but he wasn't. He was smart too, played varsity basketball. Saturday nights when there was a home game, they'd all go just to watch that boy run and make baskets. They say he never missed a one. That can't be right, but it did seem like that's how it was. Played good enough that they said he could of had a scholarship to play ball at Carolina.

Then he went to work down at the hosiery mill like everybody else. Not that I ever saw him. They started all the young boys off on third shift and kept them there as long as they could take it. Anyway, it was that little redheaded Caveness girl that Donald Ray married. She didn't have that white-faced surprised look like most redheads. And she had brown eyes; that alone was enough to make her stand out. But there was something else about her. Even when she was real young, back when I would see her buying soft drinks at Elvin's after the school bus let her off, even then, her eyes were so dark they made you think she'd seen a thing or two.

Donald Ray must have noticed it too. She wasn't but sixteen when they got engaged; it was Donald Ray's last year of school. They got married a week after her brother's accident. One minute, folks were sending flowers to the funeral home, the next they were taking wedding gifts to the Cavenesses.

I heard her mother was embarrassed by the whole thing but that didn't stop her from giving in to Darlene. They went right on, marrying in the same church where they'd held the services for her brother not seven days before. It had something to do with the magnolia trees in the churchyard. She had her head set on the windows being open during the ceremony and the smell of magnolia blossoms filling the church. Planned the whole thing around the blooming of those trees. Now, almost a year to the day, she would be back there again, burying her husband.

Berta Mae says she's spoiled goods, that nobody will have her now except some old widower. Says God is getting even with her for being so self-centered and disrespectful. I don't see it like that though. Donald Ray just picked the wrong day to go fishing, is all.

Confused. Donald Ray had to be that. One minute he was sitting in that empty place before you leave one thing and go on to the next. He was probably thinking how he'd go home and spread some newspaper out on the front porch, watch the sun go low, the color of the sky changing as it went down, and listen to the scales of the fish fly as they pulled away from his knife, dropping on the paper like sleet tapping on a tin roof. And then he was knocked smack dab into the middle of death, something he'd probably never given a second thought, not at his age.

I skipped a stone across the creek listening to the different tones it made as it skimmed the surface of the water. Berta Mae was always thinking about dying. She had looked to Emogene to make her happy. From the beginning, the two of them formed a closed circle that shut me out and only grew smaller when the other children Berta Mae wanted so badly never came. Now Emogene was growing up, pulling away, and Berta Mae took the change personally.

The world was hard on Berta Mae. Part of me had been drawn to the jumpy, unsettled hurt that shown in her dark eyes and the uneasy set of her full mouth. I'd thought of the calf with the broken ankle my daddy had once left for dead. I put it in its own stall, away from the careless deliberate jostling of the herd, giving it time and the care to heal in peace. I thought I would be able to do something like that for Berta Mae, but staying ahead of the offenses and slights she saw everywhere had exhausted me.

My life had to be half over, and I couldn't speak for the last fifteen years. A panicky feeling came over me. I told myself it was just spending the afternoon with a dead man.

I thought of when me and Berta Mae were first married. I worked third shift like Donald Ray, going to bed in the mornings just as Berta Mae got up. I would roll over and bury my face in her warm pillow. Rich with the smell of her dark hair, it lulled me to sleep.

Donald Ray had to be lost and sad, cut off from lying down beside his new wife, from feeling the breeze—warm tonight like summer coming—puffing up the curtains, breathing into their room.

2

Darlene

In the dim light of the church, Darlene could almost make Donald Ray look the way he did when she watched him sleep. Just when she got things fixed, her tears carried him off. She ground them away with her fist, and tried looking outside at the magnolias instead. The blossoms. All they needed to bloom was a soft rain like the one falling.

The trees were in flower when she and Donald Ray married, she'd made sure of that. And here it was not two weeks until their first anniversary. She had had it in her head that Donald Ray would surprise her with a magnolia bouquet he sneaked in the churchyard and picked himself. The idea was so set in her mind that she'd been smelling their strong perfume for weeks.

Darlene turned back to study Donald Ray. The pallbearers had arranged themselves around the casket. Somehow her mind hadn't let her take the whole thing this far. The time had come to shut him up, carry him outside, and stick him in the ground. That same sick prickly sweat came over her, like when she was little and Pap would lock her in the closet for talking back.

"You can't close him up." Darlene was beside them before she even knew she was on her feet. "Ramon, don't you remember how your brother hates being closed up? He can't even ride in the car with the windows rolled up in the wintertime."

Ramon looked anywhere but at her. But he stepped away, motioned for the other pallbearers to do the same.

She looked at Donald Ray real good like she hadn't been able to bring herself to do. They had his hair all wrong, parted on the right and swept high up off his face like a blond Elvis. The makeup on his face and hands was orange. Whatever this was that was left didn't care if it was shut up or not. All smooth and untouched by life, he looked like something out of that wax museum they had seen on their way to Myrtle Beach.

"You don't have to touch it," Donald Ray had said, pulling back her hand from Clark Gable's face. He was wrong. Her fingers ached to know if what her eyes told her was the truth. Gable's face was as cool to the touch as the mulberry candles Ma brought out at Christmas time, the stubble of his beard worked in with a different color of wax. It was so perfect it made her want to dig her nails into him to see what lay underneath.

She touched Donald Ray. He felt as solid and cold as a piece of granite. Her fingers snagged on the rough growth of his beard. It'd been two days since they laid him out all smooth and straight in his wedding suit but those little hairs didn't know he was dead any more than she did. His beard looked like it always did in the late afternoon. She could almost feel it on the nape of her neck: fine-grained sandpaper making the red down stand on end.

She nodded thanks to Ramon and stumbled back to her pew. They had Donald Ray shut up by the time she turned around. Her chest tightened and her breath refused to come, as if it was her in that box. Behind her the murmurs of the congregation swelled, a wave ready to break. She had forgotten about the people who had come to see her husband buried. She heard them rise together, rustling, adjusting, but she didn't have the strength to stand up. Her parents steadied her arms. She shook herself free and fell in alone behind the pallbearers, their shuffle up the aisle slow and uneven under the burden of the casket. Stares, some curious, some sympathetic burrowed into her. She didn't want them here, none of them. This felt private, not like the wedding. It was one thing for people to see you happier than you've ever been and in the prettiest dress you ever saw, and something else when it was all you could do to put one foot in front of the other. Darlene hadn't so much as combed her hair in three days and she wouldn't let her mother, Beulah, near her head with the brush either. Beulah went to town for

Darlene's dress, even though Darlene hadn't let her pick out her clothes since she was five. She came back with a black dowdy thing that hung way down below her knees, not that it mattered what she had on.

She told herself if she just kept her eyes on the open doors and the drizzle falling outside, she could make it to the graveyard. The sadness was mostly gone. Looking at Donald Ray's corpse had taken all that out of her. She was lonely. Lonely for the Donald Ray left in her head.

Darlene followed the pallbearers right to the grave, ignoring her mother's frantic motioning to her from under the dark green canopy the funeral home had set up a respectable distance from the grave. Out of the corner of her eye she saw Beulah hold out her umbrella, her eyes pleading with her to take it, to protect herself. Last night she had laid close beside Darlene on top of the covers, watching her toss and turn instead of trying to sleep herself. Beulah's tenderness brought her to tears again. Maybe Beulah was just afraid that without her Darlene would get swept so far away she'd never make it back.

Darlene's white high heels sank into the wet clay right along with the lowering of the casket into the vault. She heard it hit bottom, the sound of metal on metal ricocheting off the smooth walls. It was the kind of thing she'd hoped she would hear, a sound that held the promise of nothing.

She wiped at the mist of rain on her face, smoothed the frizz it brought out in her hair. There were beads of water on the lid of Donald Ray's casket; she saw them last thing before they lowered him down. What would happen to that rain, sealed up tight in the vault? Would it evaporate and fall over and over, using the little pocket of air that must be trapped there? She pictured herself visiting his grave, standing by the headstone, breathing softly, listening for the rain.

"Teen Angel." There Donald Ray was again in her head, singing their song, holding on to each word like he was trying to hold onto the life he'd already lost.

"Turn the car around, Pap," Darlene said to the back of her father's thick neck that was grizzled with gray hair.

He shifted his bulk, looked at his wife. "Beulah, don't you let her start."

She turned around, patted Darlene's hand. "What's the matter, sweetheart?"

"We have to go to Potter, to the record store. I won't be able to live, Ma, I swear I won't, if you don't turn this car around right now."

"Lord God Almighty, and his grave's not even filled in yet." Pap rolled down his window. "I told you, now here she goes."

Beulah fanned him with Donald Ray's funeral program. "You can't mean that, Darlene," she whispered, like Pap wouldn't hear. "Not the record store of all places. You can't be seen there."

"You go in for me, Ma, you can do that," Darlene said. "Or Chrissie, she'll do it."

Beulah turned back around like Darlene would forget she was there.

"I hear Donald Ray singing this song in my head. If I don't get the record to drown him out, I'll go crazy before this night's done, I swear I will." This last part was a lie. She wanted the record to get the song right, to give Donald Ray's voice every single last word to sing back to her. But she would never get her way if she told Pap that. He didn't hold with lingering over loss. She knew that already from watching him after her brother, Perry, died. Hadn't he sided with her about going ahead with the wedding after Perry's funeral?

Fat tears swelled in Beulah's eyes. For her, losing Donald Ray must be like losing Perry all over again. When the sheriff came about Donald Ray, she was the first to meet him at the door, sinking to her knees with a loud wail when she saw his brown uniform. She had called Donald Ray "Perry" all day, and her face wore the same blank paralyzed look Darlene remembered from her brother's funeral. "Please," Darlene whispered, the word breaking in jagged halves.

Chrissie started to cry. "I hate you both, you're so mean to Darlene." Chrissie kicked the back of the front seat. "She lost her husband, and all she wants is a record."

"Give me, give me, take me some place." Pap made a U-turn, drawing big circles with his open palm on the stirring wheel. "Five minutes. That's all you get. The yard will be full of people waiting when we get to the house. Beulah, you can just stop your blubbering and think on what to tell them."

Darlene leaned over the phonograph on the floor by the bed, moved the arm back to the beginning of the record. She settled into the throw pillows, willed the tears back in her eyes. Things became softer, their edges melting. She could see Donald Ray, his blond hair all lit up with heavenly light.

He was smiling just the way he always did when he came home after working all night. By the time he got in, Pap was in the fields, Beulah was busy in another part of the house. Chrissie was out at the main road waiting for the school bus. Those quiet mornings in the kitchen the house was theirs.

Donald Ray read to her from the morning paper, the sizzle of the frying eggs and ham rising and falling against the steady flow of his voice. She turned to watch him, his head bent over the paper. Sometimes the light from the window would catch his hair and she felt the presence of something that reached beyond him that was still a part of him. A child, she decided, making itself known to those who could see. She kept what she'd seen for herself, making it a part of her special knowing about how things would work between them.

Fridays were different. Her parents drove into Potter first thing. Those mornings Donald Ray began pulling his clothes off before he was half way in the side door, letting them fall on the kitchen floor until he stood, finally, naked beside her. The tears flooded her eyes and she lost him again.

Beulah's timid knock sounded at the door. "Darlene?" She closed the door behind her. "You shouldn't be lying there like that, honey. What if somebody opens your door by mistake?

And can't you turn that record down a little? You can hear it all the way into the living room."

Beulah leaned over and moved the arm off the record. Darlene could tell she wanted to say something about her wearing red at a time like this. The bra and panties were her Valentine's present from Donald Ray. But if Beulah didn't understand why she was playing the record, she'd never understand the underwear.

"I brought you something to eat." Beulah held the plate out. "You've been holed up in here all afternoon and it's past supper time."

Darlene stared at the food. "What is it?"

"Baked ham, candied yams, and Mrs. Freeman's potato salad with pickles."

She had used the same coaxing voice to trick Darlene into eating when she was little and went through that stage where she turned her nose up at everything on the table. Darlene looked away, picked at the fringe on a pillow.

"You've got to eat something," Beulah tried again. "You can't starve yourself to death." She hesitated, her face turning red, then hurriedly added, "You haven't had a thing since that dry biscuit at breakfast."

"Well, I sure don't want to die." Darlene patted the nightstand beside her. "Leave it right here, Ma."

Darlene saw Beulah eye her mourning dress where it lay discarded at the foot of the bed. In the cedar closet upstairs were all the black dresses Beulah had worn over the years to funerals. Sometimes, when Darlene was upstairs alone, she would open the closet and stand there, breathing in the sweet dry smell of cedar, her fingers lightly running over the different materials. Heavy wools for winter deaths, thin cottons for summer ones, all worn once then put away. When Beulah undressed tonight, she would hang the rayon dress she was wearing in that closet. Here she was ready to pick Darlene's dress up and take it right upstairs and put it in that closet. Then she'd be part of it, part of the whole thing of death. Every time she walked past that closet, she'd see the dress in there, all closed up, dark and airless, like Donald Ray in his grave. Darlene's chest froze, just like it did when they had closed Donald Ray's coffin. "Don't," she gasped, fighting for air. "Please don't take my dress."

"My poor sweetheart, I'm so sorry." Beulah reached down to stroke her head.

Darlene dodged her hand. "Don't, just leave it, leave me be."

Beulah paused at the door, her hand curled up on her chest like a broken bird. "I'll check on you later."

"Get those people out of here, please, Ma. Haven't they stayed long enough?"

Beulah nodded, her chin trembling the way it did when Darlene wore her down.

In the visitors' low murmur, Darlene heard her name then Donald Ray's, followed by hushed whispers. It was as if the two of them were sleeping and no one wanted to disturb them. She stuffed the corner of her pillow in her mouth to stifle her sobs.

Since his death, nothing tore into her more than unexpected kindness. Last night at the funeral home, Mrs. Routh, her fifth-grade teacher, had appeared out of nowhere, pulling Darlene into her baby-powdered embrace. The simple, familiar smell cut through the heady scent of the roses and lilies surrounding Donald Ray to touch off a surge of memories: Mrs. Routh leaning over Darlene's desk to check her long division; sitting with Mrs. Routh after school and learning to knit and purl while she waited for the bus; her teacher kneeling at recess to clean a cut on her knee. Longing welled up in her. She wanted to be ten again, to not know about death and loss and change. What was left for her? Losing her parents, her own death? Darlene clung to Mrs. Routh, giving over the full weight of her grief. The funeral director had eased her out of Mrs. Routh's arms and whisked her away behind a wall of green velvet drapes and into a separate room until she calmed down.

She started the record over. No matter how many times she told herself Donald Ray was dead it didn't stick. They were supposed to be together, together forever; he had promised. It was like they had broken up. She had the record, she had his ring, but they were finished. She lay back, running her hands over her Valentine nylon and lace, uncertain how to begin. Her fingers fell into the familiar pattern of Donald Ray's. They made light swirls around her nipples, moved outward to take in more of her. When the pleasure became unbearable, she smiled, thinking to herself, I'm alive yet, I know I am.

3

1925

AURILLA

I don't know that I ever liked my husband. I don't think so. Not even in the beginning when I first saw him at church. He sat toward the back, looking as mournful as a tied-up dog in his starched collar and dark suit coat. Later I found out that the only reason he was there was because his mother said it was time to find a wife and church was the place to start.

I was nineteen and teaching school down at Brower. Boarded with a family near the school and on weekends came home to be with my mother and to play piano for the Sunday church service. Oh, I had some big ideas back then, saving up my money for an education. I wanted to go off and teach in a real school, not some little two-room country school. I was going to be a music teacher, leading choirs and such. I could just see myself up there, waving my arms, moving my hands slow and graceful when I wanted them to hold on to the notes and snapping my baton to cut them off.

I didn't care a lick whether I ever married. My mother had been a widow since I was a year old and my brother was three and she didn't seem to have suffered any from being without a man. Our house had been in my mother's family so we had a place to live. I was a change-of-life child, and her parents were both gone by the time her husband died of pneumonia. They didn't leave much of anything besides the house and what was in it. But Leonora McMath had her sewing machine and could make anything you showed her. She'd had a knack for sewing since I was a young girl. Made her own Sunday school clothes when she was no more than twelve years old. The women there in Potter brought in their ladies' books and she studied the pictures and took their measurements and told them what kind of material to bring her and how much and when the dress would be done. You couldn't buy a pattern that equaled what she came up with and the women all knew it and they were willing to pay so we got by.

She was always working on something, never anything for herself. Her dresses were plain but made of good material, so they showed off her skills. She saved a lot of work by wearing simple things herself. Her customers looked that much better come fitting time with her playing the sparrow to their peacock.

At night Leonora did quiet things, basting a hem, making a dress pattern from newspaper, or piecing a quilt from the material left over from the dresses she was making that season. One thing we had was quilts. She never wasted a scrap. I can look at all those quilts today and say whose dress each patch came from. She would sit there, her fingers moving soundlessly, while I banged out the chords to some hymn on the piano. I never felt more alive than when I was playing a strong hymn.

Sometime that winter a change came into the church. I would get up to play the piano, sit on the bench arranging my skirt. Right there, in that thick silence before my hands struck the keys, I knew something was different about the place, something watchful.

I'd always been aware that way. Mother said I had another sense beyond what people ordinarily have. She knew because her mother had been the same way, feeling things coming before they happened. I couldn't have been more than seven years old at the time. I was sitting at school and dropped my pencil like it was a hot poker and doubled over my desk in pain. The teacher thought it was cramps from working on my penmanship but when I got home there was Mother with her right hand all bandaged up from where she'd burned it on a hot pot.

Burned so bad she couldn't sew for a week. So, Mother listened to me when I told her about the church.

It was Easter Sunday before I could name my feeling. I got up from the piano, looked across the congregation at the pretty spring hats the women had on. They couldn't have been more pleased with themselves if they had bouquets on their heads. The bright display only pointed up his uneasiness, making him easier to spot. He sat in the back, pulled in against a window, watching me. It was like he was looking at me from a long ways away, like I might disappear if he took his pale eyes off me.

It was all I could do to get to our pew and sit still through to the end of the service. When everyone rose, filling the church with the sound of rustling dresses and bulletins being folded, I whispered, "The one watching, he's way back on the right, all by himself."

Mother turned her head, her eyes searching the crowd, like she was looking for someone she had business with. "Emma Cutter's boy, Joe," she murmured behind her bulletin, "looking right at you."

I grabbed her arm. "You'll walk on the side of the aisle closest to him, won't you?" His eyeing me so made me feel I needed something as solid and good as her between us.

"Just carry on like it's any other Sunday, Aurilla. You just listen to me talk. I made a dress for his mother once. You were just a baby then. Hard woman to satisfy, let alone impress. And I needed the business so bad I went right ahead and made the dress over twice for her when the real problem was the cheap goods she brought me to make it with. Never came back; the ones you work the hardest to please usually don't. They're a good family, tobacco farmers. But as far as I've been able to tell, they don't have much interest in anything beyond their crop."

Outside, we passed some time talking with the different people we knew. I drew my shawl tight around me, shivering despite the bright sun. The day was what Mother called a changeling day—February in the shade, April in the sun.

He stared at me, the Cutter boy, from off in the trees, down where the cars and buggies were parked on the side of the road. His hands adjusted the mirrors on his car, the wiper blades, but his eyes never left me. That's how it would be, all those years we were together. He couldn't bring himself to be close to me but he couldn't bear for me to be out of his sight.

We went on like that, him watching and me feeling stirred up, the rest of the spring. Until the Sunday he caught up to us on the church steps.

"Want a ride home?" he asked. Just like that, not taking his hat off or introducing himself, not even mentioning his mother's name.

I hung back and let Mother do the talking. "That's very kind of you," she said. "You're Emma Cutter's boy, aren't you?" She always knew just what to say. She'd been inside the rich folks' homes measuring and fitting them so much that some of their fancy ways had rubbed off.

Joe nodded and looked relieved, as if he'd forgotten whose son he was and was grateful Leonora had reminded him. I looked at him while he was taken up with her. He seemed like a fine enough boy in spite of his ill-fitting suit. His hair was black and thick and stuck out every which way despite the hair cream he'd used. His skin was already dark from spring planting. Up close I could see why his eyes ran right through things. The irises were a watery blue but the pupils were ringed with yellow. Like a hawk's eyes, they had an unblinking way about them.

"We'd be pleased to accept your kind offer," Mother was saying. "I just want to stop and thank the minister for his fine sermon."

He nodded again and was off like a shot for the car.

"Why didn't he ask me to come along? I didn't say *I* had to speak to the minister."

Mother laughed into her glove, not wanting her voice to carry. "You should have spoken up like you usually do." She took my elbow, guiding me into the line of people waiting for their turn with the minister.

If it had been one of the other boys coming around and acting so awkward, I would have snickered and said something smart, but Joe Cutter had such a stern way about him, I didn't dare. I guess I started slipping right then, even that soon, taking on a bit of how I thought he wanted me to act.

"Does your mother still raise those prize guinea hens of hers?" Mother leaned forward to address Joe, her left hand holding her hat on, her right braced against the dashboard.

"They all but died out," he answered, not taking his eyes off the road.

Mother sat back, folded her hands in her lap. It was that way the whole drive home. One of us would ask a question, the kind sure to turn into a conversation, and he'd settle it with five words.

At our house he didn't make a move to come around and open the door for us. My mother adjusted her skirt, the way you did before getting out of a car or buggy. I can still remember the rustling the taffeta made in all that silence.

"Mr. Cutter, I'm afraid we'll need your help here." He jumped again, just like when he went to get the car. The hand he held out to me was dry and hard, like unoiled leather. After all those Sundays of staring, he never once looked me in the face. He was back in the car and gone before we could thank him.

"If he had given me a chance, I would have asked him in for lemonade. He's got a dusty ride ahead of him as dry as it's been. I guess it's for the best though." Mother put her arm around me and we started up the steps to the house. She always did that when she had something special to tell me. We were like girls sharing our secrets. "He's a strange one, doesn't like to look you in the face." She shook her head, puzzling him out. "There's something there he doesn't want anybody to see, something dark. That was your father too. He died before I got to it."

She'd never told me a thing about how it was with her and my father and I waited for her to go on. Instead she reached in her pocketbook, searched for the door key. "Darkness snuffs out light. Don't forget that, Aurilla."

But watching her gloved hands struggle with the lock, I already had.

From that Sunday on, Joe drove us home from church. In the beginning Leonora tried breaking the silence with inquiries about his family or the crops. After a number of Sundays, she sat quiet, working her house key in her gloved hand.

I sat still too, holding on to the seat, my arm next to Joe's. The contact forced by our closeness felt like a shared secret. When he worked to hold the car in a curve or to take a turn, the ripple of his muscles traveled through the rough cloth of his suit and the thin cotton lawn of my summer dress. I pictured him working bare-armed in the fields, stopping to mop the sweat from his face.

Joe's darkness struck me as brooding and since that wasn't my nature or anybody's I knew, I was drawn to him. If he was tangled up inside, then I was the one to unravel him. Leonora never spoke another word against Joe. I took Mother's silence as blessing, telling myself that she saw my father in Joe.

I'd never paid much attention to what little was left of Father in the house—the enamel snuffbox on Leonora's dressing table, the photograph in the parlor. He didn't seem to figure into our lives. I found myself studying his picture on the afternoons I sat with Joe—the deep-set eyes like mine, the stern mouth under his handlebar moustache—looking for some clue. Something in him, now in me, would help me with Joe. Before long, they began to feel the same, my father and Joe. Pieces of a puzzle that fit one into the other.

My taking to Joe was hard on Leonora. She had worked all her life opening doors for me and there I was, closing them as fast as I could. I forgot all about applying to Women's College. The deadline just slipped past the way those things do when you lose interest. To her credit Leonora never said a word.

That whole summer Joe and I sat in the parlor, the breezes lifting the lace curtains, the chipped ice slowly melting in our lemonade. Outside the bay window, an occasional buggy or car drove by or the cacophony of the wrens that nested in the azaleas broke the quiet. When I grew tired of listening for the irregular tinkling of the wind chimes out on the sunporch, I would ask him some question that would lead him to talk about the things a man studies: the crops, the weather, livestock prices. Every Sunday I led him to the same topics, never listening to a word he said once I had him going.

I was caught up instead in watching him move and fill up space, that was what interested me. I'd never been courted, so I had no idea what was supposed to go on. Close as I could tell this was all—him talking and me watching. Back then boys and girls were kept so much apart, just being alone in the same room with a man was something.

The shape of him and the deep timbre of his voice carried me beyond our being together, beyond the touching of our arms in the car. In my mind I heard him say things, the kind of things I imagined a man said to a woman at night. And all of him against me, how would that be? I wondered. To feel the weight of him, the chafe of the dark hair on his arms and legs on my bare skin?

The Cutter house set back from the road, about four miles out of Potter down near Clear Creek. The big house wandered this way and that, a warren of rooms added as children were born. It stood in a clearing without so much as a bush or flower for adornment.

That first Sunday Joe took me home for dinner, Emma Cutter stood waiting inside the front door. Her ruddy skin stretched thin and tight across her bones, irritated as if from years of being scrubbed with strong soap. She wore her black hair, shot full of white, wound in a taut bun at the nape of her neck. I was plenty nervous remembering how uncharitable Leonora said Mrs. Cutter was. I climbed the stairs to meet her, anchoring a smile on my face.

Under that hard gaze I felt myself straighten. I might not be the beauty my mother was but I did have her cheekbones and her bearing. "Thank you for inviting me to your home, Mrs. Cutter," I said in my strongest voice.

Mrs. Cutter acknowledged my politeness with a brisk nod. "We're already in the dining room. The men folk couldn't wait. They were out this morning working to get the last of the leaves pulled and strung."

I thought back to Joe's talk about crops. "The leaves must have gone yellow early this year with all the heat."

If Mrs. Cutter was surprised to see I knew something about tobacco she hid it well. "Yes, and they'll have a rough time of it tending the curing barn furnace." She shifted her gaze in her son's direction. "Joe, take that car on around back."

I followed Joe's mother down a long, dark hallway that ran to the back of the house. The air was stifling hot. Mrs. Cutter strode along in her long-sleeved brown serge like the heat was nothing. At the far end of the hall a square of light shone from an open doorway. Inside, the low rumble of male voices and the giggling of children rose above the clatter of dishes.

Emma Cutter stopped in the doorway, her broad frame blocking the light. "This here is Leonora McMath's girl, Aurilla," she announced before stepping aside to let me in the room.

Joe's two brothers looked up from their places at the far end of the table long enough to nod their greeting before going on with their meal. Joe came in through the kitchen, nodding to me as he sat down beside his older brother Jay. They had the same coloring but Jay was thickset, making me think he was running to fat. Hank, the youngest, seemed slight beside them. Just a boy yet, he looked to be eighteen.

The children, three girls from two to maybe five, sat at the end of the table nearest the door. The eldest sat by the toddler, spooning gravy into the little one's mouth. The middle child chewed on the end of one of her blond braids, shooting me a grin. Their mother slouched in a chair across from them, picking at her food.

"You're right here beside me," Emma Cutter said, moving to the head of the table. "I'll fix you a plate."

A fine web of yellowed cracks ran across the surface of the dish Mrs. Cutter filled with biscuits and beef stew. My mother threw away plates like that. "Good hiding place for germs," she'd say about the plate. I watched as Mrs. Cutter served the green beans, pulled some fatback off the cooking bone and put that on the plate too.

Leonora was probably having a little roast chicken with Waldorf salad. We got by eating like that because we had no men at home to cook for. My brother had joined up during the Great War and stayed in the army, making a life of it. We ate our ladies' meals on Grandmother's white, gold-rimmed china on the sunporch with the windows open just enough to stir up the wind chimes. A longing for the world I recognized as my mother's rose up inside me, almost bringing me to tears.

Steam wafted off the food set before me, making the air in the room seem even more scarce. The odor of overcooked beans and grease rose to meet me. There was just one window down at the far end where the men sat. The August sun poured into the room bringing more heat.

"I hear you're a schoolteacher." Mrs. Cutter pulled her chair around so she could look at me straight on. "You must know something about managing children. Do you know anything about running a house?"

That stopped me. I guessed I didn't really. It had just been my brother and me growing up and he was as helpful as any girl as long as he lived at home.

Mrs. Cutter rocked onto the back legs of her chair. "There's a lot to do around a big place like this. A girl'd have to be plenty strong to step in here and do what I do every day."

I looked over at Joe's sister-in-law, sitting on her right. Wisps of light hair hung limp around a thin face flushed from standing over scalding pots of food. I didn't imagine Mrs. Cutter got much heavy work out of her.

"And who all lives here?" I asked. I was the only one that had been introduced. I thought Joe would spring to his feet, embarrassed by his oversight. Absorbed in conversation with his brothers, he had forgotten me.

My question seemed to surprise Mrs. Cutter. "Why, everybody you see here," she said, waving her hands around the table. The gesture struck me as one she must have learned a long time ago, before her hands were so rough and red. I had never seen a woman with such hands. Leonora wore gloves the whole year long and rubbed her hands with lemon juice and cream each night to keep them smooth and white. Mrs. Cutter's fingers were as thick as a man's and I found myself watching them instead of the people they pointed to.

"There's my eldest boy, Jay, and his wife, Louellen, here, and their young'uns. Then there's Joe, of course, and Hank, my youngest."

Mrs. Cutter's hands dropped into her lap, my eyes following them. I raised my gaze slowly, looking around the table to see if I had been found out. Only Hank watched me, and his acknowledging grin told me that we had a secret. His coloring was lighter than the rest of the Cutters, a trait that seemed to carry right through to his general bearing.

"Bring out those peach pies you made this morning, Louellen," said Mrs. Cutter.

Louellen leaned into the table to pull herself out of her seat. Mrs. Cutter watched her leave the table. "Louellen's a nice enough girl, but not very stout," she murmured. "Having these young'uns so quick just about did her in. All that work, and not one of them a boy."

The eldest girl held the baby while the middle child cleaned the baby's place. "These girls don't seem to be asking much of anybody," I said.

"Well, they'll never work a day in the fields." Mrs. Cutter rubbed her napkin across her mouth. "Delicate, like the mother."

Louellen came out of the kitchen, her shoulders rounded and pulled forward from carrying small children. A pie in each hand, she stopped to serve the men. She cut the pie with a dinner knife and put the pieces right on their plates, on top of whatever was left of the beef stew and green beans. I pushed the rest of my dinner to one side of my plate.

Louellen's trip to the kitchen had raised a thin mist of sweat that made her flowered housedress stick to her shallow chest. Her movements were slow and deliberate, like someone sick. The flush I had noticed earlier was gone; she was the color of ashes. Another baby, I thought to myself. I waited for her to meet my eyes; Leonora had taught me the sure way to tell.

I was the last of the adults to be served and, besides Hank, the only one to say thank you. Louellen looked at me, as hollow-eyed as they come.

Driving out to the main road I looked back, watching the Cutter place recede until it was no bigger than a dollhouse. The closed up feeling I had from the moment I set foot inside it left me. I asked Joe to drive a ways into the country, not so much for his company as for the open air. They'd finished dinner so early—Mrs. Cutter had started clearing the table before I ate the last of my pie—that Leonora wouldn't be expecting me home for a good while yet.

Back then women cooked all day Saturday just so they could sit down once a week and do nothing. But that wasn't the case at the Cutter's. By the time we left the house to drive back to town Mrs. Cutter had Louellen boiling jars and the oldest girl peeling the peaches they were going to put up that afternoon.

"What's your mother doing canning on a Sunday?" The words fell out of my mouth the instant I thought them and they sounded critical. We hadn't yet said the first thing about the visit.

Joe didn't seem to notice. From what I'd just seen, he was used to people saying what they thought. "Mama does inside work on Sundays. During the week she leaves the rest of it to Louellen. Pap died right before the war, and then when Jay had to go fight, she took his place in the fields. Liked the work so well she never went back to the house."

I looked back over my shoulder. I could picture Joe's mother without so much as a hat on in those open fields stretching out from the house, working beside the men, her hands as big and able as theirs. And I could see Louellen, shuffling from room to room in that airless house, stopping to rest whenever she passed a chair or a bed.

"Clear Creek runs right along here." Joe pointed to the woods on the left side of the road. "Nice place for wading down the bank there." He took his foot off the accelerator, waiting for my answer.

Out here, away from the church and mother's parlor, he had finally softened some. The creek seemed like a gift he was holding out to me, a part of something special to him.

"I'd like that," I replied.

The saplings growing on the embankment were so thick there was scarcely a place to step. I could hear the water running over the rocks just on the other side of the trees. Joe spread his suit coat out for me on a sandy clearing.

"I wouldn't take my shoes off just yet," he said as I began unbuttoning mine. "I'm fixing to call the ducks. They'll be expecting me to feed them and I haven't brought a thing with me. They might settle for your toes instead."

I thought this was the silliest thing I'd ever heard and kept right on unbuttoning my shoes. "These ducks know you, do they?"

"Yes, ma'am. I come to see them most every evening after dinner. I bring them a biscuit or two. They lost their mother when they were real young and I kept them fed in the beginning."

This surprised me, him coming here alone to feed ducks. As much time as I had spent with him these past months, I never saw any sign of that kind of caring. I felt hopeful seeing it.

He whistled like he was calling a dog. I could hear the ducks starting up down the creek. There must have been a half dozen of them when they came into sight, all headed right for the bank. They waddled out of the water, flapping their wings, squawking, and running into each other, trying to get to me. I pulled my dress down over my feet, waved my hat at them and sat there, squealing and laughing. Joe was laughing and running around, trying to shoo them back in the water.

"Your hat," he yelled, "it's the berries on the hat they're after."

I flung my hat in the air, not even looking at what I was doing. He caught it, pulled off the berries, and threw them out to the middle of the creek.

"That was my best hat," I said, watching the ducks head down the bank toward the ripples the berries had set off in the water.

"We can get you another hat," he said, reaching out to grab my foot, "but not new toes."

That started us laughing again. The joy passed back and forth between us, our laughter unstoppable. The moment shimmered like a new blown bubble turning over and over in the air. I kept laughing, even though my face ached and tears streamed out of my eyes, not wanting this good feeling between us to end.

Our laughter faded. The ducks called to each other somewhere down the creek. I breathed deep, taking in the sleepy rise and fall of the cicadas' song, the cadenced tapping of a woodpecker.

I turned to smile at Joe. He kissed me, just brushing my lips. He was so gentle I found myself kissing him back and liking it. There was just the faint song of the ducks, the water flowing by, and our lips touching, like we were all part of the same thing.

Before I knew it I was lying on his coat looking straight up at the trees. He was all over me and all I could see was him. He looked preoccupied, like he had forgotten I was there, like he couldn't be interrupted.

Nineteen was still pretty young back then. Leonora, not having a husband and not thinking about it herself, never had told me what went on between men and women. I knew enough to know you weren't supposed to let them touch you, but I kept thinking just this little bit more won't hurt. The things

I'd pictured us doing as we sat in the parlor flowed into the things Joe was doing now until it was hard to know where my imagining left off.

My mind had only let me go so far, but once my dress was up around my chest I got scared. I pushed hard on his shoulders, fingernails digging into him. He held my arms to the ground, a hand tight around each wrist.

I lay still then and closed my eyes. I thought of church that morning, the tiger lilies all around the pulpit, the choir singing, and my fingers pounding on the keys. I held on to the music all the time he was pushing into me. It was awful, the burning, and it went on and on. I tasted blood and realized I was biting my lip. All the time he kept saying, "No, no," like it was awful for him too. Then the tension went out of him. He rolled onto the sand beside me, his breathing heavy and uneven.

I wanted to wash, that was what I wanted most. I got up and walked the best I could into the water. I went right out to the middle where it was deepest, holding my dress up around my waist. Was this what I had wanted, thinking my secret thoughts while Joe droned on Sunday after Sunday about the challenges of raising tobacco? What had I done that had showed that wanting in me?

The last time I had been this deep in water was for my baptism. I went under the water once for the Father, once for the Son, once for the Holy Ghost. I had turned around to face the witnesses on the bank, feeling clean, even though my feet were deep in mud. Now I had to turn around and face Joe, but the worst would be Leonora. She would know what I had been up to the moment she saw me, she'd have to. I felt so changed, so far away from her, like things could never be the way they were before with us. So quick, this thing I and Joe had done, yet it had changed everything. Something was holding me to him.

I walked over to the bank where he sat, his hand cupped, pouring water over the back of his coat. A red stream seeped through the cloth. I watched the water grow pale pink then turn back to clear.

"Get on up to the car, Aurilla." He held the coat up, examined the stain in the tree-filtered light.

"What's your mother going to say when she sees how you've spoiled your church coat?"

"I won't be needing it anymore, now will I?" He smiled, not at me, just for himself. "I've found me a wife."

I turned around and headed up the hill, moving slowly against the undertow of my dress, clinging heavy and wet around my legs. It was so big, what he'd just said. The only part I grabbed hold of was having something to tell my mother when she met me at the door.

4

Darlene

Darlene was two weeks late and Donald Ray had been dead for three. She waited for a sign—queasiness, a slight swell in her flat stomach—anything that would tell her she was right. She hadn't really eaten since Donald Ray passed—just a bite here and there to satisfy Beulah—and she knew there were women that didn't eat at first. That was the only thing she had to go on. There was supposed to be a child, she was sure of it.

This would have been her and Donald Ray's first anniversary. If he were here their room would be perfumed with yellow roses and magnolias. A single magnolia floated in the rose bowl on the dresser—the only one left on the tree in the front yard—the edges curled brown from her sniffing it every time she walked past.

The magnolias had come early this year. The oaks had already begun to drop long ropy threads of pollen that broke to yellow dust in your hands and covered cars, porches, the backs of throats. Nothing was going right, not the flowers, not their anniversary.

She tore the tags off the dress she had put on layaway when the stores first put out the spring clothes. The linen sheath was yellow, bright as lemon meringue pie. Its new smell and stiffness rekindled the excitement and anticipation of first trying it on in the shop. The dress slid over her shoulders, along the length of her.

She stared at herself in the bright glare of her dress. The good feelings disappeared as quickly as they had come. The weight of the truth pushed her back down to the muffled numbed place where she didn't dream, taste her food, or feel the warmth of the sun on her skin. She was spending her first wedding anniversary with her parents and her little sister, her husband five miles down the road in the graveyard.

"Darlene, you look so pretty, just like Ma's daffodils," Chrissie said when Darlene came in the dining room. Beulah looked up smiling. Her face fell when she saw what Darlene had on. Pap glanced up from his paper, raised his eyebrows, and went back to reading.

"Doesn't she look nice?" Chrissie asked.

"Big sister always looks nice." Beulah sat down at her place and opened her napkin across her lap, palms smoothing it so flat it blended into the material of her skirt.

"Go get the pork chops from the kitchen, please, Chrissie. Everything's ready, we were just waiting on you, Darlene."

Chrissie sat the pork chops in the center of the table and dropped into her seat beside Darlene.

"Pap, we're ready here." Beulah served his plate then hers and passed the platter to Darlene.

"I like navy beans with my pork chops," Pap said, eyeing the applesauce and fried potatoes on his plate.

"They take all day to cook and it was just too warm to heat up the kitchen like that. Feels like summer's here already." Talking about the weather always loosened her mother up. For the first time since Darlene came in, Beulah looked her in the face, a light smile crossing her lips.

Darlene took a pork chop to please her, moved the platter to Chrissie's place. She put a spoonful of applesauce in her mouth. The food's smooth slide down her throat turned her stomach. She wiped at the drop of applesauce that had somehow fallen on her lap.

She felt let down, like she had been stood up. She remembered sitting on the edge of the couch in the living room, careful not to wrinkle her dress while Pap dozed in the recliner, his fingers loose on the evening paper, and her mother washed the supper dishes. Was this what all the fuss was about? she had asked herself. The looking pretty and getting boys to notice you, so they could marry you, then spend their evenings

sleeping in the Easy Boy while you scrubbed the grease out of
the roasting pan? She got up, stomped by Pap, and called into
the kitchen just loud enough to disturb him. "That boy comes,
Ma, you tell him I left a long time ago and that I didn't say a
thing about having a date."

Darlene had set her mind on something different happening
to her. She pictured herself leaving Gold Ridge; for where, she
had no idea. But the thought freed her enough that she began,
for the first time in her life, to think beyond her plans for Saturday night.

Even Donald Ray Spencer had to do some work to get her
to change her mind. He stopped by her locker between classes
or waited outside the cafeteria. She snubbed him and the girls
would about go wild, all of them chirping at once about how
she was missing her big chance with a basketball star. What
would she be doing now and where would she be, she wondered, if she'd passed Donald Ray up like she'd meant to do in
the beginning?

Darlene looked around the table. She could see her family
talking and eating, but it was like they were all a long way off.
This must be how a ghost feels, she told herself. "The weather was the same a year ago today," she blurted out, desperate
to know she could still be heard. She watched the color leave
Beulah's face.

"How would you know a thing like that?" Pap said around
his pork chop.

"Pap," Beulah's voice warned. She shook her head faintly,
her eyes on Pap like Darlene couldn't see.

"Well, I'd like to know how she could hold on to something
like that." He looked at Darlene and waited, smoothing butter
over his biscuit.

"Today's our anniversary," Darlene said.

Pap looked at her, his face blank, like he was part of this
"our" she was talking about.

"I'm talking about me and Donald Ray."

"Donald Ray's dead," Pap said.

"I think we all know that." Beulah's voice came out snappier than Darlene had ever heard her dare, and when Pap frowned at her she said, "I mean, I don't think we have to talk about that, do we?"

"Oh, Darlene, this is so sad." Chrissie had been crying right along with her for weeks and now she started in again. "You weren't going to say a word, were you?" Chrissie choked through her tears.

Darlene squeezed Chrissie's hand and that just made her cry harder.

Pap started that squirming thing he did when things slipped out of his control. "Now see here, missy, I can't keep my own anniversary straight. Why would I remember something that's not even happening?" He tore into his biscuit, his jaws swelling with the bread.

"What do you mean?" Darlene leaned forward, ignoring the small headshakes Beulah sent her way.

"What I mean is," Pap paused, spearing another pork chop from the platter with his fork, "you can't have an anniversary by yourself. Mother, get me some of that mustard sauce from the Kelvinator."

"You're going to take that away from me too, are you?" said Darlene.

For a minute he looked at her like she was talking about the mustard sauce Beulah put in his hand. "How am I going to take something away that you don't have in the first place?"

Chrissie patted her hand. "I don't think Darlene's feeling too well, Pap."

Chrissie was right. Darlene pushed back her chair and ran to the bathroom. She grabbed a wad of toilet paper, sank on the floor in front of the toilet, and waited to throw up. There was the sound of Beulah's chair scraping against the floor and Pap calling after her. "The boy's dead, Beulah. Your humoring her won't help that any."

Beulah knocked once, closed the door behind her. She flipped the lid shut on the toilet, sat down. "I cleaned the toilet today. The smell of the disinfectant alone is enough to make you sick."

"I feel like I'm going to throw up all the time. Maybe I'm pregnant." Darlene buried her face in the toilet paper while she let Beulah consider the possibility.

"Let's hope not. You're a young girl, you need to get on with your life."

"My period's not coming either," Darlene said, trying to keep the hope out of her voice.

"It's the shock has you running late," Beulah said. "The same thing happened to me when your brother died."

Sometimes, away from Pap, Beulah dared to let her good sense show. This was one time when Darlene wasn't interested. "But I want to be pregnant. I want his baby." Speaking her secret wish out loud started her crying again. "If there was a baby, he wouldn't be so far away."

Beulah rearranged the floral soaps in their dish, adjusted the hand towels on the rack behind the door. "Let's just worry about what's at hand. Maybe you should think about going back to school. It's just one year you've missed now."

School? Darlene wouldn't be able to stand it. The girls carrying on about what they were wearing to this party, who had a crush on whom, giggling over their first kiss with a new date. When she got engaged, they had all flocked to her table in the cafeteria, climbing over each other to see her ring, to hear her secrets. She was way ahead of them; she'd loved with all her heart and she'd lost a husband. How many years would it take those girls to catch up with her? She lived somewhere else, in a dark place that knew the real truth about chance and luck.

She saw how they looked at her, the ones that had been her friends, like she was bad sick with something catching, or disfigured. Donald Ray's dying had left her a freak. Nobody was a widow at seventeen. She was living something none of them wanted to believe could happen and they'd make her pay for knowing. She pictured herself sitting at the back of the school cafeteria all alone, pretending not to mind, the way fat Opal

Matthews with the harelip had to do. She needed to be some-place else, someplace where nobody knew how she was before. "I was thinking about a job at the hosiery mill."

Beulah shook her head. "There's that money coming from Donald Ray's life insurance."

"Beulah, I'm ready for my dessert," Pap interrupted from the dining room.

Beulah exhaled, her breath coming out halfway between a sigh and a groan. "Well, it seems you want a lot. Just think be-fore you go jumping into things." She touched Darlene's cheek and rose to go.

Darlene grabbed her hand. Beulah couldn't leave her, not now. Not like when Darlene was little and had nightmares and she comforted her and then left her alone with her imagination. "What if I made all this happen? What if he's dead because of me, what if I'm being punished? I'm sorry, Ma, I'm so sorry about the wedding and Perry," Darlene said, exploding into sobs. "I didn't know how bad you were hurting. I swear I didn't, not until now."

Beulah's eyes filled with tears, but she smiled a quavering smile. "It's all right, don't you think I know that? Nobody's pun-ishing you. God doesn't make cars crash." She gave Darlene's hand a reassuring squeeze. "I better go before he throws a real fit."

Darlene got up so fast she saw stars. She grabbed onto the sink for support, squeezed her eyes shut, letting her vision right itself. A familiar wetness started between her legs. Her hand flew to her crotch, touching the soaked nylon. Dark blood filled the whorls on her fingertips.

She turned on the water, watched the blood and what felt like the last piece of Donald Ray wash away.

They'd taken away Donald Ray's flowers. His grave looked ragged and raw, a wound that made Darlene want to turn her head. The Spencers had a plot for her right here beside him. Everybody else had a fine stone. The only thing marking his place was a plastic cardholder. His name was almost gone, the ink washed to a blue blur by the rain.

Darlene knelt down, the rocks and hardened clay digging into her knees. There wasn't a soul around, not so much as a hoot owl, just row after row of white stones stretching toward the place where the night got thick.

She waited to feel something, some connection to Donald Ray. Each Saturday Beulah left the house for her visit to Perry's grave. Armed with grass clippers and rake, and flowers bought in town or picked from her garden, she would stay gone for hours. When Beulah came back, she was puffy-eyed and drained, but there was a calm acceptance about her that said tidying Perry's grave and sitting with him gave her peace.

"We're here, Perry, me and Big Sister," Beulah had called out when they went to set out Easter lilies on the family graves. Uncomfortable, Darlene had stood off to the side while Beulah carried on right out in the open, delivering the week's news in the gentle melodic voice Darlene remembered from bedtime stories.

Why fuss with Donald Ray's grave or talk to him? She felt closer to him sitting home by herself. She couldn't get past the picture of him boxed up somewhere below her and the horrible quiet of that. Her chest started to tighten and she looked away, settling on the magnolia trees growing against the church, on the remaining blossoms standing out white in the darkness.

What made Beulah and everybody else think they could give the dead an address, a tidy, fenced-in place to go visit them when they wanted to feel close? The dead didn't care. Their indifference rose up around her in deafening silence. Swallowing hard, she ran for the trees, her locket bouncing against her chest. She twisted the stems of the remaining flowers until they broke, the sap and bits of bark sticking to her fingers. Donald Ray wasn't here; he would never be here. She'd try Ramsey Lake.

She rounded the last bend of the lake road, stopping the car. How could one spot be the keeper of so much bad and good?

Donald Ray had died here, right where they had parked the Saturday nights before they got married, right on the road where he'd taught her to drive. She rolled down the windows, letting in the night air. The rustle of the leaves, the cloaked flap of a bat's wing, the slap of the water against the bank; it was all there inside her, waiting to be called up. She sat very still, letting the lake do its work.

A soft wave of breezes rolled off the water and through the trees, ruffled her hair, played over her bare arms. "Water into wine," she murmured, closing her eyes. She felt Donald Ray's warm breath on her neck, heard it catch and change as his hands moved over her. His teeth were against her mouth, smooth and even, and she felt herself flowing, falling, melting into him. His lips slid across her cheek to her ear with an urgent intake of breath.

A loud ping sounded from the car's cooling engine, startling her back to the present. She cursed and slammed the wheel with her hand. Her name, she thought, tears starting. He was just about to speak her name. Could they have talked then? She had turned the words and phrases he used over and around in her head, practicing to keep the sound of him alive, but she just couldn't get the sound of his voice.

Darlene turned her back to the driver's door, let her head hang over the ledge of the open window. The topmost needles of the pine trees swayed, showing black against the deep blue of the night sky. Stars swarmed. From the openness of the pasture Pap had taught her to read the bowl of the night sky. Archer, Little Dipper, Big Bear, she heard Pap's voice in her head. Why was his voice so easy to hear and not Donald Ray's? Maybe if she talked, just talked the way she would if he was here, she could get to him. The thought of speaking his name out loud in the dark of the night was overwhelming. She scanned the heavens, fixed her eye on the steady glow of Mars, and began. "There's not going to be any baby. I thought there would be. Remember how strong things were between us that last night?" Darlene opened the locket around her neck, turning

Donald Ray's senior picture in her hand until she found enough light to catch his eyes.

"Nothing left of you but what's in my head and your clothes and things. I've been sleeping in the last work shirt you wore. At first it smelled just like you, but now that's fading too. Lord, that thing's stiff, how'd you stand working in it?" Questions were no good. They tripped her up, reminded her how far away he was. "You should tell me I'm using too much starch, but I guess it's just like you not to." The present tense, she kept slipping into it. "The mornings are my worst time. Some days I don't get up until noon. I keep waiting for you to walk through the kitchen door. I just lie in bed wrapped up in that shirt. Ma is just dying to wash it, but I keep it hid when it's off my back. Why am I running on about laundry when today's our anniversary?"

The cautious scuttle of a small animal sounded in the underbrush. Its tail dragged through the dead leaves, ruffling them in its wake. Raccoon, or maybe opossum. It stopped short, followed by the sound of furious digging. She grabbed the magnolias and climbed out of the car. The animal blew once through its nose and the movement stilled. Definitely opossum.

The surface of the lake shone like a black mirror. She knelt at the water's edge, settled the blossoms on the surface. Faded flowers with missing petals seemed right. "There. Magnolias, just like the ones blooming on our wedding day." The flowers dipped and bobbed, striking balance with the pull of the water.

There were ghosts. She'd heard tell of them all her life. They were usually victims of an accident or violence: the train conductor killed in a derailment that walked the tracks looking for his head; the girl that died in a car wreck, then roamed the field where the car came to rest, searching for her boyfriend. The unprepared, that's who they were. Yanked from life before their time, they refused to leave.

Did it take more than tragic circumstance to make a ghost? Maybe Donald Ray's will wasn't strong enough to keep him among the living. He had never mentioned death; that was for their parents with their daily reading of the obituaries and near-regular visits to the funeral home. But then Donald Ray was the kind to go along with anything—hadn't he let her run things?—so he like as not had settled right into being dead.

There was her will. The old people told that if you cried for twelve months and one day at the grave, the dead would appear and wipe your tears. He'd loved this lake; the lake would suit him fine. Out on the water the magnolias sailed on, disappearing in the shadows thrown by poplars and sweet gums, emerging in the reflected light of the moon. Donald Ray would know when he saw her flowers, he'd know to come back.

She stared at the empty driveway through the kitchen window. Friday, her worst day. Her parents went into town right after breakfast, and Chrissie was already at the road waiting for her school bus.

Other mornings her family was here, making the sounds that annoyed her as much as they reassured her. Ma ran through the house behind Chrissie, needling her about rolling her socks right, or straightening her ponytail, new versions of the instructions she had once given Darlene. Pap stayed on in the kitchen after breakfast, his plate pushed back, the paper settled in front of him. His tongue would slide over his teeth, searching out the last of his bacon and eggs, and his lips smacked as they pulled tight over the things he read in the paper.

She could remember climbing into his lap before the school bus came, her head against his barrel chest, taking in the coffee on his breath, listening to the rumblings and workings of his insides beneath his flannel shirt, the brisk snap of his paper as he turned to a new page.

When Donald Ray was living, she could hardly wait to wake up, to be in the kitchen when he came home from working all night. And Darlene would be waiting, her hair brushed, her face scrubbed, a little lipstick on just because he loved the taste. When he came home, she pretended the house was theirs.

On Fridays it was. Once the house emptied out, she would watch the hands on the stove clock approach nine, her stomach

lurching with the same excitement she felt the first night she
gave in to Donald Ray. When she heard his car, she would pull
at the neck of her robe, at the sash, feeling the air on her skin,
her breasts, the desire to be naked with him building like the
wetness between her legs.

A rapping sound, knuckles on glass. Darlene knotted the
sash on her robe, held the collar around her neck to hide the
red lines she knew her dreaming fingers had left on her chest.

Roger Sims, the mail carrier looked at her, then at his watch.
"Nine o'clock," she could hear him telling the men at Elvin's
store when he stopped in there later this afternoon for a soft
drink. "Yes, sir, nine o'clock and she was still in her wrapper."

"Piece of certified mail here I need you to sign for." If Donald Ray were alive it'd have been him meeting Roger in the yard.
"I'm her husband," he'd say, "I can sign for that," and he would
have, his big loose hand spilling over the narrow lines of the
form. She fought back a surge of tears. The threat of breaking
down was everywhere and real. What choice did she have but
to stay locked up at home where people didn't have to see her
falling apart? The mail carrier held the papers for her while she
signed, watching her other hand on the neck of her robe.

She carried the thin envelope to the table, reading the life
insurance company's name and then the name Donald Ray had
given her: Mrs. Donald Ray Spencer. She'd never seen the name
typed up before. It had mostly been her writing it on the back
of her notebook during algebra, or on the stall door in the girls'
bathroom, making the O in Donald into a heart. The name
looked different, official and serious. She pushed the envelope
away, then pulled it back. When else would anyone write to her
as Mrs. Spencer? She slid a dinner knife under the sealed flap.
Five thousand dollars, that's what they were giving her for her
trouble.

"I don't want to sign those papers," she'd said to Donald Ray
the day she went with him to the mill to change his life insurance policy. "It feels like bad luck, talking about death before
the fact."

Donald Ray threw back his head, laughing. "Lord, Darlene, it doesn't have anything to do with us. It's just a piece of paper."

Darlene sat back, rubbed her temples. The past leapfrogged over the present inside her head. She lined up the salt and pepper shakers, the sugar bowl. He was dead; it had something to do with them after all. That's why there was a check, and if he was alive the mailman would have dropped the bills and circulars in the box at the road, shaking his head when Donald Ray tore into the driveway, kicking up gravel as he stopped short beside the house.

She fanned the check against the palm of her hand. The check was supposed to finish things. Pap had filled out the claim forms, filed the papers for her. He hadn't said as much, but she knew he was waiting, willing to indulge her until the check arrived, signaling an end to the grieving that disrupted his household. It was as if she was five and a sack of penny candy could turn her around and make her forget what she was crying for in the first place.

She'd show him. She'd show them all. She was going to buy a car, she thought, realizing it just now. Something Donald Ray would like, something he'd want her to have.

"You sure a straight gear car's what you want? You might want to think about an automatic." The salesman leaned against the side of the car, hands propped on the ridge above the white stripe. "They take some getting used to."

Darlene bent down to look in the driver's window, smelling the interior, new like a Christmas doll baby.

"White seats are mighty hard to keep up," she heard him say behind her. "And I don't know about this color, you might want something with a little more staying power. It won't be any trouble to order you something different."

She remembered the night they drove by the Chevrolet dealership to see the '63 models. "There's the color was made for you," Donald Ray had said, pointing at the aqua Impala in the showroom window. "That car can't make up its mind whether to be blue or green, but I sure could have myself a good time trying to figure it out. Your red hair'd look mighty pretty against that white interior."

She got behind the wheel, her hands locked in at ten and two o'clock. "This is what I want." She cut her eyes at the salesman.

"Maybe you ought to bring your father by with you." He hesitated, rearranged the tails of his tie, his thumbnail scraping at a spot on the material. "I want to do the right thing by you, you being alone now and all."

"Speaking of alone, I'd like to be left with the car a little bit."

The salesman held up his hands, backed toward the showroom. "Absolutely. You do that, take as long as you want."

She closed her eyes, waited for a memory to rise to the surface like cream. The power of her mind for the past had surprised her. She'd never put much effort into school and memorizing, but the thought of losing her memories of Donald Ray had frightened her into a place where she could now recall an ordinary everyday event down to the smallest detail. At times she fixed so hard on keeping each one alive that lines of pain radiated out from her forehead, running around and through the things she remembered: Donald Ray's clean fresh-scrubbed blond smell, the tiny beads of sweat that formed on his upper lip when it was hot, how the upholstery bit at her legs as she slid down the car seat to settle herself beneath him.

"Let it out easy this time, Darlene." Donald Ray had leaned toward her, one hand propped on the dash.

The clutch shot out from beneath Darlene's foot. The car lurched forward then began to roll backwards.

"Hit the brake and the clutch." His face unchanged, Donald Ray glanced over his shoulder at the ditch Darlene knew they were headed for.

She drove her feet into the pedals and the car stopped, throwing them both toward the windshield. She dared to take one hand off the wheel long enough to wipe the film of sweat off the nape of her neck. "I don't think we're going to make it up this road today."

Donald Ray reached over, pulled on the emergency brake, shifted the car into neutral. He sat back, wound his fingers through her hair, holding it off her neck. "Take your feet off those pedals and rest a minute."

Darlene obeyed him, letting the full weight of her head fall back into his hand.

His fingers worked at her skull, kneading away the pain that started at the base of her neck. "I brought you out here on this washed-out road for good reasons. First, nobody comes here this time of day. Second, if you learn to work a clutch on these hills you can handle any road. Last thing is the deserted house that's up past the lake." Donald Ray paused, stared at the road in front of them, a smile pulling at the corners of his mouth. "I snuck one of my mother's quilts out of the house a few days ago."

Darlene breathed deep, stringing his words together for herself. When she hit on the house and the quilt, she began to laugh. All the quilts she had seen at the Spencer house—dogwood, tulip, wedding ring, green lightning—floated before her eyes, patterns spinning around and changing into each other. She pictured her and Donald Ray spread out on a wedding ring quilt, as entwined as the tiny pieces of cloth and strands of thread beneath them.

"Think you can get up this hill now?" His hand moved down her neck, made a lazy circle around her breast.

Darlene leaned forward to shift into first, Donald Ray's hand traveling with her.

"Want to take her for a spin?" The salesman's voice broke her dream. She shook her head no, unsure who she was answering. She had heard Donald Ray's voice. Not just the words, but the lazy, low pitch of his speech and the easy pauses that said as much as he did. Don't cry, she ordered herself. She sat up straight, afraid to let go of the wheel and her hold on the car. "This the same car was in the window when the new models came out?"

The salesman nodded.

"Then this is the car I want." She pushed at the door handle. He scrambled to open the door for her. She stared at the bottom line of the sticker on the back window because she knew she should make a show of doing so. She looked at him. His expression was lost in the sun's glare. She shaded her eyes with her hand. "Tell me how much you're taking off the three thousand you're asking and I'll make out a check right now."

His eyes widened and Darlene knew he was figuring on how she'd come to have so much money. She ran her hand along the chrome that framed the window.

"All right, Mrs. Spencer, why don't you come on in the office? I like to get things down on paper so's I'll be telling you right the first time."

Darlene turned to follow him inside, smiling when she saw her reflection beside that of the car in the showroom window.

The woman in the window at the mill personnel office looked over the application Darlene handed her. Her penciled eyebrows shot up over the tops of her glasses when she caught the name.

"It made me real sad to hear about Donald Ray. He was a nice boy, always real nice to me."

Darlene nodded, moving her arms to air the sweat building up in her armpits. She couldn't talk about Donald Ray, not and get through this interview. "I don't want to be put on third shift." Her voice came out weak and stringy. Being here was harder than she'd thought it would be. Maybe it was that the walls were the same green she remembered from the hospital morgue, or that there were no windows, just row after row of fluorescent lights strung from one end of the low ceiling to the other. Then she remembered. This was where they'd come about changing the beneficiary on Donald Ray's life insurance. This same receptionist had pulled off her glasses when he walked in the office, swatted playfully at his hand when she passed him the form.

"Taking money away from your poor daddy and mama, are you, Donald Ray?"

"Yes, ma'am, guess I am."

"Her father will have to sign that if she's under eighteen," she'd said, pointing her glasses at Darlene before she went back to stamping envelopes.

Now the receptionist looked Darlene over as if she was trying to remember how old she was that other time. "You must be seventeen, is that right?"

"Yes, ma'am. I'd be happy to work second, but I don't want to be on third."

The woman shook her head impatiently, her eyes staying on Darlene's application. "There are no women on third shift, just the men."

Darlene breathed a sigh of relief, letting it out easy so as not to draw attention to herself. She had said men, but Darlene knew she meant boys. She wouldn't have been able to take working beside the boys that had been pallbearers for Donald Ray.

"Any area in particular interest you?"

Darlene had loved the pretty, rose-covered boxes of nylons Donald Ray brought home, the perfectly creased tissue paper inside, the pressed stockings folded evenly into thirds. "I'd like to be a folder."

The woman glanced at Darlene's hands, her lips pursed, paper-cut lines showing around her mouth. "You got to keep your hands up for that. You got to keep your hands up for all of it. Short, smooth nails. You come in with so much as a hangnail and the boss man will be filing your nails himself. They drag a nylon 'cross your hands soon as you come in the door. It catches, they pull you off to the side and go over your hands with a file and clippers. You lose your time that way. Something less careful like pre-boarding, where you pull the stocking over a leg form, might be better for you. You wear nylon gloves for that anyway." Darlene watched as the receptionist erased "folder" and wrote in "preboarder."

Darlene thought of the knickknacks that filled the surfaces in her parents' house and how she had once begged her mother to let her dust them. "We'll wait until you're more careful before we give you that job," Beulah had said. Darlene had waited, finally outgrowing her interest while Beulah continued to spend each Saturday morning dusting her tiny things.

"Well, looky here." The receptionist pulled off her glasses, her eyes shooting past Darlene's shoulder. "Where you been keeping yourself, handsome?"

The bottom dropped out of Darlene's stomach. It was the same tone she remembered the woman using with Donald Ray. She heard footsteps with the stretch of a tall man and spun around before Donald Ray could disappear on her.

Blue eyes met Darlene's, then startled, like he was the one seeing a ghost. "Mabel," he said, nodding over Darlene's head.

"You doing all right, Clayton Bishop?"

"Reckon so." He took his place behind Darlene.

She'd seen him before—at Elvin's when the school bus let her off. Leaning on the wall by the door, drawing on his cigarette, he was one of the men she had to pass to get to the drink box. Clayton Bishop. That was the name the highway patrol had called over when they came to tell her Donald Ray had been found dead.

Mabel had her glasses back on and was rushing over the application, eager to be finished with her. "It'll be six months before you get on here, Mrs. Spencer. I'd not expect to hear a thing before December or January if I was you," she warned.

"That's fine, that's all right." Darlene could feel Clayton's eyes going over the back of her. She tried to pull him together inside her head from the brief look she'd just had and what she remembered from brushing past him in Elvin's. He was a day worker; she could tell that by his skin—boys on third were white as babies—and Clayton's color was deep, telling her he spent time working outside. He was old enough to be losing his hair if he was going to, but his was thick and light brown turning to blond from the sun. Whatever else he was, he was not afraid to look at her the way the boys her age were, and that alone seemed like a big thing.

She turned to go and bumped right into him. She felt the familiar stiffness of his uniform, smelled the close air of the mill on him, the oil from the knitting machines. He touched her arm to steady her. His hand was smooth and soft. She bet he was a knitter, like Donald Ray.

5

AURILLA

Heat's a bad thing for morning sickness. That first fall I was at the Cutter house was hot, hot as the summer before. I kept soda crackers in my apron pocket the whole day. Louellen and I were so busy with the house and her children, I couldn't stop each time a wave of nausea hit me. I'd just eat a cracker and keep going.

The one time we got to rest was in the afternoon while the children napped. We'd settle them in the parlor, the coolest room in the house, spreading an old sheet out on the big hooked rug. Then the two of us would go upstairs to Louellen's room. There we were, pregnant and suffering from the heat, and headed right for the rising hot air. Heat that thick can be calming, maybe that's what we were drawn to, or maybe it was just being around Louellen's things.

Her room welcomed you, even though the walls were unfinished pine like the rest of the upstairs. Louellen came from Simmons, the county seat, where her father owned a furniture store. Every piece of bedroom furniture imaginable was crammed into that room, all of it made of mahogany so fine it shone pure red in the sun. A big wardrobe with double mirrors on the doors took up one wall. Next to the four-poster bed stood a tall chest of drawers. Beneath the window was Louellen's hope chest, and nearby, a vanity with a big round mirror. Lace curtains like Leonora's hung at the windows.

Louellen was older than me by just enough that all her courting years were shaped by the Great War. By the time Jay came along, she'd already had her share of trips to the train depot saying goodbye to the young boys going off to fight. So, when they called Jay up, she said yes to marrying him, not wanting to risk waiting to see which of those boys would make it back. He went to war and she stayed with her parents in case he was one of those that didn't come home.

And still, eight years later, what meant the most to Louellen, what she shared with me those afternoons in her room, was the emotion of that time, the hope and dread that colors everything when life comes up against war. I was too young and innocent in that first war to be aware of such things. Later, I would know that feeling, the missing and the need to prove yourself still alive. How the simplest thing—the sun going down behind a stand of red maples, or the wind rattling a field of broken corn husks—would make the longing so present, so keen, it took you to the point of pain because someone you love was gone. I learned that feeling first from Louellen's letters to Jay.

Louellen wrote him the whole time he was overseas, sometimes twice a day. He never wrote back, never mentioned her letters once he was home. She found them at the bottom of his trunk—yellowed, crumpled, dirty—and took them back as hers. She pressed the tissue-thin paper flat under the weight of her bible, sorted them, tied them into bundles with a different colored hair ribbon for each month he was away, and locked them in a little cedar chest.

When she read the letters out loud, all the affection she felt for the man she had created on paper came back to her. The blood rose in her cheeks, her voice went high and thin with excitement, and she looked nothing like the girl I had just watched drag herself from one chore to the next.

She had a favorite, one she read to me more than all the others. "This is the one about the trees," she'd say each time, "those lovely trees outside my parents' house."

Nov. 28, 1917

My darling Jay,

The leaves have all blown away and the trees, left bare, look like so many arms reaching out, stretched brittle and thin with wanting.

Remember them, the oaks that reach out to each other

from either side of the street, their branches intertwining—impossible to tell where one begins and the other leaves off? We are like those trees and I feel myself drawn to you even now with you so far away. I can feel your love winding around my heart, the shoots young and tender but already so strong I can barely breathe.

When you come home, I want us to plant two oaks— one for each of us—but closer together than the ones here so they won't have such a long wait until they touch.

Your beloved,
Louellen

She had taken the little she knew about Jay—the way his dark hair swirled out from his crown, which side of the bed he slept on, how he liked his coffee—and filled in the rest to suit herself, then set out to make him real by writing to him. This man she wrote to would listen to her read poetry at night, take walks with her and admire the spring flowers or the autumn leaves, eat supper in the summertime on a blanket spread out on the grass.

In the months since my arrival at the Cutter house, I was yet to see them do the first of these things, and there sure were no trees. Louellen's writing was just her wishing it was so, like me thinking I could draw Joe out of his darkness.

The letters were folded every which way, saying Jay had once read them as much as Louellen did now. When she smoothed out the paper on her lap, her hands lightly pressing the paper flat, creases marked with dirt crossed the page like the shifting borders of warring countries. Marveling at the stained paper, I pictured Jay huddled in some trench in France, an open, ready grave he'd dug with his own hands, fingering the letters he kept in his pocket, working hard to convince himself the world he knew was still there.

Or maybe, with death all over him, the letters sounded like heaven; they were that removed from the world. *"Oh, I have sown my love so wide that you will find it everywhere,"* she wrote to him from her favorite poem. *"It will awaken you in the night, it will enfold you in the air."*

All her talk about moonlight and the wind speeding her love to him, he must have forgotten it as soon as he was safe on a ship sailing for home. But that didn't hold for Louellen. Those letters kept her going. How lonely were things for her when she first came to the Cutter house? She was there three years before Louise was born, Mrs. Cutter eyeing her up each month to see if she was carrying a boy. Like his mother and Joe, Jay worked from dawn until dark. And like them he sat silent in the parlor in the evenings, his head nodding over the evening paper as it slowly slid out of his hands.

As much as Louellen read to me, she never reached for the letters at the bottom of her cedar box. Pale blue, her writing looped across those clean pink envelopes as big and loose as a school child's, looking fresh and new and for all the world like the letters I saw her write to her parents each week.

"Those pink ones, are they some you wrote and never mailed?" I asked one day as Louellen rummaged through the box. She sat like this every afternoon, picking up this packet, then that one, until something made her settle on one.

Louellen laughed her weak little laugh, the one that came when she had done something awkward and been found out, like the time she left the sugar out of the Sunday pies. She shook her head, not yes or no. She grabbed a bundle of letters, closed the box and turned the key, and pretended to be occupied with untying the ribbon.

That was Louellen, looking off and fiddling with things when she didn't want to talk about something. I saw she wouldn't tell so I made up a story to suit myself. She was still writing letters to the boy she'd invented when the war was on and everything about living seemed urgent. She couldn't talk to Jay about the way things made her feel, not face-to-face and finally seeing him for what he was. Instead, she poured her heart out, still, to that sweet boy who never came home.

Louellen did have Hank. He loved poems and stories as much as her. He spent his free time in the barn loft with the books he brought back from the town library. She'd be off working by herself, stringing beans or shelling peas, and he'd come find her, always an open book in his hand. I would see them bent over the pages, their heads almost touching, the bowl in Louellen's lap forgotten. Sometimes she read, her voice traveling into the same register of excitement she got when she read Jay's letters. But mostly it was him, intent and interested in a way that had become totally foreign to me in my short time in the Cutter house. Looking at them was like looking into the sun. I was so cut off from my own way of thinking about and seeing the world that seeing them made the sadness unbearable.

Boiling water rushed around the mason jars, filled the kitchen with steam. The air was thick with the sweet smell of overripe tomatoes. Using tongs, I lifted a jar of tomatoes—the last mess of the season—from the canner. I held the jar to the window, looking for the orange-red color that would tell me this jar was ready. Louellen worked beside me, reaching again and again into the simmering pot of blanched tomatoes, the skins she removed piling up on the newspaper spread out on the counter. She filled each jar, handing it to me to be fitted with a lid before I put it in the canner.

I motioned to the pot of tomatoes. "How many more jars do you think you'll be able to make with what you have there?" We had waited until the children's nap time to start canning, not wanting them underfoot. The afternoon was warming up, making the work oppressive.

Louellen stirred the tomatoes, releasing more heat into the already stifling air of the kitchen. "Probably these two here, maybe one more." Holding the spoon, she used the back of her hand to brush away the wisps of hair clinging to her damp forehead. Her palm was as red as the tomatoes she stirred.

"You've scalded your hand!" I said, angered by her carelessness. "Let's see the other one."

"It's such hot work I wanted to get it over with." Louellen opened her other palm, reluctant as a guilty child.

"We could have waited for them to cool. What good did you think you'd be to me with burnt hands? Now I'll have this to finish by myself." I went to the cupboard for salve.

Louellen took the gauze and the scissors from the pantry, and waited for me at the worktable. "I'm sorry. I know I just make things harder for you," she said.

I rubbed the salve gently over Louellen's flushed hands. I looked up at her face, pale even in this heat, and her eyes, ringed with black and hollow from fatigue. I was no better than Mrs. Cutter who rode Louellen day in and out, criticizing everything she did.

"There's not an ounce of truth in that, Louellen Cutter." I tied the gauze into soft bows around her wrists. "It must be the heat making me snap like that. You go on upstairs and rest. It won't take me a minute to do up the rest of the tomatoes."

I turned back to the stove. The tomatoes had cooled and slipped easily from their skins. Louellen took the stairs slowly, stopping to rest at the landing. It was nothing short of cruel, bringing a girl that frail into this house where there was nothing but work. I wondered at Jay for making such a mistake and at Louellen's parents for allowing it.

Our afternoon's work filled a full pantry shelf. I climbed the stairs to Louellen's room, walking softly in case she had fallen asleep. Louellen lay on the bed, her eyes closed, her letter box unopened beside her. With her fine blond hair and her pinafore apron, she looked nothing more than a girl, though she was seven years older than me.

"I didn't think it'd be like this, so hard here, did you?" she asked, her eyes still closed.

I guessed I did know better than her. Louellen had married Jay never setting eyes on this place. He was just another boy in a uniform going off to fight in places she couldn't even pronounce the names of. She'd come to this house feeling she'd chosen right and that this was her happy ending to two years of waiting. I came pregnant, with my eyes wide open, and no choice to do otherwise. In my mind I saw Mother standing up for me in the office of the justice of the peace, her face as withdrawn and unreadable as Joe's. I had lost everything, my mother, my home, even my ideas about what Joe was like.

"Life is never what you think it's going to be," I said. "If it was, there wouldn't be any point in living. Why don't I brush your hair for you, Louellen? It may put you to sleep."

Jay had brought her a brush, comb, and mirror back from France—her vanity set, Louellen called it. It was all gold with blue roses painted on the backs of the mirror and brush and across the top of the comb. The gold had faded, the handles worn down to silver from her touch, the petals of the flowers chipped.

"You can have this when I'm done with it, Aurilla." The heat and the sound of the brush pulling through her hair had nearly put Louellen to sleep.

"That's silly. I'll be so old by then there won't be anything left to comb. You leave it for your oldest girl."

She shook her head, making the brush catch in her tangled ends. "No, Louise's hair is fine like mine, she won't do it justice either. Besides, I know you appreciate pretty things." She watched me, her light blue eyes waiting.

I looked around the room at all that dark rich wood, then back at Louellen, fragile as a porcelain doll, and nodded acceptance of her gift, my hand following the half-moon curve of her head.

Louellen's labor began in the dead of February. I woke before daylight to the sound of her moaning and sleet tapping on the window. "Bony fingers," my brother Arnold had whispered from his room across the hall whenever there was a winter storm. "It's the dead," he'd say, in a calm accepting voice that made me think they had hold of him already. Louellen's suffering and the falling ice came together, sending chills through me. I wrapped myself in the dogwood blossom quilt my mother had made for my hope chest, wishing she was still down the hall for comfort.

I heard talk outside, Hank and Jay, and the thin voices of the children, tired and peevish from being awakened so early. The lantern in Jay's hand swung as he tried to steady the horse. The shifting circles of light showed the deep snow and Hank lifting the children into the wagon.

"Tell the Cravens I'll come for the children tomorrow." The cold air carried Jay's voice so clear it was like he was right in the room beside me.

Louellen was having her baby today and everything was going just as Mrs. Cutter had planned. Hank was taking the children to the nearest neighbors. Wrapped in cheesecloth on the seat beside him was the smokehouse ham she was sending along to help feed them. After he left the Cravens', he would ride into town to get Doctor Frazier. I watched the wagon until it was no more than a black speck in a swirl of white. My time would come in spring; I was grateful for that.

"I don't see a thing, Louellen, but I'm sure Hank will be here with the doctor anytime." I turned from the window and smiled at her. Louellen nodded, her head dropping back to the pillow. Outside the snow was coming down thick; there was nothing to see but white. The chill I woke with lingered; not even standing by the big fire Jay had built changed that. The cold air seeped in around the windowpanes, but it was more than the cold outside I was feeling. I was uneasy watching Louellen. Giving birth looked a lot like dying to me. There was someone to wipe your head, hold your hand, but you had to do it alone.

I had never been told a thing about labor, let alone seen it. There were limits with my mother, and it was second nature with me, knowing what was acceptable talk and what was not. When I first got the curse and went to Leonora, she pointed out a stack of torn up sheets in the linen closet, telling me there'd be a fresh pile there for me each month. She never said a word about the rags that stayed on the shelf untouched the month after my day at the creek with Joe, the same ones left behind when I left the house, two weeks later, pregnant and married.

Living with the Cutters, I had come to see a remove in Leonora I'd never realized was there. All the years she had measured women, molded cloth to their bodies. Leonora must look at them the way she did the dress forms in her workroom—nothing more than shapes for draping cloth around. I remembered watching her fit a collar on a customer's dress, her mouth full of pins, her flared nostrils barely moving with the shallow breaths she took to avoid taking in the woman's scent.

"Aurilla," Louellen called, her voice faint. "Brush my hair for me, just for a bit."

I was relieved to have something to do that fit in with how we were day-to-day with each other. All morning I'd sat in the chair beside her, sponging the tiny beads of sweat on her forehead, her eyes staring off like some hurt animal that doesn't understand what's happening. I kept thinking of the rabbit Joe caught behind the barn last week. The poor thing lay there panting, its leg nearly chewed off by the trap, its eyes glazed over like they were fixed on something distant.

My baby moved, tiny fists and feet making my stomach rise and fall. I ran my hand over my middle, my palm catching on the wales of my corduroy shift. "Things will work out fine, Louellen. This baby will get here just like the other three did. Tonight, you'll be reading me a letter with it curled up asleep in your arms."

"Really, Aurilla?" Louellen's eyes were even paler than usual, the irises fading right into the whites. She saw through everything I was telling her. "I almost drowned once." She grimaced, waited for a contraction to pass. "I couldn't have been more than four years old. We were swinging on vines at the creek behind our house, my brother and me, and mine broke. The water was barely over my head, I knew that. I could see the surface cloudy with mud above me and signs of light above that. But after a while, I didn't care. My brother got to me in time, but can't nobody pull me out of this, it's like a weight is pulling me to the bottom."

"Don't talk like that," I said. "It's bad luck."

A pain stopped Louellen. She breathed heavy, riding it out. "Every child that's come there's been less of me to deal with it each time. You watch that yarrow out there, it'll be just like me when spring comes—dry, dead stalks with tiny green plants shooting out from its roots."

There was no yarrow, no garden, nothing but dirt all around this house and snow on top of that. Maybe talking about her brother had made her think of home. I thought of Anny, the colored woman who did the wash for Leonora on Saturdays, and the golden tonic she made from those tight yellow blossoms. She was like a doctor to the colored. Sometimes when she came, she had been up all night with the sick. "She saw her death," she'd say, talking more to herself than Leonora. "Yes, ma'am, she did. Looked right at it with eyes sharp as hen's teeth and named it out loud. Told me just how it was going to go. When I seen that look, I know my work's done. I seen it enough to know."

I listened to Anny's stories from my hiding place behind the pantry door, straining to catch her words above the slap of the wet clothes against the washboard. I had instructions to stay away from her. Leonora said Anny's talk was not meant for ears young as mine. Leonora was so dignified, death and dirt had nothing to do with her.

I heard the wagon and my body went loose with relief. "Hank's back with the doctor."

Louellen nodded, her eyes closed. "Hank," she murmured, her voice hardly more than a whisper. I leaned close to her mouth to hear. "A comfort…let him be…"

Louellen's voice was lost in the sounds of arrival and greeting downstairs. Mrs. Cutter asked about the roads as she led the way upstairs. "It's Doc Frazier come, Louellen." She came straight to the bed, pulling the covers right off Louellen. "Baby's turned wrong. The pains started in the middle of the night and the baby's not moving down."

She could have been out in the barn talking about a calving

for all the regard she showed Louellen. Listening to her made my face burn but Louellen was so ragged out she didn't seem to hear or care.

Doctor Frazier nodded, his stooped back bent over the wash basin. The harsh, no-nonsense smell of Mrs. Cutter's lye soap filled the room. He had brought us all into the world, anybody my age or younger. He turned around, the towel slung over his shoulder. "Now let's see if we can't change this bullheaded baby's mind."

His confident tone sounded through the stillness, like lamps going on all over the house. Even Louellen responded. Her eyes opened, focusing hard on his face.

"I don't want any marked babies in this house, Aurilla. Your time for seeing a birth will come soon enough." Mrs. Cutter rolled up the sleeves of her black wool dress, the cloth bunching around her elbows. "You go on downstairs and get the boys' dinner started."

I squeezed Louellen's hand. "See, everything's going to be just fine." I hurried out of the room, not wanting Louellen to see my relief at being dismissed.

I was one for making a big racket in the kitchen, but not that day. With Louellen's room right above, I checked myself. I put the pine knots in the woodstove one by one, and when I filled the bean pot with water I did it a dipperful at a time.

I could have fought Mrs. Cutter and stayed; I read her well enough to know when I could push her on things. But it was like being released from prison when she told me to leave the room. I listened hard, setting spoons down on the counter instead of letting them fall, telling myself if Louellen called out for me I'd rush right up to her. I heard the doctor coaxing Louellen and Mrs. Cutter demanding, but I didn't hear a sound from Louellen.

The men came in for dinner. I stayed in the kitchen picking at my food. Joe and Hank were still in the dining room when Jay brought in his plate. He scraped his dinner into the slop jar by the pantry door.

"You heard anything yet?" he asked, his eyes angled up at the ceiling. Before I could answer, he was in the mudroom shuffling into his heavy jacket, buckling his boots. "You yell for me when something happens. I'll be in the barn. You call for me right out this door."

He held the door open, pointing to the barn with his gloved hand. Drifts of loose snow blew in around his feet. I nodded, moving behind the door and out of reach of the cold air, my hand on the knob ready to close the door behind him.

Jay ignored the path the men had dug that morning, walking instead through the fresh snow. I heard each step he took, his feet breaking through the thin crust of ice to the soft snow below. The snow was over his boot tops and deeper in places. Maybe this was his way of empathizing with Louellen, as if nothing should be too easy for him as long as she suffered.

The sun broke through the clouds. Low, it hit all that white, giving off a light as blue as the veins that showed through the skin at Louellen's temples.

All my listening and waiting hit me. I was tired; my baby was using me up too. I stoked the dying cook fire with the poker. Hot cinders flew onto my hand, singeing the light hairs there. I plunged my hand into the water I'd poured to heat for washing the dishes.

This thing was going to happen to me, too, and just like Louellen said, there was no one that could save me. The days of the next three months would roll over one another until it would be me upstairs with Doctor Frazier and Mrs. Cutter, the two of them hanging over me, ordering my body to obey.

I dropped my plate and Jay's into the steaming water. They sank to the bottom, the grease from the ham rising slowly to the surface, glistening.

Joe and Hank came through the kitchen and headed into the mudroom. "You going to have supper ready at the usual time?" That was just like Joe. The house could be coming down around his ears and he'd want to know when he would eat next.

"Don't you be worried. Nobody's going to let you starve," I

answered, not bothering to turn to look at him. I heard Hank snort and Joe mumble. There was just the sound of them dressing for the outdoors and the slap of my wet dishrag on the counter.

"Aurilla." Hank stood at the door, his cap in his hand. "She's going to be all right." There was just the hint of a question in his voice but fear and pleading shone in his eyes, their liveliness snuffed out.

"Yes, she is," I lied for both of us.

With the men gone there was just the murmur of voices upstairs, the ticking of the mantel clock in the parlor. I left the dishes to soak and climbed the stairs to my room, too tired to bother with wood for the tin heater by the bed.

This time yesterday, we had headed upstairs, Louellen and me carrying a bucket of wood between us, the girls carrying sticks of kindling. After we tucked the children in under a pile of quilts on my bed, we settled down to read a few letters, her crocheted blanket pulled up to our chins. It had seemed we would go on like that forever, caught up in a rhythm of working and talking that came as easy as breathing.

At the landing I leaned against the railing, regaining the wind my baby took. Down the hall I heard Louellen struggle for air as her baby fought its way out of her.

I fell into bed and the place between sleep and dreams. Louellen was there, in the kitchen churning butter. I was just married and the two of us were pregnant. "When you have a child, you get back the part of you that's unspoiled and this time, you're the one that gets to do the loving," Louellen said. Her words came out in rhythm with the dasher hitting the bottom of the churn. The sound of clabbered milk sloshing against the clay walls of the churn made me retch. I opened the icebox and sat on the floor, my head halfway inside, breathing in the cool air until the heat boiling up from my center began to settle down. Pregnant, I felt as rooted in the present as an animal. I sat watching Louellen, unable to move, my back against the icebox. It was late morning in the dream and already Louellen's legs were swollen, her ankles pushing over her shoes. Her feet went on growing. They toppled the churn, filled the kitchen. I pushed her away, fighting for the room I needed for myself. "Don't leave without your soda crackers." Louellen managed to wave the napkin-wrapped bundle she kept in her pocket above the mound of flesh taking her over. "Have yourself a cracker and just you watch how it works."

I startled awake to a dark room and the sound of a baby crying. Mrs. Cutter and Jay were downstairs at the front door, seeing Doctor Frazier off. I heard the relief and exhaustion in their voices. The lamp was on by Louellen's bed. She lay white and still, her eyes closed, the baby in the crook of her arm. Her head dropped over to the side of the pillow as if she was too exhausted to hold it up. Her hair clumped at the back of her neck in a dark gold snarl. Through her open mouth breath came in uneven rasps.

"Louellen," I called softly, moving one step at a time toward her. The baby's eyes were closed too, the red in its face deepening with effort as it sucked hard on Louellen's thumb. Another girl. No boy came into the world looking so delicate and finely made.

"Louellen," I said again. She smiled, her eyes still closed. It could have been something else made her smile, holding her baby at last and feeling the pull of its mouth on her finger, or a dream she was in, but I told myself it was the sound of my voice and knowing I was with her that brought her pleasure.

I pulled a chair up to the bed. "This time you're going to get your rest, Louellen. I'm here and I can do all the work until you're able. This time it will be different for you." I felt cleansed saying this to her, an atonement for my desertion earlier this afternoon.

"Is she sleeping?"

Hank stood in the doorway, poised to turn and go.

"I think so, but I'm sure she'd still like the company."

He smiled awkwardly, holding up the small book in his hand.

"I thought I'd read to her."

"I'm sure that'd soothe her." I made to get up, offering him my chair.

He touched my shoulder. "No, you stay too."

He was scared, as scared as me.

I kept my seat. Hank sat by me on the bed. He began to read, his voice as hesitant and soft as the light flurry that fell outside. "Oh, I have sown my love so wide that he will find it everywhere; It will awake him in the night, it will enfold him in the air."

The familiar poem, loved so by Louellen, brought tears to my eyes. I joined Hank for the last verse, our voices rising together like a prayer. "I set my shadow in his sight / and I have winged it with desire, that it may be a cloud by day and in the night a shaft of fire."

It was still dark the next morning when I woke to Jay shouting for his mother. With trembling hands, I lit the lamp and woke Joe. It was something bad, I knew it, and little help that he was, him being with me meant I didn't have to go see alone.

Mrs. Cutter held the baby, bouncing her, the rough motion making the child's cries come out in choked gasps. Jay stood at the foot of the bed, the legs of his long handle underwear soaked with blood, his hands hanging limp. He stared at the baby, listening hard as though the answer to all this was locked somewhere in her cries. The weak light made by the lamp I carried showed blood-soaked sheets and Louellen's bare blue leg.

Louellen had to be dead; nobody living had color like that, but I couldn't do a thing with what I was seeing. The first thing that came to my mind was—I've got to get back to bed and get some more sleep; then—I've got to change Louellen's sheets, she'll catch a chill from the damp.

"What are you doing just standing here?" I looked from Jay to his mother. "Why aren't you doing anything to help her?"

"She's hemorrhaged." Mrs. Cutter's voice was as flat and even as if she had said, *She's sleeping.* She looked right at me, like this was women's knowledge she was speaking.

"Then go for the doctor, Joe, go right now!" my voice came out thin and high. Unable to get my breath to say more, I pushed him toward the stairs. Joe stood solid, his eyes fixed on his mother's face.

"Why are you looking at her?" I screamed. "Listen to me!"

"Aurilla," Mrs. Cutter said, impatient, as if I was a dense child that can't catch on, "she's bled to death."

I thought again of Anny; she had birthing stories, too, and she told them in a tone as matter-of-fact as Mrs. Cutter's. "Lord, Miz McMath, my arms is sure sore today. Me and three more kneaded Mary Bingham's belly the whole night long to keep her from bleeding to death. Baby come too fast or be too big, the womb can't stop itself from letting loose blood."

I heard Louellen's words, "No one can pull me out of this, it's like a weight pulling me to the bottom." Had Louellen awakened this morning, realized she was nearly gone? I imagined her raising her hand to touch Jay's shoulder, then, in an act of immense will, changing her mind, letting it drop to the wet mattress, her life warming her as it seeped away.

"How did you let this happen?" I said to Jay. "You were right here beside her the whole night and you let her die?" Mrs. Cutter and Joe called my name in harsh whispers, like they could get me to stop before Jay noticed what I was saying.

"She never made a sound." Jay's voice faltered like he was trying to make it true for himself. "Quiet as a mouse. I didn't know a thing until the baby woke up hungry this morning."

He'd told the truth when he said he didn't know a thing and his ignorance went way past last night. I was angrier with him for never letting Louellen live than with letting her die. Her voice came into my head again. I wondered how much longer I would be able to recall it, clear and present as my own. How long would I remember what Louellen's eyes looked like, or the sound of her laugh? Sitting with Louellen last night, I had been glad she was asleep, relieved I didn't have to hear what my friend had been through. My face burned in shame at my selfishness.

Mrs. Cutter deposited the baby in my arms. "Take her on downstairs and make up a sugar teat. That's the best can be done until we get some canned milk. Joe, wake Hank and send him into town for the undertaker, and have him send a telegram to Louellen's parents. Jay, get some dry clothes on and then get me a pitcher of water and some rags. And, Aurilla, once you've got the baby settled, I want you to pick out a dress for Louellen."

I stared at her, looking for the thing that made her able to go on thinking and acting in the face of death. And then I saw it; Louellen's passing meant nothing to her, so little that she couldn't imagine it mattered to anyone else.

"Don't just stand there cow-eyed, Aurilla. That baby needs to eat."

Joe walked downstairs with me, the lamp held high to light my way. "I'm sorry, I know Louellen was good company for you." He stopped on the landing, as if he meant to say more. He gave my back an awkward pat.

"Good company?" I pulled away from him. "What would you know about that?"

He had reached out to comfort me and I had turned him away. Maybe I just didn't know how to let him be good to me. The baby started to fuss again. I stuck my thumb in the baby's mouth the way I saw Louellen do the night before. She quieted down, the pull of her tiny lips on my finger regular as a pulse. She burrowed into my chest and I pulled her closer, wanting to make Louellen's baby as safe as the baby inside me.

Hesitant, Joe stroked his finger across the baby's forehead. I thought of that day by the creek, and him with his ducks. He touched this new baby with more tenderness than I would expect from any man. "How much milk should I tell Hank to get?" he asked.

What could I say to make him touch me like he had touched the baby? Tears flooded my eyes and I buried my face in the baby's head until she stirred and began to cry. She batted at my thumb, hungry and frustrated by my dry finger.

"What about the milk?" Joe asked again.

I had no idea how much milk a baby took, no idea how long they did anything, and I resented his thinking I did. The responsibility that had dropped on me opened up wide and inescapable, demanding that I make decisions. The little I did know about babies came from Louellen. "Sugar teat is the best thing in the world to settle a little baby," she'd said, not a week ago. "Just some sugar wrapped in a piece of cloth shaped like a nipple calms them right down." I had hardly listened, figuring I'd just ask her when the time came what I needed to know. Now I tried to think of anything she might have said about feeding.

Joe watched me, waiting for my answer. "Just tell Hank to ask the clerk," I snapped. "They sell it, they must know. And have him ask about bottles, how many you need."

I lunged past him, moved toward the first light coming through the kitchen windows. I settled the baby in the laundry basket Louellen had already made up for her, cushioned with the worn pink and yellow blankets used by her other girls.

Stirring water into the sugar, I thought about a dress for Louellen. All of her clothes had been let out to grow with a baby then taken in and let out again, the seams uneven and riddled with holes made by her needle.

There were my clothes, the dresses Mother had made for me the last spring I lived at home. I wanted something covered with flowers since there would be none for Louellen this time of year. I settled on the pink drop waist with the rosebuds.

The sun was up, the light off the snow bathed the room. Exhausted from crying, the baby slept, her mouth open, tiny bubbles forming there. "Like dew on a rose," I whispered, my voice full of the power of naming, "a beautiful Rose for your mother."

6

Darlene

"There'll never be a senior prom for you if you get married this year." Beulah worked a knife around the tube pan, loosening the warm pound cake. "You can't go with Donald Ray to his prom, being a year behind him like you are, but he could take you to yours next year if you wait. When Pap let you get engaged, you swore you'd finish school before marrying. Now you're telling me you can't wait till Donald Ray graduates."

Darlene watched her mother fill the pan with hot water and soap and scrub it clean. The gleaming counters were bare except for the cake and the bowl of lemon icing. Beulah believed in totally finishing one thing before going on to the next. Darlene swirled her finger in the icing. "What do I care about missing some silly dance? I'll have a wedding, won't I, and it'll be just for me, not for a whole gym full of kids. I know I'll be the queen there."

"You're rushing things, Darlene, getting ahead of yourself." Beulah took the bowl from her and spread the icing over the pound cake with the back of a dinner knife. "Next thing I know you'll have me in the attic pulling out baby things. This time don't come back, I can tell you that much. You go right ahead and see if you still feel like a queen when all your girlfriends are up at Teen Haven and Belk's looking for the right dress and you're home scraping potatoes for your husband's dinner."

"I don't do the cooking, Ma, you do." Darlene slid her arms around Beulah's waist. "Besides," she said, settling her chin into the familiar dip in her mother's shoulder and swaying her left and right, "Donald Ray and I can dance right here in the kitchen if we want to."

That spring was here, the spring that would have been her prom time. Darlene had hardly shown her face since the funeral. The only time she left the house was to go to the lake late at night. She refused calls from her friends until they stopped trying. All except for Faye. Not that Darlene would talk to her either, but Beulah did. She heard Beulah murmuring into the phone, her voice shifting into a clipped code whenever Darlene walked past. Darlene and Faye had not been that close, but Faye had a stubborn sense of duty that kept her from giving up on things, whether it was a lab assignment, raising money for African orphanages, applying to colleges, or now, Darlene.

Soon Faye began appearing at the supper table, everybody acting like her presence was the most natural thing in the world. Darlene was too worn down by solitude and the effort of calling up the past to resist her. Faye never asked Darlene how she was feeling or holding up; she didn't steal sympathetic glances at her when she thought she wasn't looking.

Faye let her be, and Darlene let Faye, with her quiet little voice, slight frame, and unassuming manner, push her: first into driving into town for an ice cream cone, and a week later, the movies. Faye put herself between Darlene and the curious eyes that followed them from the car and back again. When people started in with "oh, honey, I'm so sorry," Faye steered the talk away from Donald Ray and condolences to the weather and idle gossip. Nobody got to her with Faye around and that gave Darlene the room to get back a little of herself.

"I could help out prom night." Darlene held a white satin dress up to Faye, hung it back on the rack. With Faye's blond hair and sallow coloring, white washed her right out. "You're the prom committee chairman," Darlene said. "If you say I can serve punch or hand out programs, then I can." The week before they'd gone to see a return engagement of *Gone with the Wind*. Darlene took it in her head that like Scarlett, there was a way for her to be at the dance, and maybe someone as brave as Rhett

Butler would ask her to take a turn on the floor with him. If nothing else, she could sit behind the refreshment table with Faye, who didn't have a date, her foot tapping away to the music.

"Faye," Darlene whispered, when Faye didn't answer. "I think I might die if I have to sit at home by myself that night."

Faye shook her head. "I don't know, Darlene. The prom theme is *Blue Hawaii*, not *Gone with the Wind*." She and Faye had spent so much time together in the last month they were developing a knack for following each other's thoughts. "There was a war going on in that movie, people were used to young widows."

Darlene moved farther down the wall to the dresses in her own size. What would it hurt to look for something she liked? Mrs. Ritter, the store's owner, had favored pastels this year. Baby blue, pale yellow, light pink. The colors repeated, only the cut of the dresses changed. Until the green tulle. She took it off the rack, pulling the netting away from the aqua satin underskirt. Iridescent sequins covered the strapless bodice. She turned the dress in the light, watching it glimmer and change like something alive.

Faye shook her head, parting dresses to look at another pink gown. "Not that, Darlene. I look horrible in green."

Sometimes Faye's single-mindedness annoyed her. "Who said anything about you?"

Faye's pale eyes took up her whole face. "You? You can't wear that thing."

Darlene's finger flew to Faye's lips. She pointed to the open door of the fitting room where Mrs. Ritter knelt fitting Martha Rafferty's white dress. Her heart pounded with excitement and a sense of danger. "Just carry it back like you're trying it on yourself," she whispered, piling the dress on top of the pink one in Faye's arms.

Darlene turned her in the direction of the dressing room, ignoring the flush that spread over her friend's face and neck. "That green's all wrong for you, Faye," Mrs. Ritter said around the pins in her mouth. "Better go with the pink."

"Yes, ma'am." Faye rushed past her to the dressing room at

the far end. Unlike the dressing rooms at Belk's, Mrs. Ritter had outfitted her spacious fitting rooms with three-way mirrors and louvered doors instead of flimsy curtains. Darlene was halfway out of her clothes before Faye had the door closed.

"Well, it is pretty." Faye held the dress as Darlene pulled it over her head.

Darlene closed her eyes then turned to look in the mirror. Somewhere the ocean looked like this, she'd seen pictures in magazines, the water almost white at the edges, then fading to a rich blue-green that showed the depth of the sea. "Hawaii," she murmured. She thought of the Honolulu Inn in Myrtle Beach where she and Donald Ray spent their honeymoon. No dress could be more perfect.

"You can't mean you'd wear it to the prom." Faye stared into the mirror, her pale narrow face the picture of horror and disbelief.

The prom. Darlene swayed back and forth, imagining how the dress would look under the colored lights in the gym.

"I thought you just wanted to try it on for fun," Faye pleaded, "to see how it looked."

Darlene fluffed the puffed voile sleeves of the pink gown over Faye's bony shoulders. The dress did soften her some. "This is the color for you. Now just tell Mrs. Ritter you're taking both dresses home, that you can't make up your mind."

Faye shook her head, disappearing under the dress as Darlene pulled it over her head. "You heard her. She'll never let me out of here with that green thing."

Mrs. Ritter was notorious for bossing her customers, not that she'd ever dared try it with Darlene. The dress was expensive, a third again as much as Faye's. And she could buy it without asking or answering to anyone. She opened her wallet, counted out the twenties. "Oh yes, she will, look at the price tags. She's as interested in turning a profit as the next one."

Mrs. Ritter stood behind the counter finishing up with Martha. She looked at Faye over her half-glasses. "What'd you decide, Faye?"

Darlene kicked the back of Faye's leg.

"That's just it, I can't. I'd like to take them both home."

"I can't see the point in that. You're much too pale to carry off that green. It's meant for someone—" She stole a glance at Darlene, then busied herself with the price tags. "Someone with more color." She punched the numbers in her register. "But then it is your senior prom, you ought to be able to suit yourself."

One short blast on the horn; Faye would respond. Darlene ran around to the trunk. She opened the box and lifted her dress out of its bed of pink tissue. The setting sun glanced off the bodice, turning the sequins a color more gold than green. She had looked at the dress at every opportunity and in all kinds of light, but she hadn't dared remove it from its careful wrappings. Shook free, the tulle and satin skirt shimmered and changed just as she remembered. Hers would be the most beautiful dress of all. She just wished Beulah could see her.

Faye came down the steps holding the tail of her dress, walking on tiptoe like she might trip and fall.

"Didn't you get that dress shortened?" Lucky for Darlene she was tall enough not to have to worry about hem lengths since there wasn't anywhere she could have taken her dress for alterations without setting off half the tongues in the county.

"Now how was I going to do that?" Faye asked. "Mrs. Ritter would be wanting to know where that green dress was. I'll never be able to shop in Teen Haven again. And why aren't you dressed?"

Darlene looked down at the navy blue shift her mother had made for her when she told her she was going to the dance. "I already am, far as my mother knows." Darlene climbed in the back seat, folding her dress in with her. "Come on, drive, Faye."

"I can't drive this thing, it's too fast." Her hands fastened on her hips, Faye had forgotten all about her dress tail.

"You want me to start pulling off my clothes right here?" Darlene reached for the zipper on her dress.

Faye opened the car door, slammed it behind her, opened it again to release her dress. "You're nothing but trouble, Darlene Spencer, that's all."

The car lurched into reverse, hurling the dress to the floor. The curtains at the picture window of Faye's house parted. Darlene saw Faye's mother watching, her eyes full of questions. Darlene waved to her and the curtain dropped.

"You worry too much about what people think," Darlene said. The car bolted forward, throwing Darlene against the seat. "This is not your mama's Chevy wagon, Faye. You don't have to press the pedal to the floor."

Faye nodded, pulling back on the gas, her hands frozen on the wheel.

"Can you reach back here and pull this zipper down the rest of the way?" Darlene positioned her back between the bucket seats.

"I'm scared to let go of the wheel. Wait until we get to a straight piece of road."

Darlene leaned forward, freeing Faye's right hand. "You don't have to turn around, I'll guide your hand."

In her mind she led Donald Ray's hand from the middle of her back to the front snap of the bra she'd ordered out of the back of a magazine. The warmth she'd felt that night when her breasts were freed under his hand started between her legs, spread out over her thighs. She needed to be touched like a woman who was used to being touched. What girl her age besides her knew this feeling? Maybe slutty Cindy Phelps who gave it away to half the football team. The rest of the girls at the prom would be fretting about what this special evening meant and whether they should let their dates touch their breasts or slide their fingers inside their underpants.

Donald Ray had made her this way, the two of them trying things he'd only read about in magazines. How surprised could she be that she still wanted it? The depth of her need rose up to claim her. She sank beneath the layers of satin and tulle that took up the whole back seat. Sometimes, when she was alone in the car, she heard him, just like she had that day at the dealership. She listened, but there was just the thrum of the dual exhausts and the steady yammer of Faye's worrying.

She pulled the dress over her head, drawing the zipper up as far as she could. "One more time, Faye."

"There's probably a hook and eye at the top like mine," said Faye. "I'll get it when we stop."

The satin bodice was cold against Darlene's chest. She could just imagine a boy's hand lowering the zipper, the satin sliding down to reveal her breasts, him pulling her to him, the tiny black buttons on his tuxedo shirt digging into her skin, the starched pleats against her nipples. Maybe Faye would forget about the hook. She sank back into her dress, ready for the dance to begin.

Color wheels in blue and green, the kind Beulah used to light her aluminum Christmas tree, glowed from behind palm trees made with trunks of wrapped burlap and fronds fashioned with clumps of ferns. A trail of smoke fizzled from the giant papier-mâché volcano filled with dry ice that took up most of the stage. Overhead, an arc of chicken wire wove in and out of the rafters twinkled with small white Christmas lights. Couples wearing bright-colored plastic leis shuffled around the gym floor with the awkward hesitation of bodies that don't know each other.

Darlene kicked at the grass skirt tacked around the refreshment table. She was a fool to come. How young was young enough to pretend the lights were stars, that burlap was bark? She was doing a miserable job of being seventeen and fooling no one.

The boys hadn't dared look her in the face, not even the ones that came mumbling, asking for punch. No one said the first word about her dress, and now, even Faye was dancing. It was as if she were invisible, no more than air that everybody looked through and moved around. She stood on tiptoe. She could just make out Faye, a pimply boy swinging her around so fast her gown filled with air, lifting off the floor by itself. Darlene thought of cotton candy swirling around and around a Popsicle stick.

"How about some of that punch?" a deep male voice asked.

Her eyes half on Faye, she filled two cups.

"I don't think I can handle more than one at a time, that is, unless you'd care to join me?"

Darlene felt her face turn red. She smiled at the new gym teacher, the one who had come this last year since she left school. "I don't think I should leave the table with Faye still out there."

He nodded, moving around the table to Faye's seat. "That's all right, I can sit here with you."

Darlene sat down, pulling her skirt in to give him room. He was tall and big with it. He loosened his trouser legs over his knees and sat down. She remembered driving by the school and seeing him on the ball field, his thick ropy thighs pulling against the blue gym shorts as he ran alongside the boys, lips pursed tight over his whistle.

"I don't believe I've seen you around." He took a sip of his punch, set the cup on the edge of the table. A trace of the red liquid stayed on his lips, making them seem fuller than before. He was handsome in a clean, square-jawed athletic way.

"Oh no, I'm not in school anymore," she said with a laugh meant to make him think she was older. She turned her ankle, pretending to be interested in her shoe. "Faye was shorthanded. I'm just helping her out."

The song ended and Faye and her partner headed toward the table. "No reason that should keep you from dancing, is there?" His eyes smiled first, the tiny white lines around them disappearing into deep creases, then his lips broke wide showing teeth big and white as Chiclets. The split between his front ones made him look younger than he must be. Darlene wondered what it would be like to put the tip of her tongue there, to feel the smooth edges of his teeth.

He didn't know she was a widow. He was too new for the

other teachers to invite him into the whispering clusters that had come together, glanced her way, then looked off the whole night long. He'd sure find out, but that would be later, after she'd had her chance to dance. "None I can think of." Darlene stood up and he offered her his arm. She stared straight ahead in case Faye tried to catch her eye.

She stepped onto the court and into the blue spotlights just as Elvis began to croon the opening lines of "Blue Hawaii." Darlene focused on the music, not the hush that fell over the gym.

"Now see there what a big stir you made in your pretty dress once you came out from behind the punch bowl?" His voice was low, next to her ear. Darlene stared into the black shoulder of his jacket. She'd seen the movie *Blue Hawaii* with Donald Ray. They'd played this very song on the jukebox in the lounge at the Honolulu Inn. Memories controlled her, not the other way around, ambushing her when she least expected it. Don't cry, she told herself, biting the inside of her cheek hard. Not here, not in front of all these people.

The gym teacher twirled her around, pulled her back in, his hand spread wide across her back. Darlene felt as light and easy to move as a paper doll. Mindful of the narrow span of her back beneath his long fingers, she concentrated on the old pleasure of feeling small with a man.

He swung her around again and Darlene saw Faye behind the refreshment table, her face white above her loud pink dress. In a moment Elvis's voice would swell like a soft wave rolling toward the last line of the song. The lights would go up, the dance would be over, and so would this moment. Darlene moved her hand to the gym teacher's neck, felt the crisscrossing lines the sun had made, the bristle of hair that climbed out from beneath his starched collar. Somebody older, somebody different, that's who she should be thinking of. It wouldn't be the gym teacher, but it could be someone else. Somebody who wouldn't make her cry for Donald Ray. She pressed herself against him as he swirled her deeper into the unmarked faces of the crowd.

7

AURILLA

The ice melted, the trees budded and bloomed, the leaves found their full growth and then faded before I was half myself again. Louellen's death was a terrible and stubborn darkness that clung to the house, falling hardest on Jay and me. He never passed another night in their room. When I would get up at night with Rose, I would find him stretched out, legs akimbo, on the horsehair sofa in the sitting room, his arms tight around the wedding-ring quilt that had covered their bed. He'd be gone when I got up at five, beating both his brothers to the barn. Mealtimes, he wolfed his food and hurried back to his work. Sitting still, even seeing his children, seemed too much for him.

Louellen's children, and Rose in particular, were my one salvation. They were my reason to get up in the morning, to keep track of time, to remember to eat. Little Rose was the last wisp of my dear friend left on this earth and I could scarcely bear for the baby to be out of my sight. I didn't want her to ever know the emptiness her sisters knew, the emptiness I felt inside me. I tried to do for me and Louellen both, making double fuss over each milestone—rolling over, smiling, sitting up, and reaching for my hand—until Mrs. Cutter declared I would be the child's ruination.

By the time Berta Mae was born in May, I was give out. Nothing came easy to my baby, not being born, not nursing, sleeping, or being loved by me. Maybe Rose being so undemanding made Berta Mae seem worse than she was.

When I held Rose, I was handed back a bit of the love that death had just snatched from me. Looking into Berta Mae's small pinched face I felt a hardening inside, a frightening and confusing shutting down. I could feel the endless chain of need take coil around her, binding her tighter to Joe. Each new stab of resentment carried a secret shame. What had I become not to be more moved by this new life I'd made?

By fall, Berta Mae was weaned, her colic and night wakings over. She still found plenty to fuss about. Meg, one of the Stokes girls who helped with the wash, stayed all day and some nights, and she was better than me at handling Berta Mae's fits. If Berta Mae showed signs of heading into a bad time, Meg thought nothing about making a pallet on the floor by her crib and passing a night that would try a saint.

I finally had my days the way I wanted them. Not that there wasn't plenty to do, but Meg was good company and we did the work together, laughing and carrying on. I taught Louellen's oldest girls—Louise, Madge, and Hattie—to play the piano, Rose balanced on my knee. Meg would join in the singing from wherever she was in the house, her big voice filling the rooms made empty by Louellen's death.

Meg wasn't the first Stokes to tend to a Cutter baby. Her mother had helped with Joe and his brothers. Meg's family had lived in a log cabin at the edge of the Cutter land and share-cropped the outlying fields since Joe's grandfather's time. When the tobacco was ready to be pulled and cured, her brothers and sisters were hired on to bring the crop in. The Cutters were so used to Stokes being around, I was able to get all the help I needed without having to ask Joe if I could.

We had been married a year. I'd given up thinking there was some grand mystery inside him that would change everything between us once I found it. We had our sex though, a raw angry secret need for each other that only came out in the dark of our room. I no longer told myself I'd grow to care for him. His vigilance—part fear, part possessiveness—was a wall I couldn't scale or break through, and by then I'd forgotten the point in trying.

Berta Mae might have been a bridge, a way for us to come

together, but she belonged to Joe, right from the beginning. I only resented him more, seeing how easily he felt what I couldn't.

Berta Mae and me would never be good up close. The distance between us began with our different natures and grew through all the hard times I had gone through. When she was four, one of those first summers she stayed with my mother, Leonora, I saw just how bad the feelings were, the truth laid out right before me, whole and unavoidable.

We'd all been to church that Sunday. After dinner Berta Mae slipped out back to the vegetable garden. I watched her from the kitchen window. With each step she took the pink silk bow Leonora had made for her flopped over her eyes. Her black hair shone blue in the sun. I caught my breath in wonder at having made such a beautiful thing. A new and unexpected feeling of love for this child came over me, a feeling I had yearned to know.

Berta Mae waved at me, her thin baby arm moving up and down. "My house," I heard her call out. "My secret house." She pointed to the butter bean tent and disappeared inside. I could just see the top of her head, the bow showing pink against the green leaves.

I felt Berta Mae's joy as pure and open as if it were my own. A child could take you back to the child you once were. But Berta Mae was usually stingy with herself, opening up just with Meg and Joe, and now Leonora. I saw a chance to undo some of the bad between us, to be a good, loving mother to her.

I hurried down the back stairs, dropped to my knees before the butter bean tent. It was a bright day and my eyes were slow adjusting to the darkness under the thick leaves. Berta Mae sat inside on the bare ground, her legs pulled to her chest. Her tiny face screwed up, concentrating, she made neat piles of bean pods on pieces of a broken plate.

"Can you show me your house?" I asked, leaning inside.

"No!" Berta Mae screamed. She fell back on her elbows, feet flailing in the opening. "You can't come in! Don't! It's not for you!"

I found myself screaming right back at her and hating myself for feeling so much anger toward the actions of a little child. It was horrible, horrible how uncontrollable my feelings were, how they held all that had gone wrong.

Loving your own child…there is no guarantee you will. They just pass through you. If you are lucky a spark catches. The only sure thing having a child meant was that you had one. Berta Mae had Joe, Meg, and Leonora. That would have to be love enough for anybody.

Sundays, I had my drive into town for church. Hank came with me now that Mrs. Cutter had decided it was his turn to think about marrying. With just the hum of the car and the wind whistling by the open window, I had time to think. Every so often I'd look his way so I would seem thoughtful but not unsociable.

I had a hard time getting my bearings around him, he was so different from the other Cutters. Finished with school, he was around most days, tinkering, fixing things. Mrs. Cutter didn't seem to be in any hurry to put her baby to work in the fields. Being the errand boy and handy man suited Hank, whose real interests were reading and tramping through the woods.

"Did you finish that King Arthur book I lent you?"

I jumped when he spoke, lost in the pleasure of having nothing more to do than watch the trees blurred by the movement of the car. "Just getting started really." I pulled my gloves off, then put them on again to occupy my hands. I'd had the book a week, opened it each night when I got into bed, then fell asleep moments later.

"If you can't think to douse the lamp, you'll have to stop reading at night," Joe said this morning when we woke, the lamp still burning, the wick nearly gone. "That thing gets knocked over, the house will be on fire." That was his way, tying the things he didn't want me to do, like reading or going to church, to something disastrous. When I was pregnant, he'd argued the ride into town would bring on a miscarriage. Since then, I'd learned to let him have his say and to quietly ignore him.

"I'm already on the second book," Hank said. "You'd better catch up before I forget how the first one went."

Since Louellen's passing, I had become the one he shared his reading with. If I didn't know the subject, he'd follow me around the house while I worked, telling me enough so I could discuss it with him.

When the children were asleep and the house was quiet, I'd be out shaking the dust mop on the back porch or hanging wash and I would think of him in the barn, nobody needing him or depending on him to do for them. I pictured me there, the quiet, a book in my hands and awake enough to get past the first page. What I couldn't see was Hank. Would he sit beside me or be off on the other side of the loft? It didn't sound right, my being alone with him in the barn. I could just imagine telling Meg I would be out in the loft with my brother-in-law if she needed me.

"I may be having trouble getting my reading done," I said, turning the conversation away from me and the uncomfortable image of us in the barn, "but not half the trouble you're having in finding a wife. What about church? You got a girl picked out yet?"

He laughed, his blue eyes dancing. "Nope. Looks like Joe already beat me to the prize."

Hank was having fun, that was all. I had seen that already the few times I'd ridden into town with him. We always arrived late for the service, living out like we did, and then stopping by Leonora's house for her. We usually came in right after the first hymn when the preacher was at the pulpit ready to speak. You could cut the anticipation with a knife and it sure wasn't over hearing the sermon. Hank's boots would sound across that warped wood floor, and I could almost see the fine hairs on the necks of the young girls in the congregation standing on end.

During the service he cut his eyes first at this girl, then that one, deciding who he'd talk to once services were over. Out in the church yard he was like a bee, flitting from flower to flower, staying with each one just long enough to make her think he wanted to stay more. When he moved to the next girl, he watched the one he'd just left from the corner of his eye, making sure she saw.

I might as well be old, old as the oldest woman there. A soft melancholy settled over me watching the girls eyeing Hank from under their broad-brimmed hats. They tilted their heads just so, making it impossible to be certain where they were looking. Each Sunday the dismal memory of my own courtship rose up to remind me just how unfamiliar I was with this kind of lighthearted play. I saw Joe pulled in against the window, brooding and serious, and me, uneasy, sensing him there long before I saw him.

"So why don't you just tell your mother marriage doesn't interest you?"

He laughed low and easy, the way I'd heard him do out on the porch at church with the girls. "You were quiet so long I thought we'd finished talking about that. You women have a way of holding on to things and snaring a man up just when he thinks he's safe."

He looked off down the road, his eyes distant. "It's all right about Mama. She's yet to ask me anything, and you'd better hope she doesn't. I tell her the truth, that's the end of your churchgoing, and then you'll be stuck at home with no one to take you to town."

We turned down Leonora's street and the stand of sturdy oaks on either side met overhead in a welcoming canopy. He reached over, tapped my nose. "Besides," he said, his voice light again, "the longer I put it off, the more of your mother's Sunday dinners I'll get invited to."

It was a dry clear morning in early October. A mist hung over the fields, blurring the line where the sky met the ground, and hiding the hills that lay beyond. Hattie, Louellen's three-year-old, picked up the sticks and twigs scattered about the yard.

Madge swept the dirt smooth. Louise, the eldest, came behind her with the rake, swirling the dirt into pretty patterns. The dust the children raised hung in the air, tiny mirrors for the low autumn sun.

I sat on the porch snapping the last of the green beans, shelling those that had stayed too long on the vine and turned tough. Rose sat beside me on a blanket, tiny hands pulling the empty shells apart.

"Girls," I said, "it's time we did something about this yard." They stopped scurrying around, looking first at me, then at their work. The younger ones looked to Louise, waiting for her to speak. She shrugged, her narrow shoulders rising up around her neck. "Aren't we doing a good job?"

"Well, of course you are." Being motherless like they were I always tried to make them feel important. "I've never seen a prettier raked yard but think how nice it would be with some flowers. Remember all that color you saw out in the woods last spring—the white laurel, the goldenrod, the pink dogwoods? We could grow those things right here."

They nodded, their eyes bright, even Hattie, who didn't have the first idea about time and the seasons.

Raking the yard had been my idea, and it helped the looks of the place some. But now that I was going to Mother's again, I realized how sad this place really was. Leonora's house stood on one of the oldest streets in town, just a few blocks from the center. The neighborhood was an oasis of green. Ivy covered the frame walls; yellow roses ran up the trellis behind the swing on the front porch. The bushes and trees were as old as the house itself, built before the Civil War. Twisting scuppernong vines covered the grape arbor out back. The flowers in the cutting garden grew so thick you had to turn sideways to get between the rows. In the middle of it all was the vegetable garden with an herb border.

Growing up, I had been indifferent, but that changed after living with the bare ground at the Cutter house. My visits brought back memories of lying under the big trees, leaves touching soft and slight, the sunlight and wind shifting and changing the patterns of light and shadow that fell across my arms. Looking at the garden from the sun porch, I could see my young self dodging the bumblebees that swarmed the sage and lavender, squatting beside the strawberry plants, my fingers and dress stained red with juice, chasing the white butterflies that fluttered over the new blooms.

What would Louellen's girls and Berta Mae's childhood memories be made of—hot, unbroken sun and cracked, baked dirt? I could bring some comfort to the place. Things were too hard at the Cutters' to have the house looking that way too.

"Tomorrow, instead of doing the yard, I'm going to take you on a treasure hunt."

"Where's the treasure, what kind of treasure?" Madge squealed as they all jumped up and down, blond hair flying around their heads.

"Flowers hidden in the woods. They'll be just like jewels when we set them out around the house, you'll see. Now go on inside and get Meg to settle you down for a nap. Quiet now, remember Berta Mae's sleeping," I called as they ran inside, bursting to tell Meg their news.

Come spring, the most I could expect from Mrs. Cutter would be money for a few packs of flower seed. She took no interest in the appearance of things, and she'd never spare a man from the farm for such silliness. It would soon be market time for the tobacco; it'd do no good to ask Joe. Besides, the days were getting shorter, and even if he did want to help, I couldn't see making him work by lamplight after packing the cured leaves all day.

I could easier make do with what grew around me, and I had the girls to help. Their tiny hands would be able to dig out the fragile roots of the new ferns growing down along the creek bank and to separate the rhododendron shoots from the parent plants. Hank, still doing mostly as he pleased, spent half his time off in the woods as it was. I couldn't see that it would hurt him any to bring some plants back with him.

The smell of hay met me before I was halfway in the barn. It scratched my ankles it was laid down so thick. The excess made me think of Mrs. Cutter's complaint that Hank went through too many bales, keeping the barn clean to suit himself rather than the animals.

I stepped on the first rung of the ladder leading to the loft. "Are you up there, Hank?"

"Come on up." He leaned over the edge, holding out a hand. "So you decided to take me up on the offer of my library?"

I shook my head, looking around at the couch he'd fashioned out of hay bales and covered with a quilt. I pointed to the bookshelves built of old planks and bricks lining the south wall. "These all library books?"

Hank threw back his head and laughed. "Now you know another story on me. Those are my books. I keep a little for myself here and there when I go to town for Mama, that's how I buy them. I'm going to be out of secrets soon."

He dropped down onto the hay, opening his book, but his teasing eyes were on me. My face burned red under his gaze. It was bad enough having a man look at me like that, let alone one sprawled out on the floor like he was. In the light coming through the loft window, he looked made out of gold.

"Your secrets are safe with me," I said, finding my tongue. "I don't have anyone to tell." People always say that and right then their minds are clicking off the names of everyone they can report the news to. But not me, not with Louellen gone. The only grown person I talked to besides Hank to say more than good morning, good night, and pass the bread was Meg, and I'd been raised well enough to know you didn't drag your private life or that of your family into conversations with the help.

"I'm sorry, Aurilla, I'm forgetting the little manners I do have." Hank waved me toward the couch, settled himself beside me. "Did you come out for something in particular?"

"Yes, I did. I want to change this place and I want you to help me." The tone I took with him still surprised me. I spoke my mind, like I was my old self.

He sat up, the laughter starting in his eyes. "Who are we going to work on first? Mama? Things ought to fall in place after we get her straightened out."

"I'm talking about the grounds around the house," I said, feeling the color in my cheeks rise. I had addressed him the way I would the grown boys in my class when I taught school. "I'm tired of living someplace where the land looks like it has just been cleared." Waiting for his answer, I ran my fingers along the rough stitches in the crazy quilt, feigning interest in the jumble of scraps.

"I guess this place does look pretty bad to you. It even looks rough to me now after seeing your mother's, and I grew up here." She followed his eyes out the window, past the scattered clumps of crabgrass growing up around the barn, to the hard red ground riddled with cracks that radiated out from the buffer the swept ring of dirt made around the house.

"Before I start agreeing with you," Hank began, "I better find out what you have in mind." He idly took my hand, turning it over the way I had seen him do the leaves he brought back from his walks in the woods. His finger traced the chained line Meg called the heart line that crossed the top of my palm. "This isn't going to cut into my book money, is it?"

I pulled my hand back. Why had I let him touch me in the first place? I stood up, the suddenness of my movement making me lightheaded. "Everything I need already grows in the woods. Louellen's girls and I can take care of the small things, the ferns and wildflowers. You could bring me the big plants—laurel, goldenrod, tree switches—and some topsoil to hold it all. We still have a month to get some things set out before the frost comes."

He stood beside me, brushing the hay from his clothes. "You are too cutting in on my book money. We'll need grass seed, anything you plant will wash away without it."

I let myself smile then, seeing he was with me.

Hank found a silver maple sapling for Berta Mae. Maples grew so fast, he said, the tree would be something live to measure her against. He put it where the road ended in the front yard. "You can have as many babies as you like," he told me. "There's room for a whole stand of maple trees."

By the time the first frost came, we had set out plants all around the front of the house. It took straw being spread out over the yard to get Mrs. Cutter's attention.

"What is the straw that belongs in the barn doing in the yard?" she called out as she came in the front door that evening. She used the front door like she was a lady all dressed up while the men came in the house through the back. From the heavy sound of her footsteps, she hadn't even stopped to take off her work boots. She wasn't talking to anyone in particular but her tone said that whoever heard her better have a good answer.

Hank met his mother in the dining room. "Best way I know of to keep grass seed from blowing away," he said.

I left off peeling potatoes and stood still, breathing in short shallow breaths.

"Where'd you get the money for seed?" I could hear Mrs. Cutter holding her anger back, letting it build.

"The yard was washing right down the road. Pretty soon we'd have been hauling topsoil in here by the wagonload just to fill the gullies."

In the silence that came, I pictured Mrs. Cutter boring holes through Hank to see if she could break him. And I knew he was staring at the space between her eyebrows, just like he had taught me to do, looking for all the world like he was meeting her eyes.

"You did the right thing," she finally said. "It's good somebody's thinking about the house. Lord knows I don't have time."

He walked through the kitchen, winked at me, his mother right behind him. I would be next, with Mrs. Cutter asking about the plantings. Joe and Jay's voices sounded outside the back door. Let Mrs. Cutter be sharp and short like usual and finish before Joe heard. He hadn't noticed the time I spent with his brother, and I didn't want his attention called to it. He'd have some reason why I shouldn't be fooling with the yard, and then come up with a string of chores to occupy Hank. Instead, Mrs. Cutter went straight to the icebox, poured herself a glass of buttermilk like always before supper, and headed into the parlor.

I had dreaded the moment she would notice our work and in five minutes Hank had turned the project into something necessary, something his mother couldn't do without. She was probably sitting there in her reading chair, pleased to know how much he was like her when nothing could be further from the truth.

It was as if I was being courted, the meals Leonora laid out on Sundays for Hank Cutter. She served her usual roast chicken and some cold dishes the first time I brought him home. But the things she'd cooked since then—a ham one week, pork roast the next, chicken and dumplings—told me how much she wanted him to keep coming around. Hank ate enough to satisfy the effort Leonora put into preparing it all, but she had to be picking at the leftovers all week long until the next Sunday came around just to keep from wasting food.

The presentation gradually became more elaborate as Leonora's fondness for Hank grew. A leaf appeared in the dining table to allow for the serving dishes that had set for years undisturbed in the china closet. Linen tablecloths and lace runners emerged from the cedar-lined trunk in the downstairs bedroom. Their imparted sweetness mixed with the spice of the yellow mums and the last of the black-eyed Susans from the garden.

I stood and stretched before I began clearing the table. "We haven't had meals like this since before Arnold left home, so I know this spread wasn't in my honor."

Spooning strawberry preserves onto the last biscuit, Hank smiled at my mother like she was one of the sixteen-year-olds he'd been making eyes at not an hour before. "Then I'd better earn my keep before you bring on dessert and I'm even more in your debt." He took off his jacket, draped it over the back of his chair. "I'm clearing that vegetable garden out back. I've sat staring at it out this window for weeks and it looks sorrier each time I come. Tools in the shed, ma'am?"

Leonora sat, her mouth wide open, her cheeks flushed. I laughed out loud seeing her like that. I couldn't remember a time in my life when I'd seen her flustered.

"Yes, well, fine," she stammered. "I'll leave the pie on the stove then."

He headed through the sun porch, pausing to run his hand through the wind chimes. The brightly painted pieces of glass collided in confused excitement.

Leonora followed me into the kitchen. "You sure he's hatched from the same hen?" she whispered, her eyes darting to the row of open windows overlooking the garden. "Those boys aren't a thing alike." When I didn't answer, she began again, stumbling over her words. "Now, I know, you do, Joe's a fine boy."

"I've been married to him long enough"—I broke into whatever Mother struggled to say—"don't you think I can see the difference?"

"Yes, of course you do, Aurilla," she murmured. "Forgive me." Leonora bowed her head slightly. She hurried off for the rest of the dishes.

I leaned against the sink, losing myself in the roar of the tap water cascading into the dishpan. I had never before seen Leonora kowtow to anyone other than her most demanding clients. What had made me speak to my own mother like a common servant? I saw Leonora off somewhere, moving timid as a mouse through her own house. I had pushed her away once for what I thought was love. What reason did I have now for growing the distance between us?

I stared into the garden, seeing nothing but Hank. I looked at the white shirt stuck to his back, at his strong arms and the assured swing of the pick. He tossed aside spent tomato vines, the woody stalks of overgrown lettuce. He broke the crusty topsoil, laid open the moist loose earth beneath. I waited for some sign, something in the way he moved that would reveal his feelings as clearly as I had just revealed mine.

8

Darlene

Rosslyn Hosiery Mill set off to itself like it was too good for Potter. A big stretch of well-tended grass separated the blank face of the masonry wall from Sunrise Avenue. Bushes pruned and shaped into neat leafy boxes broke up the long, low front of the building. No windows, just big craters cut into the stone that mimicked openings, the whole of it still and lifeless as the face of the moon.

Nothing was further from the truth. Nearly everyone in the county worked there at one time or other. Some started out with an eye on making the jump to the big pay at the Yankee factories, Union Carbine or General Electric; others never quite figured out how to leave. They hung on, thankful not to be at the shoe or the box factory.

Darlene waited in her car, steadying her nerves with these neutral thoughts about the hosiery mill. The mill whistle blew and she checked it against the clock on her dashboard. Four o'clock. The first shift workers streamed through the side door in twos and threes, their gray striped uniforms making it hard to tell them apart.

She saw Clayton's head above the crowd. He was one of the few workers walking by himself. For days now she had sat outside the mill, working her way up to talking to him. She took a deep breath, tapped the horn twice. It seemed everybody's head turned but his. When he finally looked in her direction, she waved her hand fast to make him come.

For such a long-legged man he was slow; part of him seemed to go forward while the rest of him held back. She wondered if he had come up on Donald Ray the same way.

She started talking as soon as he was in earshot. "You found my Donald Ray down by the lake."

"Yes, ma'am, and I'm as sorry about what happened as the next man." He shrugged his shoulders, part confusion, part embarrassment. His hands patted the pockets of his overalls. He took a pack of cigarettes from one, matches from another.

"There's things I need to know." Darlene lowered her voice to bring him closer. "I never got a good look at him until the funeral home and by then they'd worked all the pain out of his face. You know how they arrange things, making people look like dolls."

Clayton's lips pulled tight around his cigarette. He glanced at his watch. "I don't like to think about that day."

He sounded like Pap. No one wanted her to think about Donald Ray. She fought back the sense of aloneness that hovered inside, threatening to take her over whenever she let her guard down. She swallowed hard against the urge to cry. "That's all I think about."

He looked away, his eyes busy with the wave of people reporting for second shift.

She'd made him uncomfortable. She held up her hand, wiggled her fingers at him. "Aren't you going to offer me a cigarette?" When he hesitated, she said, "Come on, if I'm old enough to bury a husband, I think I can handle a little cigarette." She pushed in the car's lighter, held out her hand.

Clayton fumbled for his cigarettes, nearly dropping the lit one in his fingers.

"You got a girl named Emogene?" Darlene rolled the smoke around her mouth, breathed it out.

Clayton turned red, one hand rubbing the back of his neck. "That's right."

"You can't deny that one. She's the image of you. My little sister Chrissie and her are like two peas in a pod."

"Look, Mrs. Spencer, I got a field waiting to be plowed." Clayton flicked his cigarette onto the pavement, crushed it with his boot.

"Maybe some other time would be better. What about tomorrow—right after your shift—in the hospital parking lot?

That way you won't have to explain to anybody what you're doing talking to me." His face darkened but he didn't say no. Darlene turned over the ignition. The throaty purr of the V-8 engine shot over the parking lot; heads craned in their direction. "I need to know about the lake," she added for good measure.

The lot behind the hospital was big and new, deep black with sharp yellow lines all over. There was an emptiness to the place that had more to do with what had been here before than with all the unused parking spaces. Darlene remembered a row of renters' houses, the paint worn down to the wood, and children: hanging on the porch railings, running in the yard, and digging in the dirt any time of day or year.

"Where are the mothers of these children?" her own mother would say, rolling up her window against the shrill voices that tore through the car when they drove past. Darlene left hers open. The wild pitch of their screams reminded her of the sounds people made on the rides at the county fair once they gave themselves over to being whipped around. "I'm glad the church is doing something for those poor little things," her mother would say, and Darlene would think about how they didn't seem the least bit pitiful to her.

At Christmas the preacher brought out the donation box, a wooden chest he set up by the exit with "help those less fortunate" stenciled on the lid. Each year when the box appeared, her mother made Darlene go through her toys while she loaded up canned goods and old clothes. Leaving church those Sundays, Darlene would hang back to peek inside the box to see what these children were getting. Sometimes she slipped something small into her coat pocket, something that would go unnoticed by her mother: a crayon, a doll apron. When they drove past the houses, she would look for her old dresses and toys in the blur of children, waiting to be surprised by an encounter with herself and thinking about the things she'd held back from the box. Maybe some of her things were trapped under the blacktop now: the sash from a dress, a plate from a tea set.

She turned into the lot, followed the arrows up the hill. She pulled in close to the dumpsters at the rear of the hospital. People didn't spend much time looking at garbage cans so she figured the spot would suit Clayton. It was a hot day, hot enough to turn the pavement soft. In her yellow sundress her bare shoulders stuck to the seat.

"Sweat will ruin that leather," Pap had said as she left the house. "You better keep a towel behind you till you get some seat covers on that thing."

Darlene slid behind the wheel, running her hand over the cool white of the seat beside her, taking in the tiny pinpoint openings of the pores. "Cows sweat. I can't see the difference."

She had no intention of putting plastic over these seats; she liked the feel of skin on skin. Besides there was the air-conditioning when she remembered it. She directed the vents at her face and chest, drank in the cold dry air that cut through the humid air. She jerked involuntarily as the cold ran through her. She pushed back the wisps of hair stuck to her forehead, turned down the air. She knew enough about mill life to know Clayton wouldn't be able to take the cold, not after standing in air-conditioning for the last eight hours. Donald Ray was always a long time feeling the heat after he came off his shift.

Four o'clock came and went. On the street below, the traffic picked up then dropped off in perfect rhythm with the shift changeover at the mills. He wasn't coming. A wiry pain, part disappointment, part relief, started somewhere deep in her head. She closed her eyes and followed the pain as it bolted and reared in unexpected directions.

She replayed their conversation, going over the moment before Clayton stepped away from the car. She'd read his red face as embarrassment. Maybe it was anger, anger at her thinking she could just appear out of nowhere and have her way? He'd never agreed to meet her. She just heard what she wanted to hear, just like Pap always said. She ran over everybody to get her way; she always had. Donald Ray hadn't helped things any, laughing his easy laugh and going right along with her. Her face began to burn. The other workers had seen Clayton with her in the parking lot. What had Clayton said today to wash his hands of her? Did he sit in the lunchroom over his cheese and bologna sandwich mimicking the way she held her head or played at smoking?

The first-shift nurses hurried out the back door to their cars. If Donald Ray had made it to the hospital, it could have been one of these women working to save him. They had ways of reviving people, shocks and jolts that brought them back from death. Some of the nurses weren't much older than her but she didn't know how to do anything half as useful.

Driving here she had imagined she was setting something big in motion. With each turn she made, each intersection she crossed, a feeling laced with finality and regret ran through her, not unlike what she felt when they told her Donald Ray was killed. But this time the feeling had added up to nothing but more sitting, more empty waiting. She slammed into reverse, marking her spot by the dumpster with burned rubber.

Darlene had come to know the road to the lake well enough to drive it blind. By day, the dips and washed-out ruts she traveled each night rose and fell and turned over in her mind, teasing out the moment when she would take the last curve, and the calm plain of Ramsey Lake opened before her. In her daydreams she sometimes pulled the wheel hard and drove into the black water, welcoming the musty darkness that rushed to fill her mouth, her nose. Or she imagined Donald Ray waiting for her. Part breeze, part shadow, his form wavered, coming together beneath the branches of the sweet gum trees.

Darlene rounded what Faye said everyone now called Dead Man's Curve. A small red light dimmed, then grew bright—the glow of a lit cigarette. No one parked here, not since the accident. The nights she came, she had the lake to herself. She wasn't afraid, she told her pumping heart. Donald Ray had quit smoking six months before he died. She pulled off the road, cutting her wheels hard, her lights shining right on Clayton

Bishop. He shielded his eyes with one hand. His other palm moved up and down in front of his face, signaling her to turn off the lights.

She got out of the car, leaned against the door. "Where's your truck?" she asked, saying the only thing she could think of to say.

His cigarette made an arc across the lake, landed with a hiss. "Other side. I don't like advertising my business."

What did he mean, business? The uncertain light of the new moon made it impossible to read his face. "Nobody comes here anymore, nobody but me."

He let out a low laugh. "Guess my name's nobody then."

Nobody. That's who she'd told herself he was today, driving home from the hospital. She had meant not to see him again. If it was at Elvin's, she'd walk straight to the drink box like it was just her and Elvin in the store. When she got hired on at the mill, she would look right through him. He was a stranger; she would let him stay one. Look at him, standing here like he belonged. Leave, she thought, just leave.

He shook his head. "You think you're the only one, don't you? Not a day goes by I don't see this place, see him. There are nights it makes it hard to sleep. Then I end up here."

There was a long pause and just the sound of his breathing. She let the silence hang between them to see if he'd say more. He reached for the low-hanging branch of a nearby oak, snapped off the end. He held the branch in one hand, popping off leaf after leaf with the push of his thumb.

"Sometimes…" Clayton dropped the bare branch, wrapped his arms across his chest and spread his legs wide like he was steadying himself. "Sometimes I feel like it's him keeping me awake, making me know things for him."

She felt a deep lurching inside her ribs. How could he have it, the bond she had longed for, feeling Donald Ray with her, living through her? And why because Clayton was the first person to stumble onto him? In leaving this world, had some shimmering piece of Donald Ray's spirit collided with Clayton's?

She took a step forward, touched the hood of the car. The engine's warmth pulled her back to the moment, to the present that felt more dream than talk.

"What's he want?" she managed to get out.

"Nothing big. This." The sweep of Clayton's arm took in the lake, the sky. "Things I'd forgotten about noticing without knowing it. It's not easy, feeling so much."

The cicadas' song built, dipped in a big swoop, rose again. The urge to be away from everything he said Donald Ray wanted overwhelmed her. She scrambled for the car door, raised the windows, and told herself to breathe against the pounding of her heart.

Darlene ignored Clayton's urging voice outside the glass. How could Donald Ray be so simple? How could he have picked the wrong person? It was just like him really. He was mocking her, just the way he did when she got worked up over things, giving them, as he used to say, way more weight than they deserved. Things just happen, he seemed to be saying now. Look at me, looking at you through this stranger.

The passenger door flew open. Darlene screamed, lunged for the driver's door. Clayton was in the car and holding her arm before she could get free.

"Settle down, just settle down," he said, his voice soft and coaxing like he was calming a skittish animal. "I didn't mean to scare you, or hurt you, or make you mad. You look like you might be all three, is that right?"

Why did everything this man said send her reeling? She nodded.

"You wanted to know what happened here. Do you still?"

She yanked her arm free. "You didn't come."

"I never said I would. But I'm here now if you want to know."

His long legs looked wedged between the seat and the dash. "There's a lever on the side there if you want to move that seat back," Darlene said. "Chrissie usually sits there. She claims she can see better if the seat's all the way forward."

His seat popped backwards and Darlene turned sideways to face him. "Tell me about when you found him."

Clayton looked straight ahead like he was watching pictures in the dark. "I was going fishing. I had that in my head first thing that morning when I saw what kind of day it was going to be. By the time I got work over with, half the day was gone. At first, I thought Buford was down here fishing too, but then I saw how things were." He paused, looked over at her. Darlene nodded to let him know she was all right, and he went on. "From the looks of things, Buford sailed right into Donald Ray like he wasn't there. Car was clean up inside Donald Ray's. I didn't see a soul till I got up even with Donald Ray's car."

"You're just telling me what you told everybody else. I want to know what his face looked like, if you touched him."

Clayton let out a long sigh, one hand pulling down his face. "I checked his pulse." He stopped again. She looked back evenly at him. "His eyes were open. He looked surprised, that was all. I closed his eyes and went to call the highway patrol."

"No blood?"

"Only blood I saw was on the paper he'd wrapped his catfish in."

Darlene sat back and stared at the dark too.

"It was his neck," Clayton said. "Didn't they tell you that?"

"They could say anything, couldn't they?"

"He never felt a thing, that's what the man told me that day." He pulled out his cigarettes and pushed in the lighter. The glow when he inhaled lit his face. She saw the same tightness in his mouth she'd noticed outside the mill. He looked like someone who had been holding back a long time. "There was something else. He looked like he didn't mind so much, dying and all. There was this big calm over things and it was like he was part of that and not just himself anymore."

She repeated the words to herself: part of that and not just himself anymore. Like Donald Ray, they didn't seem to care whether she understood or was ready to know. They floated and drifted beyond her grasp, as impossible to hold on to as smoke.

She touched the console, running the nail of her index finger along the narrow ridges in the chrome. "You know what I love about this car?" Her hand trailed along the edge of his seat. The leather warmed by his body jolted her. "How clean and new it is. I get in here and it's like nothing's ever happened to me. Other times, I can hear Donald Ray as clear as if he was sitting right where you are."

He let out a sigh. "Comfort or torment?" he asked.

Was that Donald Ray talking? Who else but him knew the work she put into feeling him and the resistance he gave back?

Clayton still wore his mill uniform. The familiar ribbing was thick like the ticking on her bed. Hot nights, she and Donald Ray had rolled around until the bottom sheet worked its way off the corners of the mattress, the rough cloth pulling against her back as she moved beneath him. The picture flashed in her mind and was gone. She lifted her hand, brushing Clayton's leg. She felt the muscles in his thigh twitch.

"Torment," she said. They sat a while longer, the softness of the night and the lake filling the space around them until there was no room or need for talk. The thought that this was maybe peace floated through the dreamless half-sleep that settled over her, easing her past the uneasy place where she ended and the world began.

She felt his touch on her arm and heard him say, "I got to get on home, maybe you should go too."

She watched until the dark of the lake swallowed him. Life was one knotted, tangled string of chances. If she hadn't sent Donald Ray off fishing, Buford would have driven into the lake without hurting a soul but himself. If she hadn't shown up here early tonight, Clayton would have sat around doing whatever Donald Ray compelled him to do and then gone on home. If, if, if. Who was going to be hurting now?

9

AURILLA

"Just look at the size of it." Hank bent over a map of California. "158,000 square miles." He sucked in his breath, let out a low whistle. "Spring weather all year long and oranges anytime you feel like having one."

He turned more pages, passing pictures of ocean cliffs and orchards that went on as far as the eye could see, streets lined with palm trees taller than the largest oaks. Hank was hungry to know things, anything at all. In just a week we had read about beekeeping, the history of ancient Egypt. We traveled all over the world and through time, never leaving that barn. "Pity California is so far off," I said.

He snapped the book closed, the muscles in his jaw tightening. "It's not. Nothing is if you put your mind to it."

I thought of the pile of ironing waiting for me, and the children who would wake soon, their small faces irritable and creased from sleep. "Are you planning on going there?" I tried to make my voice sound indifferent.

He looked around the loft like he was making sure we were alone, then shrugged his shoulders. "I've been working for Ol' Man Rait whenever I get the chance, and I've saved what I can. How about you, Aurilla, want to come along?"

My heart lurched, then took off. I wrapped my arms tight around me, clutching my shawl to my heart to muffle its pounding. It means nothing; his attention means nothing, I told myself, hearing again the words I repeated each afternoon when I walked from the house to the barn, imagining Meg watching me.

All the weeks I had struggled with Hank's invitation to join him, I heard Louellen's last whispered words urging me to seek out his company. Had Louellen sat here in my place by the window, one eye on the house while she tried to keep up with Hank's curious mind?

I let myself look at him. The truth was I hadn't stopped watching him since that Sunday last fall at Mother's when he turned the garden. He didn't expect an answer to his question; he only meant to enlarge his own dream. He was already by the bookshelves looking for something else to dream about, the space between us widening the way it often did.

His eagerness made me feel old and out of chances. I closed my eyes and saw my dream, the one where I stood in front of a choir, their voices following the steady driving strokes of my arms. The church had asked me back to play piano after Berta Mae was born, but Joe wouldn't hear of me going into town on Friday nights for choir practice. And there was my piano out in that dark hall, shut off from the rest of the house like a secret. "This is the only place it will fit," Joe had said the day they moved my things out from town. Shamed by the circumstances surrounding my hasty marriage, I had just nodded, feeling myself slip that much further away. I was lost. I didn't belong anywhere, not with my mother, not here at the Cutter house, not off with Hank in some picture paradise. Each direction I turned, the way to being alive and loved was walled off.

Hank's back was turned. He had settled into a new book, going on ahead without me. I eased down the ladder, careful not to make a sound. I was at the back door before I heard him call out, the confusion in his voice echoing the uncertainty inside my head.

That night, lying in bed beside Joe, his breath already heavy and even, the house still, I thought, *This is all there will be once Hank is gone.* The emptiness between Joe and me took on the substance of something real enough to taste and touch. I stole out of bed, my feet just touching the swollen floorboards. I crossed the room to the window facing the barn.

Light snow had fallen, dusting the rough bark of the oaks,

the worn path to the barn. I pictured the confused tangle of my footprints unraveled by sudden white, revealing the true course of my heart.

Hank's lamp shown steadily through the warped wood of the barn. Where was he now? I wondered. California? Rome? I pressed my forehead to the cold glass, imagining I was with him.

The children gathered around the kitchen table for Rose's birthday celebration. Aprons covered them from head to toe. Newspapers protected the table and the floor. Meg and I had given each child their own cupcake and a small bowl of chocolate icing to eat as they pleased. Louise spread hers with a knife, working the frosting into swirls the way she had once raked the yard. Hattie and Madge, so close in age that one did like the other, dipped their cupcakes in their bowls between bites. Rose scooped her icing with both hands until it spilled over the edge of her saucer, a sluggish stream of brown dripping slowly onto the newsprint. Berta Mae had no taste for sweets. She stood holding onto the table with one hand while she splashed the chocolate over herself and Rose.

"I can just picture Miz Cutter's face if she walked in here about now," Meg said. "That woman would throw some kind of fit." Using the rag that never seemed to leave her hand, she wiped a splatter off the wall behind the table.

Mrs. Cutter wasn't the only reason I had waited for them all to go back to work before treating the children. Jay shied away from the girls, Rose in particular, with her favoring Louellen like she did. He'd been more distant than usual this week coming up on the first anniversary of Louellen's death.

What was painful for Jay had become my comfort. Pieces of Louellen were still alive, spread out over the four girls. Louise's eyes were brown, but the expression in them was her mother's. Madge had her mother's imagination, and Hattie her walk. But quiet, sweet Rose was her all over again.

The children had nearly finished when Hank came in,

helping himself to the plate of cupcakes on the counter. He ran one around the rim of Louise's icing bowl, laughing as she swatted at his hand. He licked the icing, then set the uneaten cupcake aside.

"It's a mighty warm day for the middle of February, don't you think?" His question was general, his tone was even, but his eyes caught mine and refused to let go. "Nice day for reading."

The blood flooded my face, roared in my ears. I hadn't been back to the barn since the afternoon I stole away. These past weeks I had avoided Hank at mealtimes and occupied the children's naptimes with chores.

I felt Meg's eyes on me. I glanced at her, and Meg dropped to her knees, busying herself with the drizzle of cake crumbs on the floor. Even though we'd become fast friends, she'd never let on like there was anything wrong with me being out in the barn with Hank. I saw now Meg thought differently. She was caught between us, between what felt right in her heart and right in her head.

I excused myself and ran up to my room, taking the stairs two at a time. Everything inside me was turning around, rearranging itself in an order I couldn't grasp. We'd stood in the kitchen, all of us together talking, day after day. I tried to sort out why things felt so changed, why it felt as if there was a decision that demanded to be made.

I thought about the afternoons I'd left Meg in charge of the children. I tried to picture her face; how she looked each time I told her I was going to the barn. I saw Meg's dark eyes, clear and open and meeting mine, not like today, when she dropped to her knees, training her attention on the floor.

I played the whole scene in the kitchen out again, Hank settling in against the counter, his words, his look. The difference was him being there, his saying it, and what Meg saw pass between us.

I stood by the window, grateful for the cold air that leached around the panes. The last few months flashed before me. I saw Hank's fingers brushing against mine as he read, his hand on my waist steadying me as we climbed the ladder to the loft, the two of us picking flowers in Mother's garden for the Sunday table. I'd watched him for a sign that afternoon at my mother's when my answer had been with me all along. Maybe it had been safer for me to pretend the feelings were only on my side. My one experience with courting had been so peculiar, nothing about my time with Joe resembled what I'd been doing with Hank.

Who else knew? Each night I lay in bed beside Joe, reading his brother's books. I even saw the faces of the congregation turning to watch us come in to the services late, their eyes following us to a pew at the back of the church. What did Mrs. Cutter think about all Hank's months of churchgoing and not the first mention of any girl?

Hank passed beneath the window on his way to the barn. I moved behind the curtain just as he turned and looked up. I saw the owning in his eyes. In running away from him, from them, I had confirmed his right to me.

I lay in bed, my heart beating along with the ticking clock on the bureau. Louellen was in my thoughts, making me take the long view of my own life. What was left stretched out still and even before me, nothing singular to mark the unbearable ordinariness.

I got up, thinking I'd just look for Hank's light the way I did each night. Instead I found myself heading for the door. Mrs. Cutter's room was away on the third floor. A heavy sleeper, she had never gotten up in the night but once, and that was when Louellen died.

I moved to the stairs, straining to remember which steps creaked. I heard Jay stir on the parlor sofa and held still to make sure he was only turning in his sleep. If anyone was restless in the house tonight it would be him, lying alone on the anniversary of Louellen's death.

My blood pumped so it drowned out anything else I might hear. My deliberate journey downstairs was as long as the crossing of the ocean. I knew that by taking this walk I was consenting to everything that would come after. But the fear of dying without having lived was stronger than the fear of getting caught. None of it mattered, not the shame or the punishment that would surely come.

My toes felt for the bottom step, feet moving carefully off the last riser. I made my way along the wall, hand over hand, until I reached the coat rack by the front door, grabbing the first wrap I laid hands on.

Outside the sharp black sky was dusted with stars. I ran from the cold and the house that was like an all-seeing eye boring in my back, each step carrying me closer to loving Hank.

The barn was still. One of the horses stirred, then settled again. I climbed the ladder to the loft, my breath coming in short gasps that sounded in time with my heart.

He was asleep, a book in his hands. One last jolt of reason traveled through me. I could turn around, run for the house, and everything would be as it was. Left alone without encouragement, Hank would get over what he would come to see as unrequited feelings.

In that same moment defiance, daring, and danger connected, pushing me past the remnants of hesitation and doubt, and forward with sweet and terrifying certainty. I eased the book from his grasp. He stirred, his fingers tightening. I kissed him the way I kissed the babies to send them back to sleep. He murmured my name, my presence becoming confused with his dreams. I kissed him full on the lips, pressing for passage to the dream. He opened arms warm with sleep, taking me in.

"I'm going with you when you go." The words I had practiced for weeks were finally said. We lay beneath the crazy quilt. I watched the low afternoon light play across my dress, draped over a rafter above our heads. I felt light, joyful, and carefree. I had said the words I'd longed to say and the world had not ended. Each time I traveled from the house to the barn I crossed farther into a careless, emboldened place where there was no thought of consequences. Fear and guilt had lost their power over me, locked away in some dark part of my mind.

Hank turned, pulling me to him. He pressed his nose against my forehead and inhaled. "You could do that?" he whispered. "Leave everybody and ride in boxcars and maybe the back of some pickup truck all the way across the country?" He smoothed the hair back from my neck the way I'd seen him do the horses' manes when they were jumpy.

Boxcars and trucks didn't sound like anywhere you could take a little baby. In my mind I saw Rose, not my own child. I closed my eyes against the truth of how easily I could leave Berta Mae.

Hank's fingers moved to my temples, traveling in soft open swirls. "Don't think," he said, the length of him pressed close.

Thinking was all I did at night. I would lie beside Joe after refusing his advances, so tense with expectation my body almost levitated above the mattress. I listened for the steady open-mouthed breathing that signaled his deep sleep, my mind traveling back over Hank's every word, look, and touch until I trembled with desire. When I was sure Joe slept, I let one foot slip to the floor, then the other, inching my way out of bed. Each night I escaped, my footsteps grew more careless. The dark was like the barn; it was easy to pretend nobody mattered but us.

I willed myself back to that forgetting place and relaxed my body into his. Hank read my every muscle, every feeling that crossed my face. When we made love his body followed my lead, his eyes never leaving mine. Each time he came to me I felt all the life in the world draw breath through us and I let myself feel it now.

"Looks like you'll be able to get into town for church this Sunday." Mrs. Cutter strode down each line, gathering pins and pulling the clothes Meg and her sister had washed the day before. Hattie ran along behind her grandmother, the clothes-pin bag held wide open, her chest puffed up with importance. "First time in more than three weeks these clothes haven't been froze solid when they come off the line."

I looked at the shirts she piled in my open arms, afraid to let her see the joy I felt at the thought of Sunday and time alone with Hank. With everyone kept inside these past weeks by bad weather, I had done my best to avoid Hank, telling myself surely anyone who saw us talking would know.

Mrs. Cutter made staying clear of Hank easy. She kept me busy, complaining about the state of the house as she worked beside me, watchful of my every move. Mrs. Cutter had the girls working too, all but the babies. Louise helped cook; Madge and Hattie swept and dusted and took turns folding the laundry.

Mrs. Cutter paused to admire the whiteness of a sheet. "That's more like it. You can't sit in the house leaving the help to their own devices. The sheets would be plumb gray before they'd trouble themselves to wait for the wash water to boil."

She had stood in the mudroom, her shawl wrapped tightly around her, arms braced against the broad shelf of her chest, watching while Meg and her sister did the wash. If a piece of clothing wasn't boiled, rinsed, or scrubbed to her standards, she rapped her knuckles against the glass, signaling her dissatisfaction.

I listened to her berate Meg and her sister and admired the sheet like it was fine dress cloth. Mrs. Cutter already thought I was too easy on Meg, my taking up for her would do nothing but confirm Mrs. Cutter's suspicions and possibly convince her to let Meg go.

"I know you'll be glad to see your mother," she said, her lecture on managing help apparently over for the moment. "You must miss her."

It was the most personal thing she'd ever said to me. She worked on, heading down a new row of clothes with Hattie at her heels.

"Well, the mail does get between here and town no matter what the weather, and Mother has been good about writing." I was sorry I had mentioned the letters as soon as the words were out of my mouth. Hungry as I was for adult conversation,

I had let go of something private. The three letters hidden away in my handkerchief drawer were the first I had ever had from Leonora and they'd kept her real for me during these long weeks away.

Her letters came on Wednesdays, lavender onionskin scented with her gardenia sachet. The words marched across the page in lines as straight as the seams she sewed. She wrote me on Sundays after church, and her letters were just like the visits we had then. She told me who she'd seen at services that morning, what they had on, and how the dresses she had finished the week before turned out. She always reserved judgment until she saw her clients dressed in her clothes and moving about in a natural setting like church. There would be a line or two about the sermon, if it had lifted her spirits, and then she would tell me about the work she had planned for the coming week.

Writing back had been hard. I couldn't get past knowing I loved Hank; it took up my whole mind. I only had one thing to tell and I couldn't share it. That was part of my punishment for what we were doing. I remembered girls in school giggling and carrying on when they found the beau they'd been waiting for, and that was just how I felt, but I couldn't let on, not even with Hank, not now, being shut up with the others the way we were.

"Maybe your mother could help Hank out," Mrs. Cutter said as we turned back toward the house.

It was as though she had read my thoughts, mentioning the two of them together. I nearly dropped the clothes I carried.

"I know I'm not much of an in-law," she went on, "but if she could introduce him to some of the girls she knows from her work, I'd be grateful. He's been up and down that road to church since before Berta Mae was born and I've yet to hear him mention a soul. You see him eyeing anyone, doing any talking?"

I shook my head, swallowing the jealousy I felt. "I can't speak for Hank, Mrs. Cutter. I go to church to hear the Lord's word."

Mrs. Cutter laughed, her breath showing in the damp air. "Get on in the house, Hattie, and tell Madge to clear the dining room table for the clothes. Church," she said, lowering her voice as she watched Hattie skip to the house, "like everything else in life, has more than one use. You seem smart enough to know that."

We were at the back door. Mrs. Cutter stopped and looked me in the eye like she was seeing through to something that caught her attention, something she hadn't realized was there. "Yes, I think you know it as well as anybody might." She added the clothes she carried to mine, the pile nearly covering my face. "I want to see how that field behind the barn is thawing out," I heard Mrs. Cutter say, her tone back to business. "You better get the beans going for supper."

I fumbled with the door handle, struggling to see her over the mound of clothes. I watched her stride across the yard, unsure what she knew.

"How much longer do I have to stand still?" The March wind whipped my suit around me, threatened to take my hat off my head.

Hank stood at the end of Leonora's front walk, stared into the viewfinder of the borrowed Kodak, his hair blowing across his face. "Just four frames left," he said, without raising his eyes to look at me.

He had insisted on shooting his roll of film while the sun was still high, telling Leonora he was practicing to see if he should buy a camera. To make his story hold he'd had her pose first, photographing her on the porch swing, then the steps, and finally standing by the front door, until she tired of it, insisting she had to finish preparing dinner.

"I need a picture of you," he had whispered the night before as I put away the last of the supper dishes. One eye on the dining room door, he ran his finger across my cheek, traced the line of bone beneath the skin. "Hard as I try when you're away from me I can't call up the shape of this." His hand glanced down my face, curved around my chin, then dropped when a chair scraped against the floor in the dining room.

Hank moved closer, his eyes never leaving the camera. "Stay this way, Aurilla," he called, his voice low and coaxing. "This is the way I will always see you."

10

DARLENE

She watched Clayton light up, pull smoke in his lungs. He leaned back on his elbows on the hood of her car, exhaled a string of rings that grew larger and looser as they floated out toward the lake. She watched the circles turn wispy in the car's headlights, then dissolve in the night air. In her mind she saw the magnolias she'd sent Donald Ray bob and weave in the water, drunk with her desire to connect with him.

Donald Ray had answered her, but not in any way she could have imagined. She stole a sideways glance at Clayton. It was usually him staring at her with that slow regard that was new but familiar and made the world feel tipped on its side, made her wonder who was doing the looking. "Don't do it again," she whispered.

"Do what?" She felt his eyes narrow in amusement.

What would he say if she told him about the magnolias, about her wish to be haunted? Talking to him was like walking the eye beam of the barn. She knew she was going to fall. It might be onto the square bales of hay stacked along the barn floor, or further out, over the stalls with their thin, soft carpet of spread hay. These past weeks, she had found herself looking forward to the nights, to seeing him, and to the disorienting surprise of what he might say next.

"Tell Donald Ray anything else."

"What, about you and me? Don't you think he knows?"

The thrill of believing that part of Donald Ray was beside her rippled through her again. Clayton's question didn't need answering. It was enough to let the possibility float between them, charging the air.

"Can you think of any reason why the boys don't notice me anymore?" she blurted out.

Clayton looked at her like he couldn't believe what he was hearing. He burst out laughing. "I reckon they're trying to show you some respect."

"I think I'm too young for that. I think what I need is to stop brooding and have me a good time."

"I wouldn't know about that." His face settled into a loose lopsided smile.

"What is it you do know about?" she said, pushing for some kind of reaction.

He sat up, flashed a glimmer of the old wariness she remembered from their first talk at the mill. "Running a knitting machine, farming, not much else."

"Nothing about women?"

He laughed, shook his head. "Can't say I do, and that's something, long as I've lived with one."

She threw her head back. A wispy cloud scudded across the full face of the moon. Overhead the stars showed white in a charcoal sky. She couldn't remember a night in the middle of summer so clear, so perfect. She looked away. The empty beauty would make her cry if she wasn't careful. "Don't you want to know?"

"Maybe I'm too far down the road to be thinking about that."

Maybe; he had said maybe. "You could think about something new happening to you." There was an open, yielding silence between them and Darlene waited. He stood up, making her think she had misread these past few moments.

"You going to be here tomorrow?" he asked, leaning his frame over hers. He smelled of tobacco, soap, and sunshine. The shirt he wore had dried on the line, hung there by his wife. She pushed this last thought aside. Clayton, herself, Donald Ray. There were too many people involved already. The desire to be overwhelmed, to be taken up by something, by someone, was unbearable. Longing rose in her throat, filling her mouth with the cloying taste of maraschino cherries. As a child she had drained the sugary red syrup from each new jar in secret, eager gulps, making herself sick. This hunger felt like that—forbidden, excessive. She touched his face. What was he thinking? The moon shone just behind him. Like Donald Ray, he could be transparent or impossible to read.

She didn't want to think anymore, she wanted to feel. She pulled Clayton to her, eager kisses ranging over his mouth, his face. His hands settled first on her shoulders, then traveled over her back, under her blouse. He touched her like he already knew her body. He unclasped her bra, held a breast in each hand, the side of his thumbs crossing back and forth over her nipples. No one had touched her like this but Donald Ray. Was he guiding Clayton's hands, whispering directions? Clayton's index finger trailed along the waistband of her shorts, the tip of his finger just grazing the skin below her navel.

Not the lake, she thought. Too much had already happened here. Anything else and she might drown.

"Not here," she said, gasping.

"Tell me then."

She stilled his hands so she could think. Where was there for them? In her mind she saw a flash of neon and the image of a man in coat and tails leaning over from the waist, his arm and hand extended in welcome. The Sir Robert Motel, that's where they'd go.

Darlene slowed down, forcing the driver just behind her to pass. All the way from the lake Clayton had kept his distance, staying back a few car lengths. Her eyes checked the rearview mirror, making sure he was still there. At any moment he could change his mind and disappear, leaving the road behind her dark and empty.

The motel was a mistake. What had made her think this thing between them was strong enough to hold together through the drive into town? When they arrived, they would have to start over. She went limp just thinking about his hand glancing off her stomach. Touching him had felt familiar and different all at the same time.

She turned in at the motel. He slowed down, and then turned in after her. She flashed her lights and he veered off, heading for the side of the building.

She watched him hurry down the sidewalk to the office. He wanted her, he did. How else could he walk into the only motel in a community he'd lived in all his life and ask for a room?

After what felt like way too much time, he passed through the door and strode across the parking lot to the opposite building and the last room, next to the road. In her rearview mirror she watched him turn the key in the door, slip inside.

She sat back and closed her eyes. She could leave now, leave and never go back to the lake. But the thought only felt like more dying, more loss. Nobody but Clayton let her talk about Donald Ray, let her speak his name out loud without turning away. No one but him knew her now, the her after Donald Ray, not even Faye. He knew her because he understood what it meant to be haunted. She grabbed her pocketbook, told herself to get out of the car and cross the black ocean of pavement to Clayton's arms.

The moment at the lake was gone. They were left with the awkwardness of strangers. He threw his hat on the bed, stood beside the picture window that looked out on the highway.

The room felt used up. The sheets showed through the worn pile of the green chenille bedspread. The beige paint on the walls was yellowed from the smoke of cigarettes smoked alone in the dark.

"You ever seen blackout drapes?" Darlene pulled the curtains and the room went dark. "See? They've got this heavy rubber on the back that keeps all the light out. The mill ought to give these to the boys on third, don't you think? Issue them right along with their uniforms."

The air-conditioning unit below the window kicked on, its roar rattling the glass. Clayton laughed an uneasy laugh. "That, and maybe an air-conditioner." He stared into the wall of black the window had suddenly become.

"Maybe you ought to call, let her know you won't be coming tonight." The words were out of her mouth before she could get them back. She had only meant to ease his discomfort, not remind him of home, of responsibility.

She could feel his surprise through the dark. The idea of staying with her hadn't occurred to him. "I got animals to feed. There's nobody to do that but me."

Her eyes had adjusted to the dark. She could see him standing there, spinning his retrieved hat in his hands. "What's Donald Ray telling you to do right now?" she whispered. What had happened to her ability to breathe? It was as if all the air had been sucked from the room. The thump of her heart made her ears feel like they would bleed.

"He says…" Clayton paused as if he were listening to someone talking far off. "Just stop it."

"Stop what?"

Clayton turned to her. He reached out, tracing the line of her jaw like he was memorizing the shape of her face. "Stop expecting and just start feeling."

Darlene's heart lurched, then began to race. He touched her lips, then kissed her, and the ugly airless room melted away. What could she do to make the moment even better? Holding on to him, she stepped backward toward the bathroom.

"What are you up to?" he said, his mouth just at her ear.

"A shower, let's take a shower."

He pulled back, his bashfulness returning. "You go ahead. I'll wait for you."

She closed the bathroom door behind her. Donald Ray's laugh sounded in the squeals made by the hot water pipes behind the crumbling tiled wall.

They'd put a clear shower curtain in the downstairs bathroom that her mother pretended not to see. The water streaming down the inside of the curtain made Donald Ray look like he was melting, all the colors that were him—blue, gold, and white—dissolving behind sheets of water. She was glad the motel shower curtain was white and thick: impossible to think she was seeing anything in the room beyond. She turned the water from hot to cold, shuddered when it changed over. Mouth open, she stood under the shower head, the water pouring in, out, and over her, her nipples hardening. She turned off the spigots, threw back the curtain. Donald Ray couldn't hold her towel, wrap her close, rub her down. She couldn't bear his being disembodied; it was like something she shouldn't see, something that took away from his having been a man.

Their last night together he'd stayed in the living room to watch the news, the first time he had missed her shower since they were married. She took a bath instead, loading the water with oil. She left herself wet, the moisture giving her skin the luster of a pearl. She stepped naked into the hall, the risk she was taking warming her all over. She came up behind him, clasped her hands over his eyes. His hands flew to hers.

No, she'd said. *You can't touch until you have all your clothes off.*

He had dressed for work, the creases and lines in his uniform ironed deep into the cloth by her. He tossed each piece in a mound on the couch without so much as a glance at the stairs that led to her parents' room.

What is it you've done? he whispered, angling the shade on the lamp, turning the light on her. *Your skin looks alive.*

Lie down. She dropped to her knees, holding herself over him, drawing out the time it took them to connect.

He touched the oil pooled in the hollow at the base of her neck then lay still waiting for her. So smooth she had flowed into him, moving effortlessly when he arched his back to meet her.

                        ❧

I lay in bed listening to the water spill over Darlene. I closed my eyes and tried to picture her, but fear got in the way. Nobody but Berta Mae had seen me all-out naked, not since my physical for Korea. Boys had walked around talking like they were fully clothed. I hung back in a corner doing my best to cover myself and not look deliberate about it. And the examiner tying a blue ribbon around the biggest cock after we'd all had a turn at being poked by his fingers and coughing for him. The boy kept the ribbon on, saying he'd leave it for his girlfriend to find that night. The honor wasn't mine by a long shot; the sideways glances I took told me that. Still I tried to imagine it was so and then Berta Mae discovering the ribbon, reaching out when it brushed against her thigh, but the picture wouldn't come.

I even failed the physical. The doctor joked about how I'd be dead by the time I was thirty-five the way my heart raced. Here I was, a year away from that and my heart going at it, so this just might be it. Right here in the Sir Edward Motel with a seventeen-year-old, half-crazy girl who actually believed there was a ghost in the room.

How could she be anything else? Darlene was in a world of hurt. She loved that boy, loved him with all of her at an age when she had no business knowing what love was, and she would never get over him, no amount of living would change that. And now she thought she could use me to get Donald Ray back, and I wasn't so sure she was wrong.

Nothing had been the same since finding Donald Ray. There was the sense of everything being new and urgent, and the need to feel all I hadn't bothered with or had been afraid to notice for longer than I remembered. And there was Darlene herself. Each night I left the lake I told myself I had lost my mind thinking I was doing the living for two and bringing peace to a third.

The only thing in my life that came anywhere close to this moment was eloping with Berta Mae. I tried putting the excitement of the night we left for Spartanburg beside the daring I felt lying here waiting for Darlene. But that instant with Berta Mae was so short and so unlike the rest of my life with her I couldn't touch on a thing that would bring that night back to me.

Berta Mae was soured on life all the way around. I couldn't begin to count the blue skies I'd shown her, or the fields green and full from just the right amount of rain and sun. If it had beauty it was lost on her. She saw the worst in things and each time I caught myself seeing the world her way, a little more life went out of me.

I'd been dead a long time. I couldn't blame Berta Mae or the nameless hurt in her that blocked me out. I went along, never questioning the way she was with me, never asking how it made me feel. I got by, telling myself things wouldn't be much different with someone else. I had believed it, too, until Darlene looked at me for the first time, her eyes brimming with life and her husband not dead two months. A man might risk a lot to find out what fired up those eyes of hers.

❧

Darlene closed the bathroom door behind her, clutching the knob so tight her fingers ached. Clayton was in bed, covered up to his neck. He reached for the lamp and the room went black.

"What'd you do that for?" The sound of her own voice gave her a start. She was glad for the dark, glad for the extra time it'd take her to work her way across the unfamiliar room. For Clayton she said, "It may take me longer, but you'll know when I get to you."

Would he? She had no idea what touching him this time would do to her. Donald Ray had come back like she asked, and he was waiting with this other man, waiting to give her a second chance. Her hands shook so hard she dropped the towel. She could just make out the contours of the lamp, the white rectangle of the bed. Clayton felt like a door, an opening she needed to go through to get free of her fear of living beyond Donald Ray. She pulled back the covers, held her breath as she dove into him. She had to know he wasn't Donald Ray, she had to. She closed her eyes, reaching deep inside herself, loving Donald Ray anyway.

❧

I grabbed for air like a man struggling in water. I was never baptized. Maybe this was my time and my immersion was Darlene.

She was all around me, flowing through me. Tears streamed down my face, for Donald Ray and all he had lost, for Darlene, for me and the deep loneliness of my marriage. I felt cleansed, forgiven somehow, for all the time I'd lived a coward.

11

AURILLA

The gold chain dropped onto the dining room table, coiling like a snake around the tiny cross I had worn since I was saved at fourteen. My hand flew to my neck before I could stop myself.

"You lose this?" Joe asked. "I found it out by the barn."

"I must have," I said, murmuring thanks. The room spun around me. I trained my eyes on my plate, hoping my chair would anchor me, not daring to look in Hank's direction.

"That's a piece of luck," I heard Mrs. Cutter say from what seemed like a long way off. "You'd better check the clasp before you go wearing it again."

I heard the sound of Jay's voice, Hank's laugh, and the chatter of the girls, without hearing a single word. Berta Mae's high chair was pulled in tight beside me. The gentle kick of her legs against my arm brought me back to myself. I swirled the spoon in the mashed potatoes, held it to Berta Mae's mouth.

Joe hadn't found my cross in the dark. How long had he carried it? Since dinnertime? Since this morning? He would have known it was mine. He must have watched the glint of gold shift against my skin as he moved into me time and time again.

I waited for him to say more, but knew he wouldn't. He was never one for talk while he ate, and these were already more words than had passed between us in weeks. I watched the pot roast disappear off his place in regular steady bites. He took no deep breaths to calm himself; there was no pulsing vein in his temple.

My secret was safe for now.

How many clues would Joe need before he knew? If he came home early and saw me coming out of the barn would that be enough? If he woke at night and didn't find me beside him, twice, four times? The many ways I could be found out multiplied faster than I could follow the possibilities. But the lies I told came just as easy and fast, growing between us, pushing us even farther apart.

Fear crept out of hiding to find me. Thick as cotton batting, it wound itself tight around my head, layer on layer, smothering me. I cared for the children, worked beside Mrs. Cutter, and lay down with Joe, and no one seemed to know this was my false life. No one except Leonora. I kept the letter she sent. I knew it by heart, like I knew the Lord's Prayer or the twenty-third Psalm; it was my mother's epistle to me.

Dear Aurilla,

I'd never write this if I didn't know it was you getting the mail each day. With Hank sharing our Sunday visits there's been no chance to speak openly.

I didn't say a word with the first Cutter, but now that you're going around with another one, I've got to speak up. It's nothing against Hank, let me say that right off. Arnold was his age when he left home and having him around feels like having a son again.

It breaks my heart seeing the difference Hank makes in you, but you chose something else and your choosing is done. I pray you haven't let things go past friendship. It's a lot, right there, more than I ever had with a man. There's nothing I'd like more than to see you with someone like him, but that can't be. Even if the two of you could find a way to be together the disgrace would eat up whatever happiness you had. And think of the shame it would heap on Berta Mae.

Seeing you these last few Sundays I know you're worried enough to understand what I'm saying. He's just a boy, Aurilla. He doesn't need the trouble loving you would bring him.

I hope you don't hold my speaking up against me. I just don't see a way things can be changed to let you have the life you need, sorry as I am for that.

Burn this when you're done with it.

Love always,
Mother

I am still not done with it. Why else had I kept the letter all these years, first saving it from Hank, then moving it from this hiding place to that one, until I settled on the loose brick in the hearth in Louellen's old room?

I thought about that letter plenty when I was in the hospital after my stroke, not knowing if the doctors were lying when they said I'd live. Anybody in Louellen's room, moving things around would be sure to notice the brick—it stuck up above the rest—maybe that's what I wanted all along.

Lying there in that hospital room, everything white, the life bleached out of it, I pictured me dead and Berta Mae upstairs tagging things for the estate sale, looking in every drawer to make sure there was nothing she was giving away for free. Her heel would snag on the brick, an edge of faded lavender looking up at her. That would be the best I could do to account for the way I had been with my daughter and how Berta Mae's life had gone in part because of it.

Leonora didn't know the power she had over me; if she did, she never would have sent that letter. From the day it came until the day Joe died, she had me convinced there was no way I could have Hank. Finally finished with the business of being a woman, of feeling obliged to put everybody else before me, I don't believe Leonora for a minute.

That letter was the only thing in my mother's long life I hold against her. Leonora was too proper to live. I mean the kind of living I did those three months with Hank, when I loved with all my life from a place that had nothing to do with anybody but me and him. Not Leonora, not Joe, not Berta Mae, just me and him.

"And Queen Guinevere said to King Lancelot, 'Sir, what seek

you here?' And Sir Lancelot replied, 'I seek thee, lady. For ever art thou present with me by day and by night and never art thou absent from my thoughts.'" Hank paused in his reading and looked over at where I sat by the loft window. I was watching for Meg's signal, the open shade on the girls' bedroom window that would tell me the children were up from their afternoon nap. I smoothed my skirt, my mother's letter rustling in my pocket. I had carried the letter three days, keeping it in the pocket of whatever I wore, reading it whenever I got the chance, waiting for the right time to show it to Hank.

"The queen said, 'Ah, Lancelot, it is vain to seek me here for ever my heart is here in this place and here it will always remain.'" We were close to the end of the last volume of *King Arthur*. All the months we had read these books, I had imagined myself some kind of Guinevere, and it was never truer than now. I was as bad off as the queen herself. This farm was no convent but, like her, I knew I'd spend the rest of my days here thinking about my joys and sins and how tied together they were.

"I'd like you to read something else." I held out the letter. He must have thought it was a love letter from me the way his face lit up. That changed soon enough, his face hardening. "You believe in disgrace, Aurilla?" He pulled a match from his shirt pocket, struck it on the sole of his boot, and lit the edge of the letter.

I was so worn out from worrying that none of it made sense to me—not his question, not the fire that caught the lavender paper, making it twist, curl, and turn black. I knocked the letter out of his hand, dropped to my knees, and smothered the fire with my dress tail. I made sure my mother's words were safe before I looked at him.

"If there's any disgrace here, it's with you and Joe." He slammed the window shutter against the wall. "You're not married to him. I see me all over you." He took off for the other end of the open loft, his boots hitting the floor so hard I thought he'd fall through. "I can see that," he yelled back to me.

"Why can't your mother, why can't you?"

I imagined Meg, her ears perked up beside an open window somewhere, and I closed the shutters.

"What's happened to you, Aurilla? It's like you're scared to move."

The late afternoon light in the loft was dim. I couldn't make out his face, but I heard his disappointment. He was right, I was scared. There were nights I'd lain awake beside Joe thinking of all the hurt that would come about if I left with him: Mother tainted by my scandalous actions and losing all her customers, her livelihood; Berta Mae being raised grudgingly by Mrs. Cutter, then whispered about, mocked by the other children; Joe hunting us down, killing me and maybe his own brother.

"You want us to stop?" His voice was quiet and he moved toward me where I knelt at the edge of the loft. "Is that what you want?" He dropped down beside me. "You want me to leave without you?"

I hadn't let my fears carry my thinking that far along. What would it be like to watch him move around me each day, seeing him and not having him? Or worse, him gone, on to a life that had nothing to do with me? A boundless emptiness began inside me, making me grateful for the coming darkness that shadowed my face.

But Hank hadn't learned the trick of hiding his feelings. I felt all of him in the hands holding my face, demanding I look right at him. He kissed me deeply, pulling me close. I dug my fingers into his hair and cradled his face, drinking in his love for the last time.

"Is that what you want?" he asked again, whispering, his voice thick with tears. His trembling hands still held my face as I rocked back and forth. But I felt my mother, Berta Mae, and all the rest of the Cutters behind me, pulling on me. I might as well be in deep water with bricks tied to my waist. And there was Hank, free to float right up to the light. I was trouble, nothing but dark trouble holding him back.

What if he died instead of leaving? Each day that passed

making it easier to put the loss behind me. Death completes us, giving us a fixed beginning, middle, and end, like a piece of music or the well-told stories in his books.

I wanted this to stop, the talking, the worrying, the choosing. I kept my eyes closed, unable to breathe, unable to bear seeing what my answer would do to him, and nodded yes. And then I must have pushed him. I felt his hands fall away and the only thing saving my life was let go.

For Hank to miss supper, lost in his books, was nothing to remark upon. No one mentioned his absence at breakfast the next morning either, but I knew. I sat there, spooning cereal into Berta Mae. The dry toast I tried to eat caught in my throat, choking me. All I could see was Hank's twisted neck and the deep look of absence in his open, still eyes. Hank, waiting for his brothers to find him there, limbs splayed, on the dirt. The everyday talk and sounds swirled like gnats, coming together in a low mocking roar.

I managed to stumble back to the kitchen, carrying my burden of knowing. Time had slowed to a low crawl. Meg stood over the steaming dishes, the water shining on her dark arms. Berta Mae hung on her skirt, her stream of babble low and continuous. Rose lay on the floor, her finger chasing the changing pattern of sunlight coming in from the window. I heard the big girls clearing the last of the breakfast dishes in the dining room. I saw all this, but I was outside, watching from someplace far off, a scrim of pain and loss between me and the rest of the world.

My legs gave up on me. I sank to the floor by Berta Mae, overwhelmed by a wish for love and to love my baby. I reached out for her and just that quick there was the tightening, the arching back, the pulling away that was Berta Mae with me.

"Stop it!" I heard myself roar. "Don't you dare pull away from me."

The strength that had left me flowed back as quick as it had gone. Berta Mae's little head snapped back and forth, her face full of fear and surprise. The more terrified she looked, the harder I shook her, my teeth clenched so tight my jaw ached. Meg called my name, her voice low and even, like she was calming a wild animal.

Meg's sure touch on my shoulders stopped me. I looked around and saw the other children huddled together by the pantry door, eyes wide in fear, and I let go. Berta Mae came back to herself and began to cry, burying her face in Meg's legs.

Tears welled in Meg's eyes, spilling silently over her face. "Why don't you go on upstairs for a while, Miz Aurilla? I won't have no trouble tending to things while you get some rest."

In spite of what she'd just seen, and the larger trouble she must suspect, Meg spoke in the same caring tone I heard from her every day. I put one hand on the counter and pulled myself up. The scene around me that had seemed so removed just a few moments before closed in on me so I could scarcely draw breath. Everything in the room had come alive—the table, the stove, the butcher block—all of it taking up air, making my own breath come in jagged gasps.

I went through the parlor, too ashamed to face Louellen's girls. I stopped at the door to Hank's room, taking it all in one last time. When Mrs. Cutter realized he was dead, she was bound to clear his room, put it to some practical use. But that room would stay just like he left it until the day Mrs. Cutter died. Except for the bookshelves she had Joe build for Hank's books, she wouldn't hear of anybody touching it. Like she thought he'd wake from the dead and return to her shrine and be the same.

Each day I woke, I had to face all over again what I'd done, remind myself that I'd get through this day putting one foot in front of the other just like the day before. I ate the first peas from the garden without noting their sweetness, saw the grass Hank sowed come up tender and green and felt no desire to touch it.

Bit by bit, I made his plan for leaving into something big and grand, the moment in my life that everything could have changed. And there he was, on the other side of that afternoon in the barn, flawless and unending, like God himself, removed from chance and change.

The first days after my stroke, before I got hold of myself, Hank was with me. I saw him by the door, peeking in, grinning the way he always did when he was somewhere he wasn't supposed to be. I spoke his name right away, not that anybody could understand what I was saying. It'd been years since I had said his name out loud and garbled as my words were, the longing still had the power to break me.

Berta Mae stood over the bed, talking loud the way she does to sick folks, holding out a pen and paper for my good hand in case I had something to say. I waved my arm, knocking the pad out of her hand. I didn't even look her way when she gathered her pocketbook and magazines to go. I watched Berta Mae walk right through Hank like he was air. That's when I knew he was a ghost and that I was close myself.

"You come for me?" I asked. He moved toward me with that swaggering walk of his. He was the same, committed to nothing, smiling, working his way around things. And like always, that was enough for me.

He reached out and circled his fingers around my temples the way he used to when my head would be about to burst with worry over us. I closed my eyes and I could have sworn I was back in that barn loft. The smell of fresh hay and the faint vanilla smell of old books rose all around me. "I've been sorry a long time I pushed you away. You going to stay with me now for good?"

All the time I was running on he kept rubbing my forehead. I smelled loamy, turned earth on his fingers. He was always bringing me something green, a sapling, some goldenrod. By the time he died we had about dug up that whole yard with our planting. "Those dogwood switches we set out? They nearly cover the front of the house now."

"Rest, Aurilla," he said. "We don't need talk, you can rest."

I felt spring then, hearing his voice. It was like someone had thrown open the sealed windows, letting in the same sweet air and sun from that one spring, the one I'd had with him long ago when I was so alive just looking at the bright green of new grass was enough to make me cry.

As I got stronger, he got weaker. First to go was his talk, then his touch, until he was just the barest trace of a shadow hovering over me. Three days later I woke to nothing.

Nobody dies alone, that's what I know. The dead forgive and they come for their own. Hank came for me once; he would come back again. Knowing that is solace enough to carry me through to the end. Everybody gets their own heaven. I know that too. My mother was so prim, hers was right by the book. Angels, that's what Leonora saw when she was dying, wings and harps and all. She laid there, a calm woman all her life until the moment she knew their glory. She claimed they were all around the bed, lifting her up, their singing drowning out her pain. She didn't seem a bit sorry to be dying.

I will be here a long time yet; my people don't die under ninety. But the day I wake up and I am back in Hank's arms, I will know the waiting is finally over and I won't be sorry either.

12

DARLENE

The trailer sat off by itself, the chrome edges of its porthole windows glinting in the sun.

"That's the one," Darlene said. She watched Clayton's eyes fly around the lot. She could tell he didn't see it; he didn't see it at all. She closed her mind to this disappointment and the nagging thought of how he had begun to fail her in other small ways.

"Over there." Darlene took off for the back of the lot, Clayton following along in his slow cautious way. "This one has portholes." She stood on tiptoe, patted the curved glass.

He peered in the window, his hands cupped around his face. "This thing is old, Darlene, and small to boot."

She forgot how tall he was until she saw him towering above her, easily seeing what she couldn't. "Lift me up." She wanted to feel his hands around her waist, setting off the sweet little pain she knew his fingers pressing into her ribs would bring.

"Thing's bound to be unlocked, they've got to want to get rid of it."

"Let's go in then," she said, sidestepping the let-down feeling she got whenever he didn't want to go along with her.

He stayed outside while she moved through the tiny kitchen, past the two-burner stove and the bowl-sized sink, into the living room, where a scuffed-up chair and couch were bolted into the floor. Straight back was the bathroom, no bigger than her closet at home, and a bedroom with drawers built into the wall and a three-quarter bed jammed between the walls with the porthole windows. It was small but she liked the directness: here you would eat, sit, bathe, love, and sleep. Darlene stared at the bare mattress with all the fascination she would feel coming upon somebody naked.

"I don't like the smell of this thing." Clayton had given up and followed her in. He stood behind her, the toe of his shoe picking at the cracked linoleum.

"That's nothing. A little Pine-Sol will take care of that." Darlene opened the portholes. A breeze teased the ruffled yellow nylon curtain covering the full-sized window over the bed.

Clayton's eyes roamed over the stained mattress. "I don't think it's got as much to do with cleaning as it has the number of folks that's dragged through here."

Darlene ignored him. She did this when he got in her way. The motel was ruining things. They needed a special place, she'd decided. She'd already rented a secluded little lot right on the water down at Badin Lake. She glanced at the floor, at the swirls of pink cabbage roses beneath her feet. What did it matter if the trailer was small, if things were run down? This was her playhouse and she would make it into whatever she wanted. "Now who'd think of putting yellow in a room with a rug like this? Pink, that's what this trailer is crying out for, you'll see." Darlene looked out a porthole and waved at the salesman across the lot. "With these windows it'll feel just like being out on the lake in a boat."

❦

Sardine cans, that was what Berta Mae called trailers. Lying on the narrow bed, I hit on one more thing she was right about. I pressed my feet against the wall scarred with black heel marks until the aching muscles in my calves stopped me from trying to prove her wrong.

It would be daylight soon. Through the window above my head came the random twitters of the birds just beginning to wake up, the soft lapping of the lake at the shore. I sat up, looking into the circle of fading darkness held by the window. This poor excuse for a window got Darlene started on this trailer in the first place.

"This one has portholes," she had said in that chirpy voice

that told me her mind was already made up. The trailer, run down, and ten years old if it was a day, sat at the back of the dealer's lot with nothing but the trash dumpster to keep it company. "It'll feel just like we're in a boat out on the water, hearing the lake through these windows."

Despite all her scrubbing, the smell of strangers still came at me from every corner. Whether it was skin or hair or sweat, I couldn't say, but it was so strong it was almost a taste, and it made the trailer feel public the way motel rooms did.

The thought took me back to the Sir Robert Motel. Each time my mind returned, it was always to the same night, the first night, to the shock of feeling all of her against me. Her desire—for me, or for Donald Ray, it hardly mattered which—had been so present it was like being in the direct path of a tornado. To feel so much. I wondered the burden of it didn't kill her.

I turned toward Darlene, took in her peppery scent. Every redhead I had known well enough to get close to smelled like this. They were as exotic as another race. I breathed her in. There was something else, a sweet smell as faraway and wavering as lost chances. A trace of it had greeted me when I got into her car for the first time. I smelled it that night at Ramsey Lake when I first kissed her. It made me want to take her in my arms and rock her until it disappeared.

She lay on the edge of the narrow bed, her left foot and hand dragging the floor. I threw my leg over her, started to crawl out of bed. I was taken by the urge to enter her, unguarded and unknowing as she was. How quickly she could move me to wanting her, how completely she had taken me over. Everything in me strained toward that soft center where I couldn't think of a thing but how right she felt. But she was sleeping as deep as a baby and that was about all she was. Just six years older than Emogene. I sat back, sobered by the two of them coming together in my thoughts.

"Time to start home," I said. Saying things out loud helped me make things real but the word *home* had lost its meaning.

I leaned over Darlene, reached for my shoes and socks, not wanting to set foot on the cracked linoleum floor without them.

Was this home, this used up trailer pulled up to the water? Looking at Darlene didn't give me any answers, though in the beginning it had. I kept coming to this awful place because I couldn't stop, because this was what I needed. I wanted to shake her awake, make her own up to her share in this.

After months of following unfamiliar impulses, I felt less driven to go along with Darlene. She felt the change; I knew she did. To her it meant Donald Ray's retreat, and that made her more desperate to prove him here and more impatient with me for standing in her way. Last night, after sex I heard her whisper, "We could leave, go somewhere new, somewhere nobody knows us." I laid still, letting her think I was already asleep. I may have drifted back toward my old self, but I couldn't begin to think of giving her up. Life didn't make much sense. There was Berta Mae about eat up because I didn't want her, and here I was, eat up with wanting somebody I had no business with, somebody I wasn't even sure was real.

Darlene's hurt was real, I knew that. I saw it deep inside her. It had become a part of her, like the color of her hair or her eyes, like the hurt I'd first been drawn to so long ago in Berta Mae. Where was it lodged, I wondered, Darlene's grain of grief?

❧

Clayton bent over the outboard motor of the boat. His forearms were brown while his upper arms, chest, and back were a sickly white. Darlene never noticed it when she saw him undress, but out here on the lake, with the light bouncing off the water and the silver boat bottom, she couldn't focus on anything else.

"Looks like you still got your shirt on," she yelled above the roar of the motor. He nodded the way he did when he heard her voice but wasn't bothering to listen to what she was saying.

She looked away, concentrating on the gray-green water that gently rocked the boat. Donald Ray's skin had been smooth and pale. Working third shift he slept until three or so and it was usually five o'clock before he was out of the house. That all turned around during their trips to Myrtle Beach. He spent the first day sleeping on the beach and by dark he was red all over, the hairs on his arms and legs bleached blond. At night the skin covered by his swim trunks lit up like phosphorescent sand.

"Can't this thing go any faster?" she yelled at Clayton.

"Could, but it'll scatter the fish and I aim to catch a mess of bass today." He was guiding the boat to the inlet where he thought his luck was best.

Darlene readjusted her cushion on the hard seat and saw her day roll out before her, same as every other Sunday they had spent at the lake this summer. They would sit out here on the most deserted part of the lake, away from the speedboats and swimmers. The smell of bait would get stronger as the day got hotter, the caught fish flapping and then finally lying still in the bottom of the boat. The days were her price for the nights with him. Inside the close walls of the trailer there was room for nothing but their desire.

Another bass landed at her feet. The fish were Clayton's alibi. She didn't mind them so much. She knew that when the pile was big enough, she could talk him into taking her over to where she could watch the skiers.

A boat, bright as red nail polish, cut through the flat surface of the lake. It set off swells, pitching Clayton's boat from side to side.

"That was as good as any ride at the county fair." Darlene wiped the spray off her face. The boat circled around and came towards them again. She turned to watch the girl on skis move out in a wide arc.

She had seen them all summer, the girl and two boys, taking turns skiing. Today the girl wore a bright-pink two-piece swimsuit. Darlene thought her own suit, the green one she'd bought for the lake, would look better behind that boat. She'd only worn it once, though, feeling like a fool with Clayton in his cut-off work pants.

The boat roared by and the girl was so close Darlene could almost touch her. She held the towline with one hand, pushed her black hair back from her face, and waved at Darlene, a full arm wave like a beauty queen in a parade. The two boys—one steering and one looking back over his shoulder at the girl—were smooth and brown all over, their hair white from the sun. Eighteen. The number came into her head. She bet they were eighteen like her.

Clayton never watched the skiers; fishing seemed to take everything out of him. His back to Darlene, he sat slumped over his paper at the stern of the boat. He snapped the newsprint, fighting the corners that hung over wet and limp, heavier than the rest. She watched as he tried to turn the page, waiting for the clicking sound he would make with his tongue when the pages stuck together. "You think you could be more careful with this thing next time?" he called over his shoulder. "Floor of the boat's no place to leave the paper."

"I never realized they were so young," she said.

"What's that?"

He'd been expecting her to say something about the paper, about how she wouldn't let it happen again. He was always looking for her to account for things.

"The skiers," she said impatiently.

"Who else would act like that, cutting so close to another boat?"

It was like he had forgotten how young she was. "Well, they're no younger than I am."

"You've never been that young, Darlene."

Maybe he was right, maybe that was what she was doing here with him. Being a widow had ruined her for young boys. She watched the boat head back up the lake. As it swung around to follow the piney shore, the line snapped out of the girl's hands. She screamed in delight and fell backward, her skis floating beside her like pieces of driftwood.

The noise from the boat's motor dropped off. Clayton looked up from his paper. "Good way to get hurt."

Darlene's father had said that about just about everything when she was small: climbing trees, walking fences, swimming in the creek. She could see him coming across the yard, hitting his hat against his leg to let her know she was in for it.

"Just looks like living to me." Darlene stood up and waved to the boys who were circling back around. "You need some help?" she yelled.

"What the hell are you doing, Darlene?"

She didn't have to turn around to know she was embarrassing him. He was talking in that hushed, hissing tone he used with her when she got out of hand. She waved her hand behind her back to cut him off and yelled again. Maybe the boys would slow down when they swung by Clayton's boat, saying everything was fine and would she like to come for a ride for being so thoughtful. But when they passed her their eyes were fixed on the skier. She sat down to watch again, wishing she had on that green suit.

One boy pulled the girl into the boat while the other one held up a white beach towel. He ran the towel over her in a way that said he knew her body. They were laughing. She could see their teeth, white and new, like the terry cloth.

In her mind she saw another day. The stiff ocean breeze was cold, the sun hot in the blue sky. Donald Ray walked to the water's edge, a big white hotel towel spread wide in his arms. He wrapped it around her, pulled her to his chest. He was warm from the sun and smelled of coconut suntan lotion and salt. Grains of sand bit her arms and legs as he rubbed her dry. They were all the same thing: him, her, the ocean, the sky. She had kissed him, breathing him way deep inside her.

Laughter followed by a shriek sounded across the lake. "What the hell kind of craziness is that?" Clayton asked.

The girl flew out of her boyfriend's arms and dove into the water. Darlene wiped her face, tasting the salt of her tears. She was too young to know what she knew. Donald Ray's death had cleaved her life down the middle. She could act like her old self, but she was as far away as Donald Ray. She was just going through the motions; maybe she would always be going through the motions. Nothing else she would ever get could be enough or make up for all she had lost.

The boy pulled his girl out of the water, all for the pleasure of wiping her down again. Darlene turned away as he reached for the towel. "I want to go back," she said. "Take me back now."

13

AURILLA

"I don't know which going to happen first, Miz Aurilla, you turn blue from freezing yourself to death, or the ice all melt from the hot air in this kitchen. Iceman just come yesterday and Miz Cutter be expecting that chunk to still be here come next Saturday."

I pulled my head out of the icebox. I leaned against the wooden door, the metal hasp digging into my back. Satisfied she had done what she could for me, Meg went back outside to her sister and the boiling washtub of clothes.

How could May be so hot? I rubbed a piece of chipped ice over my temples, watching the water run down my forearm in tiny streams that parted and came back together again. Hank had been dead three weeks and I was carrying his baby.

When my time came and went, I told myself it was the shock of losing him, that my body was running around in circles like my mind. But a few days later when I was living off soda crackers and ice, I had to face the truth.

That meant moving off the edge of the bed where I'd slept for the past six months, catching Joe, exhausted from a day of spring planting, before he fell into deep sleep. My body had betrayed me, responding to his touch with the same animal heat that always flared between us. As I came, I closed my eyes against tears and told myself this pleasure was my punishment.

I steadied myself with the edge of the kitchen table, then moved over to the stove to stir the green beans boiling for dinner. The gamey smell of fatback hit me full in the face. Meat gray, fat white, it floated on the surface of the greasy water. I fell to my knees, retching into my skirt. I heard Meg take the back stairs two at a time, then the sound of a towel sloshing in water, the drops raining into the bucket as her hands wrung the towel. She dropped down beside me, pulled the skirt away, wiping my face and then my dress in sweeping strokes with the towel. "A baby ain't the worst thing," she whispered. "It'll be some company to you in all this."

I figured God would let me die having this one. I spent a lot of time worrying how it would come to pass and settled on the baby's refusing to be born, staying inside me like the secret love that brought it about.

But Malinah came into the world as easy as any baby could and she was born the image of her father. Seeing the likeness, Mrs. Cutter cried like a baby when she sponged her off, making Doc Frazier swear she was the same as her Hank twenty years before.

"I'm getting married."

A silence fell over the supper table. Only Malinah kept on gurgling where she lay in her basket behind my chair, her tiny feet pushing against the wicker. Louellen's girls looked first at their father, Jay, who sat red-faced, bent over his stew, like he'd never spoken, and then at me, confused and questioning. I looked at Mrs. Cutter. This was her house; she should be the one to speak.

Mrs. Cutter wiped the last of the gravy from her plate with her biscuit and ate it before she spoke. "Bringing her here, are you?"

Jay shook his head, his eyes still glued to his plate. "She's got a farm in Troy and two near grown boys working it."

"And what about my fields?" Mrs. Cutter pushed her chair back from the table, locking her arms.

"There's always sharecroppers. What about that woman who works around the house? She got a husband?"

Meg. The woman who had helped me raise his daughters this past year and he didn't even know her name. Hattie left her place and climbed into my lap, her plump soft arms wrapping around my neck. I buried my face in Hattie's hair. Blond and fine, it smelled of sunshine. I pulled her close, my fingers catching in the knots at the nape of her neck. "What about the girls?" I asked.

"Esther's looking forward to having their help around the house." He looked at me, saw my arms tighten around Hattie. He lifted his hand then let it drop, as uncomfortable with me now as he'd been the day of Louellen's labor. "It's a real big house," he mumbled, filling his mouth with more stew.

I looked down the table at Louise, who sat staring into her lap, and at Madge, slumped over her plate, picking her biscuit apart with her fork. Orphans, Louellen's girls would be nothing more than orphans if I let him take them. "Where'd you meet this Esther, the obituary column?"

"Aurilla," I heard Joe caution me, his voice low and gruff, but the thought of Jay carrying the girls off on top of losing Hank made me bold. "She's so old you'll be the one that ends up with all that land her first husband left, that right, Jay?"

Joe's fist came down hard on the table. Berta Mae and Rose began to cry.

"I've heard enough out of all of you," Mrs. Cutter said, but her eyes narrowed and stayed fixed on Joe. He glared at his food, stabbing his beans. The table fell quiet except for the sniffling of the smallest girls. I put a finger to my lips and handed them my handkerchief to share.

"That's more like it," Mrs. Cutter said, her eyes moving over all of them. She stood up to leave the table. Holding on to her chair back, she steadied herself as she bent over to lift Malinah from her basket. The baby batted her fists against her grandmother's rough cheeks. Mrs. Cutter let out an unexpected laugh, full of joy and pride. She moved down the hall to Hank's old room where she would play with Malinah until it was time to put her down for the night.

I lifted Berta Mae from her high chair, taking her in the kitchen. Louise carried Rose; Hattie and Madge trailed behind them. On the other side of the swinging door I listened, waiting to hear what the men would say next. Louise stood beside me, her ear pressed to the door.

"How many acres you coming into?" she heard Joe ask, his voice calm, even.

"I didn't think it'd be proper to ask, but from the looks of it, I'd say three hundred fifty. Boys already got the wheat sown. Her man put in mostly corn last year. I figure I'll give those fields a rest and plant some milo."

There was more but I couldn't bear to listen to them going on like nothing was at stake here but crop yields. I moved away from the door, pulling Louise with me.

"I won't go," she hissed, her whisper defiant.

Madge and Hattie stood beside Louise, following her example, their faces set. I would be doing them no favors to fan their hopes of staying. Jay was taking them; they were part of the bargain he'd made. "Troy's not so far," I began, handing them each a dishtowel. "And you heard your daddy, it's a great big house…"

Seeing the disappointment, the sense of abandonment in Louise's face, I knew I had already lost them.

"Hattie, bring me the brush on my bureau." I undid Louise's hair. Hattie took off down the hall, her new dress shoes sounding against the bare wood floor. It was Louise's eighth birthday, and I had let her decide on her own celebration. She'd asked to go to church to hear the choir, and she'd made up her mind she was going with braided hair. Louise loved singing and music as much as I did, and she was fixy, too, fussing over what she wore, combing her hair and her sisters' every which way. It hadn't been more than an hour since Madge had braided Louise's hair and already tiny strands had worked their way free, opening the plaits that narrowed at her waist to a few hairs, and threatened to send her into a fit of tears.

The brush had been Louellen's. Just this morning I wound pink and yellow ribbons around the handle where the gold had faded from her touch, tying them so that when Louise brushed her hair, they would swirl around her arm like streamers on a maypole.

"Louise, look," Madge said, the ribbons hanging to her knees. "It's a brush for a princess."

Louise had kept up a steady pout these two weeks since Jay had announced his wedding plans, outlasting Madge and Hattie both. For the first time a real smile crossed her face.

"Happy birthday, Louise." The child threw her arms around my neck. I buried my face in her warm hair, pulling in all the breath I could hold. She smelled of the outdoors, and beneath that there was something faint and sweet that brought back all those afternoons I laid beside her mother, drawing this very brush through her hair.

"This belonged to your mother," I began. There was more I wanted to tell Louise—about Louellen, and what the brush meant to her, and how much she loved her oldest daughter— but my voice quavered, filling with tears, and I stopped, not wanting to spoil her pretty time. Instead, I ran my hand down her hair, smoothing the wavy folds set by the first braiding.

"My mother had so much hair and lots of curls," Louise said, her voice filled with pride. Somehow her mother and the princesses in her fairy-tale book had come together, blocking out the real Louellen with the stringy blond hair.

I tried to see her and the only image that would come was of Louellen's hair spread out over her pillow that night she had Rose. Gold as the wedding band on her finger, that was how I remembered it. I knew it couldn't be right, but it was such a pretty picture, I couldn't see the harm in letting Louise have her picture, too. "Yes, thick and gold," I said, the brush releasing a smell so like her mother I closed my eyes and drank deep.

That night after I doused the lamp, I lay watching the shapes of the bedroom furniture emerge from the darkness as I gathered the courage to speak. The slow even pulls of Joe's breath told me he was beginning to slip into sleep. "I'd like to keep Louellen's girls here with me." I had finally spoken the words that had been repeating over and over in my head since he came to bed. I pulled the covers tight under my chin. Asking him for anything made me feel naked. I dug my nails into my palm, willing myself to lie still while I waited for his answer. When I wanted something from Joe, I tried to put some distance between it and me before I spoke.

"That's the mistake you're making right off," he finally said, his head still buried in his pillow. I pictured the red crease running down his right cheek each morning from pressing his face into that pillow. How could I know something so private and not know him at all? "Louellen's dead. Those are Jay's girls now."

In no time his back rose and fell, easy with sleep. In my mind I held each of the girls. When I got to Rose, I had to stuff the sheet in my mouth to keep from crying out.

The losses kept coming like ocean waves, one right after the other—first Louellen, then Hank, now the girls—and nothing I did changed it. I trembled with a rage that had nowhere to go but deeper inside me. Its fire smoldered in my heart until the walls turned to black ice.

14

CLAYTON

I watched the road, waiting for Darlene's car to streak by. From the well I could see all I needed to see. The red-dirt road beyond the cow pasture wound out and back around itself like Darlene's hair spread across her pillow. I'd come to see her in everything. They said that about God, but for me it was true about her.

I took the tin dipper from its hook, plunged it into the bucket of cool water I'd just drawn. The taste of iron stayed in my mouth, coated my tongue. Berta Mae said the iron tore up her stomach. She poured drinking water into quart mason jars and let it stand overnight, claiming the iron settled to the bottom that way. Like most things she worried over, I'd never been able to see that her going to all that trouble made any difference.

It was almost seven. The sun had already fallen into the line of trees behind the barn and a splinter of a new moon hung in the sky. I started back to the barn. Away from Berta Mae's banging in the kitchen, I could listen for the roar of Darlene's dual exhaust telling me she was on her way to the trailer.

That car had it all. "Loaded" she called it, right down to the power windows and air-conditioning. I couldn't bring myself to set foot in it, knowing where the money came from. Maybe I had taken advantage of Donald Ray as it was, finding him dead and then ending up with his wife. The car might be pushing my luck. Although what I felt was the exact opposite, like Donald Ray wanted the two of us together, wanted Darlene looking for him in me.

A car backfired. I focused on the road. Darlene slowed down at the gravel drive that led to my place. She looked up at the barn, the sun on her face. I felt her eyes on me, like she knew I was there watching. She wore the same self-satisfied look when she caught me staring at her. I stepped into the shadows, checked my watch. She would be at the trailer in an hour.

I started toward the house, reminding myself to act as worn out as I usually did this time of day. It would be pitch dark before I could leave. Berta Mae thought I was going frog gigging with some boys from the mill. The long night of chasing down bullfrogs by flashlight, spearing them, and then cleaning them made for a good excuse. The biggest part of frog gigging was the breakfast the men went out for afterward. That gave me until sunrise with Darlene and until eight or so to get back home. The thought of that alone was enough to get me through supper.

"Food's cold," Berta Mae said, her eyes spiked with tears. She pointed with her fork to the plate she had served up for me. I took the evening paper off the counter.

"I got three ticks off Fifi today, Daddy." I didn't have to look up to know Emogene was perched on the edge of her chair, waiting for some sign that would tell her I was willing to be distracted. "They were this big around," she tried again. "Look, Daddy, they were this big." She made a circle with her index finger and thumb.

"I guess we'd better get Fifi on up to the vet for a blood transfusion. Sounds like she's been sucked dry."

"I can't stand to hear such talk while I'm trying to eat." Berta Mae put down her fork. Her unshed tears brimmed, making her eyes bright.

"Aw, Berta Mae, it's just a little bug we're talking about." I knew it was more than that. She wasn't good at keeping the things that bothered her separate. The ticks got tossed right in with my staying gone and her moving into Emogene's room. That had started a few months ago with Emogene's nightmares, but we both knew she wasn't staying in there because of Emogene. She was afraid she had nothing to come back to.

I ate a few forkfuls of beans and a biscuit to hold me until a late supper with Darlene. "That all you're going to eat?" Emogene asked.

"Got to be light so's I can keep up with the frogs." I hopped my fingers across the table, grabbed her nose.

She burst into a fit of giggles, the way she did when she was little. I could no longer see that child in my mind and the laugh echoed inside me like something precious lost. The Emogene I had known was gone and in her place was this awkward long-legged stranger who spent her time on the phone or holed up in her room. She swung back and forth between what felt like ten and eighteen; tonight, she seemed closer to ten. I reached out to ruffle her hair, but she dodged my hand, squealing in protest. Would I know her any better if all of me had been here as the change happened?

Berta Mae stood at the sink washing her and Emogene's plates. She held the sponge so hard I could see the veins in her hands straining. I leaned closer, caught the metallic tang at her damp temple, tasting her fear as plain as if I had kissed her there. "You know not to worry about my breakfast tomorrow." I scraped my plate, held it out to her.

"I don't ever worry about it." She jerked the plate from my hand, squeezed green dish soap in circles that grew together and took over the plate.

"You think you got enough soap there?" Once I could say that kind of thing, pointing out how carried away she was, and it would bring her back to herself, make her smile and soften a bit. She slammed the plate in the sink and turned the water on so hard it shot clear up her arms.

"Daddy, you want to see how I can make Fifi chase her tail?" Emogene jumped around me, willing me to look at her instead of Berta Mae.

"Can't you see Daddy's got other things on his mind besides you?" Berta Mae slapped her dishrag on the counter and headed for the den. "Go on out and play, Emogene. I need the quiet. I'm lying down awhile on the couch."

I stayed at the sink, caught, reeling between them and their need. Berta Mae had never said anything like that before. What had she meant? She had to know about Darlene. The tension in the house never went away anymore. Sometimes, like now, it threatened to swallow us whole.

The soles of Emogene's tennis shoes pulled against the linoleum floor as she dragged out her leaving. What did she want me to do or say? Berta Mae was usually all over her about scuffing up her wax; she heard that kind of thing no matter where she was in the house. But all of her was taken up with me. I could feel her listening for my steps out the back door, listening for what I might say to Emogene.

Instead, I perched on the edge of the counter and filled a glass with water. I drank it down, filled it again. I waited, thinking Berta Mae would say something about the water, how it was the water tying my stomach in knots. I knew better and wondered if she didn't too. I was restless, stirred up. This thing with Darlene had me going all 'round the clock.

I looked out the open window. Emogene sat on the grass, Fifi spread across her lap, belly up. Her fingers inspected every inch of that dog. Maybe she was looking for something else to tell me, something that would make me stay. Until this summer, I could count on one hand the nights I'd been away from her since she had come into the world. The trailer had started something that changed all that.

Emogene said the dog's eyes were violet. Hard as I looked at that dog all I could see was brown. It was all part of making a stray into the poodle she'd really wanted, just like that fool name she gave the dog. Just like Darlene and that car she said was aqua. Nothing more than blue, gaudy as they come, but still blue.

Emogene, though, had some queer ideas; she was born not quite seeing things the way they were. It had made me uneasy, her wanting things to be different, better, burdened with feeling and meaning. Maybe I'd been put off by it because I was seeing a part of myself I couldn't own. Inside me, the same urge had waited for the right moment to spring loose; with Donald Ray's death it finally had. I no longer stumbled from one thing to the next, feeling nothing. Everywhere I looked I saw people hurting, disappointed, weighed down with longings they couldn't name. I thought of Berta Mae's tears, the fear I had tasted. Long ago, in the beginning, I had been able to read her feelings like I did tonight, taking on some of what she felt and being opened by it.

And what about Emogene? She knelt beneath the hickory tree gathering sticks for Fifi to fetch. She was confused by the anger she felt around her, by the distance it had put between us all. If I wasn't careful, she would make it into something she could understand: into her own fault.

An urge to protect her, to do right by her, rose up in me, along with shame over how rarely I put her before me. I'd needed a lie to leave tonight; now I needed another to stay. Berta Mae had heard me drink the tap water. I could complain about my stomach, say I felt off. That would be enough for her.

I called Emogene's name, the love rising so thick and sweet in my throat it choked me. "You got that dog taught to fetch yet?"

15

DARLENE

Gray clouds churned, closing off the sun that had warmed her earlier. Darlene sat up, her body catching the full force of the cool wind stirring up the sky. It chopped at the surface of the lake, broken now into whitecaps that slapped against the pilings of the pier Clayton had built behind the trailer. Leaves tipped with red had begun to fall from the water maples.

She picked up the watch she'd taken off to keep from getting a white mark on her arm. One o'clock and still no sign of Clayton. He hadn't come last night; he wouldn't be coming today either. It had happened enough by now; she knew the signs.

She couldn't even say he should have called. There was no phone in the trailer or her parents' house if he'd wanted to tell her last night before she left for the lake. She pulled her beach towel around her, leaving her face open to the October sun.

She had nearly frozen last night, winding the bedspread tight around her and cursing Clayton each time she woke. This morning, frost had laced across the bottom of the portholes; this was probably the weekend the trailer should be closed for the winter. There were things she couldn't do herself—turn off the gas and water lines, close the septic tank. It wasn't that Clayton was unreliable, he just had a hard time holding it all together: her and this trailer, Berta Mae and his little girl, his job, the farm. She was beginning to figure out she came in somewhere after Emogene and the farm.

Maybe like her he was thinking of ending things. She kept putting it off, waiting for the moment when Donald Ray would reveal himself again. It had been four months since that first night at the motel when even the air she breathed seemed to be

Donald Ray. Why would he push her into someone else's arms to be with him again only to disappear?

Lately, too many things about Clayton got in Donald Ray's way, from the way he walked to how he held his fork. It was as if she was looking at Donald Ray through a shifting, distracting crowd.

An outboard motor sounded in the distance. It was too cool for the skiers to be out today. She rolled over onto her stomach, one eye on the lake as the roar grew stronger. The familiar red prow cut through the water and she was on her feet waving her towel above her head.

"Hey, help!" There was just the one boy. He looked back in her direction, turned the boat in a wide arc toward her.

Darlene kept jumping, afraid that if she stopped, he might change his mind. The approaching boat set off swells that slammed against the dock, sending a fine spray into the air. The motor dropped to a hum. Darlene waited, wanting him to speak first.

"Something wrong?" He looked like somebody who wouldn't know firsthand what the word meant. He wore a pale-yellow windbreaker and madras pants. His head was gold, pure gold like Donald Ray's. It'd been so long since a man under twenty-five had had the nerve to speak to her, she'd forgotten how untried their voices sounded: deep, but like something just made.

"I've got to shut the trailer down, and I don't have the first idea how to do that."

He threw her the line. She ran it through and around the hooks Clayton had screwed into the green wood.

He leapt onto the dock. "That's just what my folks are doing today. I was on my way to the marina for some things. Your parents didn't come down?"

His smile was so open she could fall right into it. He didn't even think of her as being old enough to be married, let alone widowed and carrying on with somebody else's husband. She shook her head, worked her wedding band off her finger beneath the towel. "I left home early so I could get some sun. They're supposed to be here already. Now I'm afraid they're not coming." A picture of her parents came into her mind, her father in plaid shorts, his white socks pulled up to his knees, her mother with her hair anchored by a chiffon scarf. She bit her lip to keep from laughing. She started up the hill, thinking how she would explain the tiny trailer. The trailer wouldn't let her play the part of a young girl any more than all she had lived through would. She slipped the ring back on her finger. "Some weekends my husband and me come out here. We trade weekends with my parents."

He turned to look at her, his face lit up with interest. "You're married? You don't look any older than me. What are you, eighteen? Class of '63, right?"

Darlene nodded, wanting his questions to stop.

"There's a gas line for the stove and the heater," she said, holding open the door for him, "and there's the water and electricity."

He knelt down by the stove, his brown fingers tracing wires and hoses.

"You know I think about getting married sometimes. I've got this really great girl—"

"She the skier, the dark-haired girl?" Darlene followed him around back to the place where cables and lines came together in a hopeless knot.

His face broke into his wide smile. "How'd you know?"

Darlene shrugged. "That boat of yours stands out."

"It's her dad's. He tells me if I marry her, he'll get us one just like it."

Darlene thought about her parents' double bed, the one they'd given her and Donald Ray when they married. The middle was sunken and Darlene was sure it was from all the nights her father had held on to her mother. It was reassuring to think that even though her parents seemed mindless of each other in the daytime, in the dark they were drawn to each other sure as magnets. She was conceived in that bed and she had loved the circle of making love there with Donald Ray, making babies of their own. She couldn't see the meaning in a new boat. "Well, maybe you ought to do that," she said finally, not knowing what else to say.

"Your husband let you drive down here alone? I don't think I'd let somebody as good-looking as you drive down here all by herself."

He was smiling again, and it was starting to wear on her, the smiling back making her head ache. "His work gets him stuck in town sometimes." She'd heard the women say that on the daytime dramas, and it sounded right to say, though she didn't have any idea what it meant. How could you get stuck? The whistle blew and your shift was over; somebody fresh came in on your heels to pick up where you left off.

The boy nodded like he knew exactly what she was saying. "Try to keep him from working so hard." He held out his hand, as uncalloused as a hosiery mill worker's, except his daddy probably owned a mill somewhere.

"I appreciate your help." Darlene watched him scramble down the hill, one hand waving behind his head, the light catching his hair. Something felt lost and unreachable, something gone long before. The broken face of the water and the dense close green of the trees was suddenly too horrible and too big to endure. She swallowed against the wild urge to call out to him, to try and make him stay.

How had it happened that everyone else did the leaving? That was supposed to be her, off somewhere living a new and different life that no one she knew could imagine. How she would leave and where she would go didn't matter—just being free.

The thrum of the outboard motor faded and was lost in the relentless slosh of the waves. Being with Donald Ray had changed everything. Her love for him got so big she had no longer thought about leaving. The wish to escape had hidden all this time beneath the calm she felt with Donald Ray, the sense of home. She squeezed her eyes shut against a surge of tears even though there was no one to see or care. She had buried her contentment with her husband. Clayton couldn't give it back to her any more than he could give her back Donald Ray.

16

Aurilla

Mrs. Cutter poured boiling water into the bowl of dried mustard. "If there's anything will keep that child's chest loose tonight it's my mustard poultice," she said. She briskly stirred the hard lumps of powder until they dissolved into a smooth, steaming yellow paste. Watching her sure movements made me feel hopeful that Malinah really was out of danger.

Heating the stew left over from last night's dinner, I shifted the spoon from one hand to the other, my fingers so thick with exhaustion they could hardly hold the handle. I leaned my hip against the stove, comforted by the sight of Mrs. Cutter in her stocking feet padding up the stairs to Malinah.

Before daylight the baby had wakened coughing, a raw barking sound that made her whimper with pain. Mrs. Cutter and I carried bucket after bucket of hot water up the stairs, taking turns sitting by her crib, lifting the flannel sheet we had draped over the top to catch the steam.

Children died over nothing. I saw the tiny headstones in the graveyard behind the church, listing, broken, the ground beneath them sunken, the carving faded. Babies known only by their last names and their sex, the giving of their Christian name held off until they proved themselves, living past the age of likely death. People buried their pain and went on, the memories of the dead baby blending in with those of all the sons and daughters that came after, like so many insurances against loss.

I could never make Malinah over. Watching her draw each breath, her tiny face red with the effort, the child's singularity threatened to overwhelm me until I could scarcely breathe myself.

By late afternoon, Malinah's cough had loosened and she was

able to sleep. Only then did I notice how my shoulders ached from carrying water, that my hand was stiff from gripping the white metal crib rail, my arm weak from holding up the sheet.

A cold wet rain began to fall, the kind that turns the last green things brown. The house would be damp tonight. I moved the stew off the fire, put on bricks to heat for the children's beds and a tub of water for the supper dishes.

"It's ready," I called out to Joe and Berta Mae. They were in the parlor, him reading, her playing at his feet, making a tent from the sections of the newspaper he discarded. I watched Berta Mae follow her father into the dining room, seeing her for what felt like the first time today. The child dug into her stew with uncommon interest. I was too exhausted to remember when Meg had fed her last.

I handed Joe his plate. His fingers stayed on mine, his touch intentional. I knew he'd be moving to my side of the bed later. Anger surged in me. Here I'd been nursing a sick child all day, his for all he knew, and he hadn't asked the first thing about Malinah, or expressed the least bit of concern for her.

Berta Mae finished her dinner, climbed into Joe's lap, and started in begging for his. Watching him feed her, all his attention focused on her face, my feelings settled into a hard, tight ball in my throat. A small, sweet smile crossed his face as tender as that of any young boy in love. I had to look away, surprised by my jealousy. I thought of our courting days, the time I'd invested in opening him up, in finding him out. I tried to remember the last time he'd looked at me with half that sense of caring, and I knew it had never been there, not even in the beginning. This small sour child had bested me.

"Malinah's better." My words hit the air and rang back at me, hollow and empty. I ran the handle of my fork along the crack between two of the pine boards that made up the table, unsettling the crumbs left from a hundred suppers just like this one.

When Joe did look up from his plate, his eyes met mine, holding them. "That's good, maybe we'll be able to get some rest tonight."

We passed the rest of the meal in silence. I watched for Berta Mae's interest in eating to wane so I could pack her off to bed and get back to Malinah. Berta Mae didn't handle change well, not even the ones that happened day in and out, like waking up and going to sleep, or, like now, ending a meal.

Mrs. Cutter's steps sounded on the stairs. "Aurilla," she said, "I believe that poultice is working its magic already." She fixed herself a plate, leaned against the stove as she ate. "She's sleeping, and her breath's coming easy. Still, I'd take her in with you tonight. It's a cold night when the window lights fog up this early in the year." She drew her finger down the pane in a hard straight line, no hesitation about disturbing the steam, perfect and whole as new snow. She scraped her plate, dropped it in the dishwater heating on the stove. "I'll be going upstairs." She paused, her solid frame filling the doorway. "You holler up if you need me in the night. Don't be shy about raising your voice, I don't hear a thing once I drop off."

"You coming out with me tomorrow to the pack house to check the tobacco leaves?" Joe asked. "Market opens next week."

"All depends on how that little girl of yours is doing in the morning. You might try showing some concern yourself." Without the distraction of Hank and Jay, it was as if Mrs. Cutter had finally looked at Joe and found him lacking and deserving of the ill temper she had previously doled out in equal lots.

I stood up, using the strength of Mrs. Cutter's exit to make my own. "Time for bed, Berta Mae." I moved around the table, gathering the plates. Berta Mae hung back, burying her head in Joe's lap. "Daddy," she said. "Daddy, not you."

"Do as your mother says," Joe said, pushing her gently off his lap. "I'll finish the paper and be up after you have her settled."

Hearing again the suggestion in his voice, I kept my eyes trained on the crumbs I swept into my apron. "Bring the bricks with you when you come." I walked briskly toward the mudroom, my apron held tight against me. I opened the back door to shake out the crumbs. The rain hit me full in the face, sending a chill straight through me. I closed the door against the wind. The baby was sleeping with us tonight. It didn't matter what Joe's plans were.

"That's a good way to bring rats," Joe said, "shaking crumbs around the house. You'll lead them right in the door."

"Take it up with your mother, she's been doing the same for thirty years." Snapping at him usually led to a fight, but it wouldn't tonight, not when he wanted me. I picked up Berta Mae, ignoring her pleas to walk. Left to her own devices, we'd be twenty minutes climbing the stairs, with her stopping to examine every dust mote and crack in the wood that caught her eye.

Malinah was sleeping deep, her breath even and untroubled. I reached out to touch her forehead. Finding it cool and dry, I unraveled, the full weight of relief and exhaustion loosening every joint and muscle in my body. I undressed Berta Mae quickly, concentrating on my fingers, willing them to move one after the other, then settled her under a pile of quilts. I wrapped Malinah in the blanket closest to her body and carried her to our bed. What could Joe say? His mother had stood right in the dining room, saying the child needed to be kept warm.

I heard him coming, taking the stairs two at a time. I moved closer to Malinah, wrapping both arms around her. He stopped at our room first, his face falling when he saw the baby in the crook of my arm.

"You're not keeping the baby here tonight," he said, no question at all in his voice.

"You heard your mother, she needs the warmth."

"These bricks will do just as well." Bundled in heavy rags to protect his hands from the heat, he held them out like an offering. The posture of giving weighed on him, pulled his shoulders down, making him seem less powerful. His knuckles strained white in their hold on the bricks. It would do no good to fight him. He raised the bricks, shaking them. "This is more than enough warmth," he said, going next door to put them in the girls' beds.

I drew Malinah closer, wrapping her blanket tight around her, traced the curve of her forehead, the curve of her father's.

Joe crossed the room. "I'm tired of the store you put in this one." His voice was low and even, just this side of rage. "There's no call for any child getting this much attention."

"Joe, please." The word came so easy, the word I was too careful and proud to ever use with him. I drew Malinah to me.

He grabbed the covers, pushed me onto my back. The sudden movement startled Malinah awake. She began to cry, arching her back in resistance. He'd never shown any interest in Malinah, and it was odd to see him hold her. I had regarded his indifference as a blessing; seeing him carry on like he was her father would have been one more pain to bear. From over his shoulder Malinah's eyes locked on mine the whole way out of the room.

I could hear the baby's cries, low and broken, the whole time he was on me. Worse was my body responding to his touch, joining him in the heat that was us. Each time Malinah coughed, I told myself she was all right, she was better, Mrs. Cutter had said so herself. Malinah's voice faded into a hoarse whimper. I pictured her, mouth parched, open, and sore, like a baby bird tired out from crying for food.

Afterward, I laid staring straight up, seeing nothing but darkness. Joe sprawled over me, his weight holding me there with him. I pushed against him, lightly at first, then harder when I realized that even in the depth of his sleep his muscles were coiled with a will to keep me here. I couldn't make out his face, but in my mind, I saw him, hard and determined, pulling Malinah from my arms, and the fight left me.

In Hank's room a picture frame full of butterflies hung on the wall, all pressed flat and even by the glass that covered them. I pushed the heels of my hands into my eyelids and watched the swirled colors of their wings fill the room.

The bits and pieces of that next morning are as broken as the patterns on those butterfly wings. The beginning I knew from

Mrs. Cutter. She said she found me on the floor by the crib, Malinah held tight between my legs and chest. She couldn't get me to let go, but she could see Malinah was blue with death.

It took Mrs. Cutter all morning to talk me into giving Malinah up. I do have some memory of that, her firm voice and her rough hands on my arm kneading the muscles that cramped from holding Malinah so tight. It was like Malinah was being born again, the pain inside me was just as crippling, the fear of letting go and giving in to the suffering just as strong.

My hate for Joe was finally whole. I could feel the shape of it deep inside, pouring into every hollow and crack, freezing solid, like water on a cold night. I knew that once Malinah was let go, the hate would fill me up, take me over.

There was this horrible knowing that if I had fought him, insisted she stay with me, or if I had taken her to Mrs. Cutter, that we'd all be downstairs now. I pictured Mrs. Cutter dressed for the fields, Malinah hanging on her hip, her arms wrapped loose around her grandmother's neck as Mrs. Cutter scrambled the eggs Joe had brought in from the hen house and set on the counter without so much as looking at either one of us, sullen from his comeuppance the night before.

Joe had the sense to stay away. I read his distance as his owning the guilt for her death. He came in once to take Berta Mae. The child's high-pitched cries were so lost in my own anguish I didn't recognize the sound as Berta Mae's until he carried her out and the room suddenly went quiet.

Mrs. Cutter followed him into the hall. I could hear her issuing orders in the calm, firm voice I remembered from the morning Louellen died. In my mind I saw myself making a sugar teat for Rose, then holding her in one arm while my free hand ran over the clothes in my closet, searching for the dress that would be Louellen's last.

Mrs. Cutter closed the door behind her. "I've sent Joe into town, Aurilla." She stood by the dresser near the window, the sun of late morning showing the fullness of her grief. It wasn't even daylight when I found Malinah. How had I sat here so long, held in that one moment? "I know you were waiting on her first birthday to get her picture taken. I think we better do that today, don't you?" Mrs. Cutter wiped her eyes with both hands. She opened Malinah's drawers, took out her tiny clothes, just as I did each morning.

I had judged Mrs. Cutter cold when Louellen died, mistaking her ability to put aside pain and sadness for indifference. Watching her lay out Malinah's clothes, I felt the potential for salvation that came through connecting with the plain and everyday. Just thinking about dressing my child allowed me to find the strength to finally get up and put Malinah in her crib. I knew how to dress my baby and I could do that now.

Mrs. Cutter silently handed Malinah's clothes to me, one piece at a time, her actions deliberate and encouraging. Caring for a baby, making sure they're rested, fed, warm or cool enough, one's hands get used to working. The familiarity of dressing Malinah was a comfort even though her little body was stiff and impenetrable as a doll.

The Catholics have those rosaries, beads they work with their hands, each one holding a prayer. I had my baby's clothes. Handling the tiny white socks edged in lace, the crocheted booties woven with pink satin ribbons, worked the same. "Leggings," I called to Mrs. Cutter, "she'll need some leggings."

"Malinah's just fine the way she is, Aurilla." Mrs. Cutter handed me one of the dresses Mother had made Malinah last summer. Bright yellow, the print was of a little girl in a red bonnet and smock bending over a patch of white flowers, a blue watering can in her hand.

"You don't think it's too gay?" I turned the material over in my hand. The little girls fell into diagonal lines then shifted into circles and squares the longer I stared at them.

"She's a baby, Aurilla, that's how things should be with her."

I knew why Mrs. Cutter had chosen this one over the others. I undid the buttons that ran from neck to hem and the dress opened wide as a fan, slipping easily over Malinah's rigid body. Mrs. Cutter handed me the hairbrush. I pulled it gently through

Malinah's tangled curls, lifting her head to spread her hair out on the pillow around her.

There wasn't a thing left to do but take her picture and put her in her coffin. I felt helplessness returning. The damp of early fall raised gooseflesh on my arms and legs beneath the material of my summer gown. I'd had nothing to eat and my hands were weak, shaking, my bladder heavy and aching.

"Come on now." Mrs. Cutter put her arm around my shoulders and pulled me toward the door. "Joe will be here with the other men soon. We best get dressed."

I stopped at the foot of the crib. I covered Malinah, tucking the blanket tight around her legs the way she liked it.

For two days the house was full of folks coming around with their cakes and hams. Through it all Joe stayed to himself, carrying Berta Mae around like a shield. Whenever a mourner cornered him, he turned sheepish, then moved away, leaving them talking mid-sentence so it was me receiving their condolences. The horrible thing was not a soul among them knew all of what I had lost. Nobody but Meg. She was there each day setting out the food and cleaning up after the visitors and tending to Berta Mae. That evening, she dragged out finishing her chores, waiting for Mrs. Cutter, my mother, and Joe to go upstairs.

"You don't mind if I sit awhile?" she had asked the first night, pulling her chair up close to Malinah's coffin. We stayed like that, sharing a quilt for warmth, neither one of us talking, the sounds of the night filling us up. Then she said, "Lord knows that sure was a pretty baby in every way. Don't you feel glad to have had her for a while?"

"What?" Nobody had asked a thing of me for two days, let alone to feel something. Not even having Louellen's girls here had been able to reach me.

"You got to find some joy in this, or you going to kill yourself."

"Sounds just fine to me. Then I won't have to worry about hurting anymore." I pulled the quilt tight around my shoulders, hid part of my face.

"Let me see that hand." Meg turned my palm over, flattened the fingers. She ran the nail of her index finger along the deepest lines like she was following the twisting roads on a map. She settled on the line that crossed the top of my palm. I closed my eyes and saw Hank take my hand that first day in the loft, trace the same line.

"This heart line broke bad, right here." I leaned forward, drawn by the low rasp of Meg's whisper. "That break be happening right about now. Things ain't never going to be like they just was again."

I pulled my hand back. "Then I might as well die."

Meg grunted. "They won't be no dying for you. Not for a long, long time." She grabbed my hand. "Look at all that time. You here to hoe a long row. You want to spend it dried up inside?" She pressed her thumb along the arc of a deep double line that swooped down to meet my wrist. "This here's what they call a double life line. Anything bad comes your way, you'll outlast it. Brittle, that when you hurt the most. Being mean won't bring that young'un back. Won't bring that man back either. You got to learn to bend. You done gone through the worst storms of your life, can't nothing ever be this bad again. You got to take some comfort in that."

"I didn't fight him," I said, giving voice at last to my awful secret. "Joe insisted Malinah sleep in her room. I didn't fight hard enough for her to stay. I gave in to him and let him keep me from her. I killed her, just like—"

Meg squeezed my hand so hard it stopped me from going on. "Don't be thinking like that, any of that," Meg said. "That child's croup had already broke come nightfall. Maybe God's mind was already made up. Maybe there was nothing you could have done. Maybe there never was."

We stayed there the rest of the night, not another word passing between us. Coming in and out of sleep when a cramped muscle twitched, I would wake thinking, at first, that I'd dozed off sitting by Malinah's crib. Then it would come to me where we were and what had happened, and the burden, sick and slow, settled over me again. Reaching out through the darkness I'd come at last to Meg. Feeling her warmth, hearing her breathe, deep and untroubled, I matched my shallow breath to hers, drawing in more and more air, loosening the fear that held my chest tight until I slept again.

Malinah's tiny coffin was like a jewelry box. Smooth bronze lined with white velvet, a satin pillow cradling her tiny gold head. I sat in the front pew, my mother on one side, Mrs. Cutter on the other, both of them holding my hands. The black kid of Mother's glove was cool while Mrs. Cutter's hand was bare and warm. I held on tight, fearful that if I let go, I'd float right up to the bare wood rafters, insubstantial as the dust showing in the sunlight.

All the Sundays I'd sat in this pew, waiting to move to the piano, a pile of sheet music on my lap, my foot silently tapping out the rhythm of the next hymn. A little over three years; that's all it had been since the winter I first saw Joe Cutter. Not two years since I sat in the back with Hank, watching his eyes to see which girl they settled on. A few of those girls were here today, married since, and showing off their new station in life, doing a community service by being seen at that poor Cutter baby's funeral. If they only knew whose baby they'd come to see buried.

The preacher called for the last hymn and I stood out of habit. The pianist's hands froze on the keys, her eyes expectant, waiting for me to get ahold of myself and sit back down. Instead, I walked toward the coffin and the pianist struck up playing "Amazing Grace," her fingers stumbling over the opening notes.

I lay my open hand over Malinah's face, ran my fingers lightly over her eyes. Every night she'd been in the world I'd stroked her eyelids as she fell off to sleep, felt her lashes flutter against my fingertips as she stirred, her breath warming my hand, a tiny pout of a smile crossing her lips. All that came back to me now was deep hard cold given off by unending emptiness.

I had done this terrible thing. The hate I felt for Joe was nothing compared to the disgust I felt for myself. I hadn't been strong enough to risk his anger, and now my baby was dead. My weakness didn't begin there. I had been afraid to resist Joe in the beginning, afraid to stand by Louellen when she needed me most, afraid to leave with Hank, afraid to let him leave without me. God had tested me again and again, as sure as if I'd been dangling from a cliff, and he had raised my fingers one at a time. And now I had fallen, fallen beyond the world, beyond all hope.

The hymn ended. I turned around, my eyes settling on Joe and Berta Mae. They stood with everyone else, ready to move out to the graveyard. He carried Berta Mae, her face pulled into his chest, hidden in his suit coat, his brown hand smoothing her unruly hair. There he was with the one that meant the most to him in all the world and all I had were photographs of a dead baby and a dead man.

They lowered Malinah into a hole beside Hank's grave that was hardly big enough to hold the roots of a good-sized shrub. I watched the men fill in the opening, shovelful by shovelful. I heard the dirt rain on the metal below, but what I saw was Hank digging up the yard, his arms and face smeared with dirt and sweat that rubbed off on me when I bent to help him settle a plant into place.

The smell of fresh-turned earth was thick on my tongue like it was me being covered with dirt. Part of me was going in the ground with Malinah, all that was good and kind and took an interest in others. The day would never come when smelling a plowed field didn't make me think of Hank and our baby's grave and the part of me that was dead.

That was the true thing in all this, not that "time heals," or "prayer brings understanding," like everybody said. The best you could hope for was accommodation, to know sorrow could come on you sudden, at any time, full, like at the first, and to be able to go on about your business, knowing grieving is a part of things just like getting up every morning and doing what you have to do.

17

DARLENE

The announcer broke into the radio program, breathless, like he'd run all the way from the newsroom. Darlene knew the news was something bad before he ever said, just like she'd known Donald Ray was hurt or dead when the law pulled in her parents' driveway.

Chance and bad luck, somebody as powerful as the president wasn't even immune. Darlene rolled up the windows, locked the doors and began to shake, arms crossed, fingers dancing up and down the pattern of raised cables on the arms of her pink mohair sweater. She stared at the radio while the announcer told her the same thing fifty different ways.

The first-shift nurses came out the back door of the hospital. The older women hurried to their cars, but the young ones stood together by the exit, laughing, lighting cigarettes, looking for all the world like her and Faye had when they got out of school. They didn't know—they couldn't; not to be acting like this. She stared at the nurses, fascinated by the difference between what she was hearing and seeing.

An insistent tapping sounded through the car, cutting into the news report. She brought her hand down hard on the dash, the way she remembered Donald Ray doing in his old Chevrolet when the radio acted up. Clayton leaned over the windshield, his fingers lightly hitting the glass. He got her out of her car and into his truck. They drove to the motel without speaking, her edging up the radio volume. She stayed in the truck listening while he got the TV going in the motel room.

She sat on the edge of the bed in Clayton's usual spot, the TV cart wheeled in close, the chenille spread pulling against the strip of thigh beneath her wool jumper. She watched Jackie crawl over the trunk of the car, the nubby fabric of her pink suit soaking up blood easy as a terry cloth dishrag.

"I think it's indecent the way she refused to change clothes." Beulah shook her head over the picture on the front page of the morning paper.

Darlene's eyes were so swollen from crying all night she could barely make the picture out. It took all her energy just to raise the piece of toast in her hand to her mouth.

That blood had to make the whole thing real for Jackie; it gave the president's death a certainty she had never felt about her own husband's dying. He'd left the house fine and the next time she saw him he was laid out at the funeral home in his wedding suit, not a scratch on him, looking for all the world like he could get up and come on home with her. At Johnson's swearing-in ceremony, Jackie stood beside the new president, her face dead as stone, the blood on her suit dried brown like old scabs. Anytime she thought it was all a bad dream she could look down and see the truth splattered across her lap.

"I wish I had something with Donald Ray's blood on it." Darlene swirled her toast through the runny yellow of her fried egg. "I wish I'd been with him when he died."

Her father stuffed a link sausage in his mouth, shook his empty fork at her. "He didn't bleed, the highway patrol told you that. I thought we were done with this." He turned his fork on her mother. "I don't want her watching any more of this Kennedy mess, Beulah, you hear?" He stood up, buttoning his flannel shirt over his long underwear. "Let sleeping dogs lie, is what I say."

Beulah nodded weakly, stacking the breakfast plates on top of her own. The kitchen door closed behind her father. Darlene wandered into the den, settled herself in front of the TV.

Beulah lingered at the door and teased the flounce on her apron. "You'll turn that thing off when Pap comes in for dinner, won't you?"

Darlene nodded, staring straight ahead at the set. Out of the corner of her eye she saw Beulah hovering by the door, her unsteady form as distracting as the black specks that sometimes floated across her eyes, settling somewhere beyond her field of vision.

There were no pictures taken of Darlene right after Donald Ray's death, but watching Jackie on television, seeing her in the papers, she didn't need pictures to know this was how she had looked. It was too easy and felt too familiar copying Jackie's numbed expression. Shock and strain, these were the words the television announcers used to describe Jackie's condition, the same words murmured over Darlene as she'd floated past the mourners, her mind off someplace where none of it had ever happened.

Part of her still couldn't believe Donald Ray was dead. The knowledge hid somewhere between the past and present, allowing her to believe he was still here. Not even her nightmare made it real, the one she'd had again last night. She watched the pallbearers close Donald Ray up before they turned to her and put her inside the casket beside his. The only sound was her fists beating against the lid, the tufted fabric muffling her pounding.

What nightmares was the First Lady having? Did she sit paralyzed, watching the life drain out of her husband, or did she maybe drown in a sea of his blood? People were always urging you to write your congressman; she would write Jackie, tell her the things she felt.

She got out the fresh box of note cards her mother had bought her to write thank-you notes for Donald Ray's flowers. Her mother had hounded her so about sending the cards that finally she told her she did and hid the box of stationery away beneath her underwear.

Dear Jackie,

Having just last spring lost my husband of less than a year in a car accident, I'm going through the whole thing again with you. We were living a fairy tale, just like you and the president, and I know how it feels when dreams end but you can't wake up.

Sincerely,
Darlene Spencer

Faye's ongoing prattle broke into the last refrain of "Teen Angel." "This is the most morbid thing I ever saw." She lay on her stomach crossways on Darlene's bed, the scrapbook open on the floor. Darlene swiveled her vanity stool around to see what page Faye was on. She had already passed the heavy black pages filled with newspaper clippings about Donald Ray's basketball games, his graduation announcement, the envelope full of movie stubs, their wedding invitation, his obituary notice, the pamphlet from the funeral home. She was into the section on Jackie, the newspaper clippings about the assassination showed white against the black. A card from Mrs. Kennedy's secretary saying how comforted the First Lady had been by Darlene's sharing of her personal loss and acquaintance with grief was wrapped in Saran Wrap.

"Haven't you had enough dying without borrowing somebody else's?" Faye's fingers played at the edges of the plastic.

Darlene started the record over, turned back to the mirror. "You can't understand," she said to her reflection. "It's the same. It's the same with me and her."

An endless line of steel legs, toes tilted upward toward the ceiling, paraded toward her. Darlene never wore a watch to the hosiery mill, seeing the slow sweep of the hands only made the time drag more.

She'd come on the job in the dead of winter and at the time it didn't seem so bad. There were no windows but there was nothing outside to see or feel but gray and cold.

She hated the brown hairnet that dulled her hair, the being made to dress like everybody else. She changed small things that would slip past the floorman's eyes, one day a butterfly pin on the lapel of her uniform, on another a colored belt to cinch the uniform's shapeless waist.

But the uniform held the smell of the sealed mill—the smell of yarn running through oil on the knitting machines—that made her memories flow like nowhere else. At each stoplight on her drive home she'd bury her face in her sleeve and breathe in the traces of oil clinging to her uniform, the same scent that had been on Donald Ray when he came through the door each morning.

She had been able to watch Clayton, too, seeing more of him than she had this whole time they'd been together. She had only known him the way he was when he was alone with her. When she first saw him on break, talking with a group of men by the drink machine, it hit her how odd their situation was. When they were together, they only talked to gas attendants, waitresses, and ticket sellers.

In the beginning she'd liked that her time with him was all hers. But she found herself missing the common intimacies, the simple and familiar ways to know someone, not just how they were with you, but with the people you loved.

Donald Ray had worked alongside her father during evening chores and helped Chrissie do her lessons after clearing the supper dishes with her mother. She thought longingly of the light that came over his face when Chrissie came in the room, the loud laugh that he only let out when her father told one of his dirty jokes, and the careful politeness he reserved for her mother. Watching Clayton around the curves of the leg forms, she looked for something she didn't know, something that might make him more real and lovable to her.

There wasn't much to see while they worked. The fixer roamed back and forth between twelve knitting machines, his tool belt swung low on his hips. He stopped to issue an order to a knitter, or to right a machine that was giving trouble. Clayton seldom called on him. He was careful. She knew that already from the cautious, thought-out way his hands moved over her in the dark. Most times when he passed Clayton, the fixer just nodded, his face full of satisfaction as he watched

Clayton's loping stride carry him from one end of the sixty foot machine to the other, or him remembering to cream his hands before taking a finished pair of stockings off the machine.

Breaks and dinnertime told her more. Breaks were staggered by job, and the knitters were let off first. Clayton liked to lean into the wall by the drink machine, one foot propped behind him, his RC resting on his knee. The men shared packs of Nabs, candy, or passed around peanuts to sprinkle in their drinks. Clayton usually stepped up to the machines to treat the rest of them, his hands rambling through all his pockets before he located his change. He spent more of his time handing food to the others than he did eating. Lunchtime everybody filed into the employees' lounge, a room that with its brown folding tables and chairs looked like the church basement used for suppers. The men stayed on one side, the women on the other, with courting couples keeping to the tables at the back.

Clayton carried his food in a paper sack. Berta Mae didn't seem to put much effort into what she sent with him. A can of pork and beans or Vienna sausages, a few leftover biscuits, maybe a piece of chicken, store-bought potato salad, or coleslaw. He ate in a big hurry, washing his food down with tap water. She would watch his Adam's apple move as he drank, and see him gulping for air when they were in bed. Each day when he finished, he would wad his bag into a tight ball, throw it into the trash can by the water fountain, and go outside.

"It's because of me you leave the lounge every day, isn't it?" she had asked him last night as they dressed to leave the motel. She was already mad because he wouldn't go eat supper with her, so she pushed, knowing he'd be gone in a few minutes anyway. "What's the matter with you?" Darlene waved her hands around the room, taking in the glasses wrapped in paper on the table, the stack of small fresh soaps on the dresser by the bathroom door. "Right here is fine, but you can't take it out in public?" Clayton had turned up the sound on the TV, pretending to be interested in what the newscaster had to say, his hands busy with the laces on his shoes.

"That one can put his shoes under my bed anytime he pleases," Shirley murmured as Clayton walked by their lunch table. "I wouldn't mind being wrapped up in those long legs." The other women tittered.

Marge pushed aside the stocking order form. It was payday and it was understood that everyone had to buy at least one box of stockings. "I think you done missed your chance." She wiped the sweat off her drink bottle with a paper napkin, her eyes openly on Clayton.

Marge's seniority made her an authority on everything. Marge was a supervisor, had spent half her life at the mill, and wore her twenty-year pin on the collar of her starched gray-striped dress to prove it. Darlene had been assigned to work alongside her on her first day. Hands hovering, stocking stretched over her open fingers, she dropped the nylon quickly over the hot steel form, easy as a spider trapping a fly. "Not a single burn in twenty years," she'd said, handing a pile of stockings to Darlene, the smug look on her face daring her to match her safety record.

"Used to be," Marge was saying, "he was at least friendly. Lately, he don't even look in the direction of this table. He's putting it to somebody, all right."

"Who do you think it is?" Shirley leaned closer, her plump cool arm pressing up against Darlene.

"I tell you who it's not." Marge paused, lighting her cigarette, her face grimacing in the sudden plume of smoke. "And that's that wife of his. I don't believe I've ever seen anybody more dried up than her."

Darlene wanted to say that it was her Clayton was putting it to, that she was why he spent half his dinner break in his truck. But she'd kept her distance from the women she worked with. Afraid they might put two and two together about her and Clayton, she let the women's stories, the details of their lives wash through her as easily as water poured in a sieve. If she'd acted differently—shown some interest in the pictures of children and grandbabies, read the recipes they shared, tried that new lipstick on the back of her hand like everybody else before she passed it on—she could tell them what she'd been up to these last six months. They'd all suck in their breath and laugh, surprised to learn the truth about Clayton, and they'd probably have some advice.

"I tell you what," Marge said to Glenda, the young girl across the table who had just confessed to seeing a married man. "You better have a good time now, get all you can out of him. I don't care what he told you, he won't be leaving his wife. She owns that land they live on, her daddy deeded that to her when she married." She tapped her cigarette ashes into her half-empty drink bottle, crossed her arms over her chest. "They don't leave, men. They never do, except in some extreme case."

Darlene had been half paying attention, the way you listen to strangers talk, until she heard this last thing. She thought about Marge's husband, a checker who stood at the door each morning examining the arriving workers' hands. He had pulled her aside more than once after dragging a stocking across her hand, making her wince as he jerked his file across a rough nail. The tight pleased set of his mouth told Darlene while Marge might be the boss here, it was otherwise at home. The woman had probably seen firsthand enough marital disappointment to make her an expert.

Extreme case. Darlene wanted to ask what that meant. What did Berta Mae have that Clayton couldn't give up? She couldn't ask, so she stared at Glenda, waiting for her to do the asking for her. But Glenda slid down in her seat, worrying the buttons on her cardigan, cowed by the older woman's experience.

"You're playing with fire." Marge dropped her cigarette in her drink bottle, the sizzle of the butt emphasizing her words. Her eyes settled on Darlene. "See you don't get burned."

Darlene studied the clutch of little red scars on her hands. She had already burned herself plenty. There'd never be a twenty-year pin for her.

A spray of ice hit them as the waltzing couple banked a turn. "See," Darlene said, nudging Clayton, "I told you it was worth the extra money for these front row seats." Clayton wiped his face with his handkerchief, offered it to Darlene.

She pushed his hand away, leaned over the railing. The pair flashed by on blades fine as razors. Tiny shards flew off their skates, glittered like jewels in the colored spotlights roaming the white ice.

Outside the coliseum, the sleet that had fallen last night, threatening their trip to the *Ice Capades*, was melting, turning the ground to soft mud. But here the fantasy of a winter paradise was safe. She drank in the beauty of the perfect glinting expanse before her, blocking out the giant air-conditioners that hummed just beneath the music.

The skaters spun in a series of quick turns. The girl twirled inside the circle of the boy's arms, her short white dress turning from blue to green under the lights. Darlene felt the crowd stir and braced herself for the building roar of approval that would send chills all through her. Skating backward, the pair bowed, spun around, and landed on one leg. They glided toward the exit, disappearing behind the heavy red velvet curtain.

"Looks like the last act is coming." Clayton threw his program on the floor beside his empty popcorn box and shifted on the metal seat. "I'm about ready for this thing to be over."

"Don't you want your program?"

He glanced at the floor, shook his head. "What am I going to do with that? Leave it somewhere so Berta Mae can come across it?"

"Give it to me," Darlene snapped. She held out her hand, her eyes on the curtain on the other side of the rink. *Sleigh Parade*, the program said. *Members of the audience will be selected to join the procession.* They'd pick her, she was sure of it. Whoever was doing the choosing, she'd stare them down. She'd never had any trouble getting noticed once she decided she wanted to be. Besides, they'd have to take people from the front; they couldn't go running up the stairs on ice skates.

A trumpet sounded and the audience fell quiet. Two little girls in red and green pulled back the curtains and six men dressed like elves came through, pulling the sleigh by red satin ribbons.

Clayton snorted. "They're no more pulling that thing than I am."

Darlene ignored him, holding her breath to see what would come next. A wave of skaters dressed in red velvet and white fur fanned out behind the sleigh, swirling toward different parts of the rink. The girl who had danced the duet headed for Darlene, the smile on her lips so neutral Darlene couldn't tell if she was seeing her or not. Her pulse shot up and she leaned forward, ready to take the girl's hand. When the skater reached the railing, she turned her blades sharply, stopped at the little boy seated beside Clayton.

Darlene collapsed against the back of her seat, the metal bars digging into her back. "Now why are they just taking kids? I wanted a ride in that thing."

"What are you thinking?" Clayton's eyes spun around the audience. "Anybody could be in this crowd."

"And what of it? You think any time I'm seen somewhere folks automatically think of you? You could wait for me outside, or not. It's not like I don't have my own car here."

Clayton pretended to be interested in who all else was getting picked but she knew by the white line of his lips that he was angry at her for bringing up the separate cars again. "I don't see why we can't go in one car," she'd said to him at the hospital parking lot before they left today. "I ride with you when we go to the lake sometimes."

"That's a different direction, we get right on the highway then." Clayton had glanced over his shoulder, like he felt eyes on him. "Now we'll be cutting right through town."

He was burdened by the two of them; he saw people watching him everywhere. Even the way he looked out of his eyes had changed. He used to take the world straight on, his eyes clear and open. Now they moved side to side, always checking to see who was around him.

The sleigh parade ended. The lights went up. The music died away. Clayton moved up the aisle with everybody else, but Darlene hung back until she was the last one left.

Soon there was nothing but the endless cycling of the air-conditioners, the silvered gleam of the scarred ice. The charged emptiness reminded her of the nights she spent alone at Ramsey Lake, keyed up and waiting for the world to open again.

She clung to the rail, steadying herself against the sure awareness that inched its way through her. She knew this place. This still coldness was her heart. She had felt like this inside since Donald Ray died, she had felt like this for so long she couldn't imagine ever feeling any other way. Even her memories of Donald Ray were lost to her, encased in a filigree of ice that each day grew more elaborate.

She had needed to believe something extraordinary could still happen to her. That wish, she had lived on that wish, but she had never stopped to think what she was wishing for. She only knew that when this thing happened, the pieces of her life would shift mysteriously, like the bits of glass in a kaleidoscope, into a pattern she would recognize at once, and everything would be changed.

She had imagined Donald Ray's death as a kind of bridge between her and Clayton, a way out. To what, she hadn't let herself think. Clayton was not the answer. She had known, she realized, in the trailer waking up next to him, in the boat, at the lake by herself, here with him this afternoon.

She had told herself a thousand lies. Now, the largeness of the truth and the despair that followed threatened to escape her head and take over the whole of the coliseum. What had she done to him—what had she done to herself? Why did he go on with it, why did she? She wasn't ready to leave him, she knew that. But she didn't know where else to go, how to do anything but what she was doing.

A service door opened. A growling Zamboni moved onto the ice, clearing away the traces of the dancers and the sleigh. She turned from the ruin of those perfectly etched circles and spirals and ran, each step she took toward the exit pushing her thoughts farther down inside, back where they belonged.

18

BERTA MAE

Whenever Berta Mae was worked up, she took a scrap and just stitched. She felt Grandmother McMath's hands guiding her fingers, her touch smooth and soft like a baby's. Pushing a needle through cloth, making a straight line of even stitches, each just like the one before, brought reason to the world.

Life had first turned right for her during the summers she spent with her grandmother. She remembered her father arguing to keep her home, his voice coming through the walls of her parents' bedroom loud and harsh, and Aurilla's, low and insistent, quiet as a hissing snake. For years Berta Mae thought Aurilla sent her away because her father liked her better. Maybe the best Aurilla could do for her was sending her to her mother, getting her out of that house and away from the two of them.

Grandmother McMath didn't live a thing like the Cutters. Each morning she had come downstairs in her seersucker wrapper, fixed her coffee, and drank it on the sunporch while reading the Bible. She sent Berta Mae out with a colander in one hand and a basket in the other, looking for berries and flowers. "Now mind the roots," she called out, her eyes fixed on her reading. "Pinch the flowers off the plant, don't pull them." Every blooming thing imaginable was in that backyard. In June, fat bumblebees drunk on nectar buzzed over mounds of blue and yellow columbine, jack-in-the-pulpit, and the purple and white clematis running up the trellis that screened off the basement steps. Then came yarrow: yellow, white, pink, and coral bells, and right before Berta Mae left for home, the stonecrop, deepening each day from rose to red, and mums yellow and orange like autumn coming. Always in order, always the same; she never wanted to leave.

"Every girl should know how to arrange flowers," Grandmother said. She spread newspaper on the counter by the sink. Berta Mae cleaned the lower leaves off the stems. The vase kept on the table in the sunporch was fashioned out of three white calla lilies, the flowers' trumpets holding the blossoms, their heart-shaped leaves forming the base. Grandmother placed the flowers in one at a time, then stood back to "take in the whole effect," trimming a stem here, moving a flower there, until a look of contentment would drift across her face, her hand passing over the flowers one last time before she carried the arrangement to the breakfast table.

"Tiny hands for delicate work," Grandmother said as Berta Mae rinsed and capped the berries. They went in the prettiest porcelain bowl, woven just like a basket. Berta Mae ran her fingers along the webbing, popping the beads of water that filled the openings like tiny gleaming mirrors. "Portuguese." Grandmother's finger tapped the rim of the bowl. "It was my mother's and someday it will be yours." Berta Mae had no idea what Portuguese meant, but she could tell from the pride in Grandmother's voice that it made the bowl precious and rare.

After berries came soft-boiled eggs served in china egg cups rimmed with gold. They sat dipping toast into the creamy yellows and Grandmother talked about her Bible reading. She told Berta Mae the stories of Joseph and his many-colored coat, David and Goliath, Moses in the bulrushes. Other adults didn't talk, they gave orders, and here Grandmother was, talking to Berta Mae all day and listening to what she said.

That berry dish was still here somewhere, probably in one of the high cabinets where Berta Mae put the fragile things when Emogene was little and into everything. She had to fight Aurilla for that bowl when Grandmother McMath died, Aurilla telling Berta Mae, she'd be welcome to it when she was done with it. But Berta Mae was going to have that bowl if she didn't get anything else, which was about how it turned out. She had pictured herself with a daughter someday, the two of them sitting down to breakfast like she'd done with her grandmother.

Of course, no such thing ever happened. Emogene won't hear of eating a thing in the morning besides pickle-loaf and mustard sandwiches washed down with Pepsi. Besides, nobody grew berries anymore. She couldn't see putting those big things with the white hollow centers and no taste in that bowl, it'd be an insult to Grandmother's memory.

Berta Mae did have the embroidery designs Grandmother made her; a drawer full of the things. "Shake your hands, shake your arms, now jump around in a circle." That was how Grandmother began Berta Mae's morning embroidery lesson. "You must be loose if you want your stitches to flow." When she put herself back in Grandmother's sewing room, she saw the one of the Lord's Prayer with lambs all around the border, their fluffy coats made up of looped stitches of white thread. The faithful flock, Grandmother called them, the ones Jesus would lead into heaven.

Heaven was right there, watching her grandmother pin dress patterns to fabric on the long mahogany dining table, her fingers arranging the pins in tight neat lines. The bolts that lined the dark paneled room emitted the smell of new cloth. Spools of ribbons and lace covered the mirrored sideboard. Everything in that room was old, passed down, but the furniture never took on that faded mildewed smell until Grandmother died and Aurilla sold the house and took everything for herself.

Each new dress was like life starting over fresh and unspoiled. As Grandmother's customers changed, so did the dress forms that stood by the double windows. "Morning, Mrs. Staley, Miss Staley, Mrs. Watkins," Grandmother would say, nodding briskly in their direction as she opened the French doors. She'd go on like that, talking to each one as she tacked on a skirt or pinned a hem. She moved back and forth, Berta Mae following, plump red tomato pincushion in one hand, a pin ready in the other, waiting for her grandmother's nod and outstretched hand. "Suck in your stomach, Mrs. Staley, or I'll never get this waist set. You always bring me blue no matter how much talking I do about warm colors. Washes you out, that's what this color does."

Berta Mae saw it as a game and she fell right in, offering the dress forms tea, fanning them if it was a hot day. Now she knew that talking to them was Grandmother's way of filling up that big quiet house.

"Have you been a good girl for Daddy?" Chill bumps came up on Berta Mae's arms even though her neck was moist from the heat of the August afternoon. He stroked her hair, his rough fingers catching in the curls her grandmother had set the night before.

They sat on a bench under the grape arbor, the air thick with the sour smell of crushed scuppernongs. Her parents had come into town to church that morning, staying for dinner at Grandmother McMath's. Mama and Grandmother were in the kitchen. Berta Mae heard their voices through the open window overlooking the back yard; Grandmother's low and even, each word blending into the next, and Aurilla's, harsh, like the pots clattering in her hands.

She had never seen her father like this, combed and shaved all at once, stiff white collar rubbing at the brown skin of his neck, and she told herself maybe he was different, maybe he and Mama were different together.

Berta Mae felt sick, knots of pain marching across her stomach. She didn't want to go home, not now, not ever. Grandmother had just said this morning that it was more than a month before she had to go.

She looked up through the bower, past the leaves and clusters of amber-green fruit, to the kitchen window. Mama's dress, a blur of pink, moved from the table to the sink. Berta Mae pleaded silently for her to stop at the window, to come running down the back steps to join them, the porch door slamming behind her. She wanted her to be with her father, for Berta Mae not to be the one taking him away.

Mama paused at the window. Her eyes moved slowly,

appreciating Grandmother McMath's flowers. Berta Mae took shallow breaths, waiting for her eyes to reach the arbor. She looked right at them; Berta Mae knew it even through the fluttering leaves of the grapevines. She looked a minute longer, her face indifferent, unchanged, then turned back to the kitchen. Mama didn't want Daddy; she didn't want her.

The curtain puffed up with the breeze, filled the empty window. Yellow gingham. Berta Mae had chosen the cloth herself from all the bolts at the dry goods store. Her grandmother laid the material out on the dining room table, guiding her hand as she marked the cloth with chalk. Grandmother pinched the starched gingham between Berta Mae's fingers, setting the pleats. "You're such a good little seamstress," she heard her grandmother say. "I bet next summer you'll be able to do this all by yourself." She closed her eyes and the smell of new material came back to her, fresh and sweet.

Berta Mae first heard Clayton's name whispered in her college dorm room late at night. A group of girls, shoulder-length hair bobby-pinned in curls flat to their heads, huddled excitedly around a Ouija board. There was only one question, repeated and building in power like a chant as each one took her turn, "Who will I marry?" The other girls got Bill, John, or David, strong recognizable American names. C-L-A-Y-T-O-N, the Ouija board spelled out at Berta Mae's turn. She was sure the girl whose fingers helped hers guide the pointer over the board with its letters and numbers, its yeses and nos and goodbyes, made it spell out this old-fashioned name just to make her look bad. She made the other girls each take a turn with her, and each time the pointer glided seamlessly over the same improbable combination of letters. Even the stubborn drag of her fingers on the pointer would not change its course.

High above the county fairground, yellow and white lights on the Ferris wheel spun big circles of gold, wedding rings in the black sky. This was the first thing Berta Mae saw and she took it as an omen.

She dragged Vinnie to the ticket booth at the foot of the ride, forgetting to be careful of her ballet slippers in the mud and straw. They took their seats; the Ferris wheel spun backward, stopping as each bucket was filled. Berta Mae pulled the red jacket of her sundress—red like the camellias appliquéd on her full white cotton piqué skirt—close about her shoulders.

Swinging in space, the ground beneath her gone, she heard a girl's voice say the Ouija board name. It was not what she expected, the "a" held long and sweet as spilt honey before it puddled deep in the rest of the word. Clayton. The two syllables held promises of something she can't begin to imagine or lay name to, but she recognized them in the lazy tumble of the name. The girl called out again. Berta Mae located her in the crowd milling below. She saw the tall boy with the broad open face move toward the girl as she spun away, backward, into the sky.

"That one of your admirers there?" Berta Mae's father nodded in the direction of the boy standing by his car at the gas station.

Berta Mae looked up just as the car swung a wide left, her eyes running straight on with the boy's. They were clear and sweet, unmarked, like his face. He looked hopeful.

"Take advantage of you, that's all any of them are after."

She didn't believe it, not this time, not about this one. He'd been watching the school playground during her class's afternoon recess since she saw him at the fair. She'd waited for him to cross the road, hoping and dreading the moment when he would come, leaning into the fence like the rest of them, calling her pet names in a voice that said he was sure of himself, then turning nasty when she ignored him. But he kept his distance and she'd grown comfortable with his presence. It was almost like he was watching out for her.

"You're lucky I'm here to protect you from all that," her father said.

Berta Mae bent over her open pocketbook to escape his hand as it moved along the back of the seat. For as long as she could remember, he'd reached out to stroke her head, fingers rubbing her neck through the tangled hair at her nape. She'd never seen him touch Aurilla, only heard them late at night when she lay in her bed half asleep, the sound of his rhythmic deep breaths jolting her awake. Aurilla had made her pay and pay for Daddy loving her the best. She must have done something to make him choose her, something she wished she could undo. She took out her hairbrush and pulled it through the knotted curls, her eyes watering as the brush stopped and started.

Fifteen minutes until the teachers' meeting. Berta Mae took off across the road for the filling station. Her eyes swept the parking lot; he had to be here, he'd been here every afternoon for a month, puttering, watching. She'd just buy herself a nice cool drink and get a better look. There was a drink machine in the teachers' lounge, but he didn't know that.

At the edge of the lot a group of boys bent over the open engine of a pickup. Clayton was with them, his tall frame curved under the hood. One hand rested on the side of the truck, while the other pulled hoses, jiggled wires. He straightened up, a slow unwinding motion. She trained her eyes on the ground. The boys talked, voices rambling over each other, and she listened, trying to pick out which one was his.

Berta Mae hurried into the empty station, eyes fixed on the drink box at the far end of the room. She tried the lid. Expecting it to open easily, her hands flew upward, spread open before her in the moment before she realized the lid had resisted her. She let her arms drop to her side, looking over her shoulder to the service bay. The mechanic went on with his work, unaware of her presence. She pulled at the lid once more, just like she'd done for years with the drink box in Vinnie's parents' store, but cautiously this time. Again, it refused her.

Locks and fasteners were her lifelong frustration. "You'll need to jiggle the knob a bit while you work the lock; won't take you long to get the feel for it," the principal had said last fall, handing her the key to her classroom. Her new heels sounding on the freshly waxed floors, she told herself if she could get through four years of college, she could handle a lock in a rundown schoolhouse. She struggled with it for what seemed like an eternity, her damp hand slipping on the key before the janitor finally came along, opening it with one try. Here it was May and the lock fought her still.

"You look like you could use some help."

Berta Mae jumped. So soft, his voice sounded like he was right at her ear, but he stood by the door, waiting. She nodded and he was at her side in two strides. His hands moved with confidence along the rim, locating the latch she'd missed.

Smiling, he held the lid while she chose her drink. She was so stirred up she took a Brownie drink, one of those sickeningly sweet things Vinnie adored. She was too embarrassed to mention her mistake. He closed the lid and settled against it, his hands resting on either side of him. They were big hands, broad with thick fingers. They seemed out of place with the rest of him, narrow and full of angles. Even his teeth were small, his eyeteeth pointed as a young child's.

"You teach school, don't you? I've seen you out on the playground."

"Third grade."

He nodded, his eyes looking past her to the wall lined with candy bars and cigarette cartons. He was younger than her— just a boy—like the ones she saw in the upper grades when she took her class to the library over in the high school building. Like them, he had a child's face and the start of a man's body. There had been no boys on campus her first two years of college, just older men, or injured GIs back from Germany or the Pacific. Their faces were marked with all they'd seen, old and hard as her father's in some ways, lines running from their noses to their mouths. Looking at this boy's smooth face, his eyes unclouded as those of the children in her class, the blue bright and unfaded, she felt safe somehow.

"Your drink's getting hot," he said, nodding toward her hand.

Berta Mae positioned the cap in the bottle opener, her hands slipping on the sweating glass. The cap came off suddenly, throwing her off balance, and she chipped the lip of the bottle.

She raised the drink to her mouth, hoping he wouldn't notice.

"You shouldn't drink that," he said. "You don't know where that piece of glass went."

He opened the case, brought out another Brownie. He shook the drink slowly, his big wrist moving like a giant hinge. Taking the chipped bottle from her hand, he placed it in the wooden crate half-filled with empties.

"Thanks." Her voice came out thin and dry. She turned up the drink, ignoring the sweet, focusing on the wet.

"I'm Clayton Bishop. I'd be pleased to give you a ride home one of these days." Clayton. Just hearing the Ouija board name again nearly knocked the wind out of her.

"Did I say something wrong?" she heard him ask from a long way off.

"No, it's my father. He comes for me." Berta Mae paused. "He expects to."

"What about Saturday? You like going to the pictures?"

She nodded. Out in the bay a car started up, the mechanic flooring the gas pedal again and again.

She moved closer and he leaned down to hear. He smelled of earth and tobacco, smells she knew from her father.

"Vinnie, my best friend and me, we usually go to the evening show."

"Then I'll meet you right out front."

Her father was set against boys asking her out. Her mind raced, trying to remember whose father's turn it was to drive them to town this Saturday. She saw the front of the movie theater, pure glass, the entire lobby visible from the outside. There was the red velvet alcove inside where they sold soft drinks and candy.

"No. Inside," she said, "by the candy."

"All right. I'll treat you girls to all the candy and popcorn you can eat."

"I got to go." Berta Mae waved her arm in the direction

of the school and backed toward the door. "I got a teachers' meeting to get to."

"See you Saturday," Clayton called after her, his voice carrying like a woman's above the mechanic's banging.

Halfway across the lot she realized she hadn't told him her name. Looking back, she saw him leaning in the door, watching her, a cigarette dangling loosely in one hand. "I'm Berta Mae Cutter," she shouted, cupping her free hand around her mouth.

The boys on the lot turned their heads, looking at her with interest. Drawing attention to herself usually made her feel the fool, but today, looking at Clayton, she felt brave and beyond caring.

She would never have dared if Vinnie hadn't pushed her. "You want to be sitting at the movies with me every Saturday night for the rest of your life?" The fat that had made Vinnie so pretty as a child had worked against her as a young woman. If she minded being passed up by the boys, she didn't let on.

Vinnie was all in favor of Clayton. Each Saturday night he bought her more candy than she could hold and sometimes, after the movie, ice cream. That was Vinnie; all she studied was her stomach. She knew a trip to the drug store soda fountain would make them late getting home, and just because nobody in her house would notice, she assumed it was the same for Berta Mae. Her father would be awake though, waiting for Berta Mae's footsteps to pass his bedroom door.

Clayton pulled over, looking hard in the direction of the house. "I hope somebody's waiting up for you." Vinnie's father thought Berta Mae's father was picking them up each night and they had Berta Mae's father convinced it was the other way around. And Clayton assumed everyone knew he was bringing the girls home. Each time Berta Mae had him drop her down by the mailbox on the main road. "Let me walk you to the door. I'll apologize for getting you home late," Clayton said.

"No!" Berta Mae's voice came out sharp. Seeing his confused look, she added, "Everybody's asleep."

"I can't let you walk down there," Clayton said. "The house is pitch black."

The bottom dropped out of Berta Mae's stomach. She put her face up to the window, searching the darkness for the porch light they always left on for her.

"Don't pull down the drive." She struggled to keep her voice even. "The lights might wake somebody up."

"I can kill the lights."

"But that doesn't do a thing about the engine."

"I don't feel right letting you out like this."

"It'll be fine." She patted his hand. At times she felt like she was dealing with one of the children in her class. "You forget about that full moon you were going on about tonight? It's light as day out."

"I want to come for you next week, meet your people."

Berta Mae pretended not to hear. She waved goodbye, turned and started down the drive to the house. She would be found out by her parents and by Clayton, despite doing her best to keep them apart. The gravel beneath her feet pressed through the thin soles of her ballet slippers. She shifted her weight back and forth from her toes to her heels so only one part of her foot hurt at a time. She moved up the steps to the front door even though she knew it would be locked. She took some white pebbles from the drain dish beneath Aurilla's begonia planter and headed for Grandmother Cutter's window.

"Grandmother," she called in a loud whisper. The stone hit the screen with a thump like a large, light-seeking moth. The wind started, rustling the leaves in the dogwoods. She waited, holding her breath, not wanting to risk calling out again. The curtains parted and Aurilla appeared at the window. "Why don't you just go back to where you were before you drug up here? Out all hours of the night like trash."

"Daddy?" Berta Mae called, then again, louder, pleading.

"Scream all you want, he'll not hear. He's dead asleep with no thought of you."

The window slammed shut. Aurilla's voice—trained on

who? Grandmother? Daddy?—rasped against the glass. Then it was quiet, the house dark again.

Fifteen minutes late. Berta Mae walked around to the front steps and sat down. How had the truth come out? Maybe the fathers saw each other on the road, threw a hand up, slowed to speak, blocking the road in both directions the way they had done for years. Her parents would know the trouble was a boy and now she'd have to bring him home. And when she did her father would sull up and go indifferent the way he had each summer when she left for Grandmother McMath's. Once Aurilla opened her mouth, Clayton would surely be looking for the door.

Right now, she had tonight to worry about. What did Aurilla think she would do? Did she care? She could sleep in the barn, but Aurilla would get too much satisfaction out of her coming in tomorrow morning in rumpled clothes flecked with broken pieces of hay. "Don't you know to brush off before you come in the house?" she'd say, her fingers picking at the hay, pinching Berta Mae as she pulled at her dress.

She looked at the moon. Dark clouds hurried across its wide face. Vinnie's was no more than a half mile away. She could walk there; it was light enough.

The woods on either side of the dirt road rose like dark walls. She picked her way down the drive, her heart jumping with every snapped twig and leaf rustle. Her toes pushed against the end of her slippers, toenails throbbing, and she cursed herself for being too vain to buy the right size. Once she hit the paved road, she took them off, the held warmth of the blacktop soothing her feet. Even in this light she could see the beginning of blisters, raised and red, coming on her toes.

The Craven house was pitch black. Berta Mae stumbled across the yard, trying to recall the location of all the holes dug over the years by the family's dogs. They pocked the yard, many of them deep enough to twist an ankle. Rounding the side of the house to Vinnie's bedroom, she heard the vague whining of Mr. Craven's bird dogs, their rest disturbed by the full moon.

"Vinnie," she called through the open window. The dogs barked, rushing out of the oil drum on cinder blocks that was their house. They danced on the ends of their chains, choking as they strained against the stake holding them inside a bare circle of dirt.

"Vinnie," she called again. Vinnie's parents' bedroom was on the third floor and they never seemed to hear noise; she'd spent enough nights here to know.

"Stirred up the dogs, did you?" Vinnie held out her hand, pulled Berta Mae in. Vinnie fell back in bed already breathing deeply by the time Berta Mae had shed her skirt and blouse and laid down beside her.

Sleep was Vinnie's second most favorite thing. Berta Mae hadn't expected her to wake up enough to find out why she was here in the middle of the night. When they were in school, Vinnie had staggered out to meet the bus each morning, her eyes open only far enough to find her way to her seat where she'd doze off, her fingers loosening around the sweet roll her mother had given her to eat on the way.

Berta Mae lay still, listening first to Vinnie, her breath even and familiar, then to the breeze that lifted the window shade, knocking the wooden pull lightly against the sill. She heard the dogs settle into their cedar shavings, the slow beat of their tails against the side of the oil drum. Further out in the night there was a comforting hum to things, low and even, like the earth spinning on through space, past this day.

Clayton arrived after supper. He sat on the low red-velvet lounge, knees angled up sharply in front of him, smiling his broadest smile. "I hear your mother can plow good as any man, that right, Clayton?" Aurilla sat back, her spine straight in the claw-armed walnut chair that had been Grandmother McMath's. "My mother-in-law could work like that in her day." Aurilla nodded her head in the direction of Uncle Hank's room where Grandmother Cutter spent her time. "Worked around the clock and she saw that everybody else did the same." Aurilla paused, leaning toward him. "I bet your mama's the same way."

"Yes, ma'am, she sure is." He sat up a little straighter, like this was some grand thing the families had in common. Berta Mae knew better. She sat stiff in her chair, her legs wrapped tight around each other. She tried to catch Aurilla's eye. She was out to show Berta Mae just how bad life would be with the Bishops.

"Yes, siree, Bob, no school in the world teaches you to work like that," Aurilla said, leading him on.

"I never put much stock in school. Too much sitting around." Clayton squirmed on his seat as if the memory made him cast about for a more comfortable position.

"Now Berta Mae here is educated, of course; valedictorian of her class."

Suddenly Clayton looked lost, thrown by the turn the conversation had taken.

"She sat over the books so much, Joe would make her stop, telling her she'd go blind if she kept on."

The loud rattle of newspaper in the kitchen where he sat reading registered with Aurilla as a contradiction. "You know it's true, Joe," she said, her voice rising, refracting off the walls. "I can't begin to count the times I've seen you throw one of her books halfway across the house."

Daddy's chair scraped across the linoleum. Aurilla turned to smile at Clayton, her face lit up by what Berta Mae knew was the prospect of a good fight. But her father headed through the dining room and upstairs. Berta Mae let out a breath she hadn't known she was holding. Aurilla had been working up to the prospect of a fight all night, serving her father leftovers at dinner, going on about the beau that was coming for Berta Mae, and all the while Berta Mae had sat next to him watching the little vein in his left temple pulse and bulge. Now that he had refused to cooperate, Aurilla would turn on her.

Berta Mae stood up abruptly, wobbly lights swimming before her eyes. "We'll miss the start of our movie if we don't get going." Clayton sprang up, his hand on her elbow to steady her.

"That's right, she's not the strongest thing. She's half Mc-Math. You know, town people."

"I'm pleased to meet you." Clayton stuck his hand out, his arm stiff and straight.

Aurilla patted his arm the way you'd do a child that was acting too old for their years.

"And Mr. Cutter too," Clayton added.

"He's a stern man, not too fond of people. Him and Berta Mae are like two peas in a pod that way."

Berta Mae pulled Clayton onto the porch and Aurilla shut the door behind them.

"She's some talker that mother of yours." He held the car door for her, bending down to adjust the tail of her dress.

Free and easy, Clayton's gait said more about him than anything else. She watched him walk around the car, looking for some change brought on by this half hour with her family. But his arms and legs swung loose, moving with a life of their own that struck her as familiar and right. She saw with relief that, somehow, he'd missed it all.

The carpet inside the lingerie department was pale beige, almost white. Everything that wasn't enclosed in glass was put away in drawers and closets. A made-up woman dressed in black stood behind a long counter of dark wood that smelled of lemons and wax.

"May I help you?" The saleslady's forehead rose and her eyebrows—twin black-penciled lines—looked like question marks.

"I need a nightgown," Berta Mae said, her voice low.

"A fancy one for a honeymoon," Vinnie added, settling her thick arms on the glass top of the cabinet, totally nonplussed by the fineness of it all.

They had taken the bus all the way to Simmons just to come to this store. They sat at the back until the bus stopped at enough places that all the people they knew from Potter finally got off. "A nightgown is a lot cheaper than a wedding dress, and a whole lot more fun to pick out, you'll see," Vinnie had yelled over the roar of the bus engine.

Now that they were here their plan felt like a big mistake. This was for girls planning big church weddings paid for by their fathers. What business did she have here? Taking every last cent she'd managed to save this past year and spending it on something she'd wear once.

"What's the matter with you?" Vinnie whispered. "You sure don't seem to be in the spirit of things."

"You'll want white, of course." The woman stared through her, her lashes clumped together with black paint. Berta Mae looked off, pretending to be absorbed in the slips in the case beside her.

"Sure, she does," Vinnie spoke up, kicking Berta Mae's foot.

The woman turned to open the double doors of one of the closets behind her. She stood at arm's length, looking at the gowns. She flipped through them, the palm of her hand held flat, careful not to catch her long red nails on the nylon. At each white gown she stopped, looked over her shoulder at Berta Mae. Dismissing each one, she moved on with an air of authority.

"Nylon," Berta Mae could hear Grandmother McMath say with disdain as she pushed away the box that held the bed jacket Aurilla gave her on what turned out to be her last birthday. "What kind of material is that?" she asked, pulling her seersucker wrapper tight around her. "Turns yellow the minute it meets up with perspiration." The trousseau gowns Grandmother had sewn for her customers were made of fine linen or cotton lawn. She spent days tacking on the heavy lace trim by hand, weeks stitching a fine design of roses and lilies along the front placket. "I am a rose of Sharon, a lily of the valley," she recited from the Song of Solomon as her needle traveled in tiny stitches across the fabric. "As a lily among brambles so is my love among maidens."

Berta Mae blinked back tears. Her longing for her grandmother always lay in waiting, ready to pounce when she least expected it. She took in the gown the saleslady displayed before her. "This doesn't look so well made," she murmured, fingering the white lace patterned with a clumsy chain of daisies.

"What's that matter?" said Vinnie. "You said yourself it would only be worn one time. This night only comes once," Vinnie whispered, squeezing Berta Mae's hand.

Berta Mae lay in the motel bed, willing herself to calm down. A truck route; she was spending her wedding night on a truck route. Lights from the big semis lit the wall, caught the mirror over the bureau, then burst like stars. Running off had been her idea. Clayton was perfectly willing to go through with a wedding, but she'd known her parents would never give her one. "City Hall's good enough for anybody," Aurilla always said when she draped white tablecloths over her head and played bride. "It's all I had, it will do for you too."

She couldn't imagine walking down the aisle on Daddy's arm, being handed over to Clayton. No, she hadn't wanted them to have anything to do with her day but here she was lying in her wedding bed, her head filled with them.

She heard the toilet flush through the thin walls, then water running and Clayton spitting into the sink. She curled the pillow around her ears. Now things would be common between them, all their patterns of eating, washing, and voiding right out with everything else.

The bathroom door opened. Berta Mae closed her eyes, the fear starting inside. He could be naked, naked and coming at her.

"Berta Mae."

She opened her eyes. He stood beside the bed. Blond hairs spread out from the tiny clump at the center of his chest. She kept her eyes above his waist, not wanting to see if there was a threatening bulge in his underwear. He reached out to pull back the sheet. She held on so tight her knuckles ached.

"You're not going to leave me out here on a cool night like this, are you?"

Was it cold? She was burning up, her face hot, her gown

wedged wet beneath her arms. It was probably beginning to yellow already.

"Berta Mae," he whispered. She relaxed her grip, the softness of his voice soothing her. He slid under the covers, a little moan escaping his lips when his body hit up against hers. She stiffened at once.

"We don't have to do a thing but lie here and get acquainted, that sound all right to you?" His voice was a whisper half-lost in the stream of transfer trucks that rolled down the highway outside their door. She let go of a breath that began with a gasp. He drew her head gently to his chest, his light touch steadily working against the tension in her neck. All the little smells she had caught from him in manageable wisps were held there, no soap or tobacco or clean clothes to mask them. There was a faint trace of salt, like ocean water allowed to dry, and something more, something sweet and rich that must be him alone. She pulled inside, away from such realness. She'd always been able to turn her head, or concentrate on the fragrance of her own cologne, or the air blowing in from an open car window. But here she was, his fingers on her neck like flies lighting, making her squirm.

She hated herself for feeling this way. Maybe if she thought of sleep. Legs and arms akimbo, mouth relaxed. Maybe then she could find the softness she so wanted to give him, the fullness she never knew when she was awake and guarded.

Clayton shifted under her, eased her closer. His hand traveled down her back, rested between her shoulder blades. The tips of his fingers hovered, tracing small circles that were more heat than touch. In and out their breath came, in and out and the same. She felt herself opening up, giving over.

She moved her hand to his wrist. Her fingers found a tiny pulsing vein and pressed deeper. A miracle, to touch and be touched this way. If she could feel this, she could be anything Clayton wanted.

19

Nothing's private anymore. Take my son-in-law carrying on with that child widow. The hospital parking lot, that's where Clayton and Darlene met after things got going with them. Biggest parking lot in all of Potter. Never mind that the front door of my church was across the street. Sunday nights after prayer meeting, I'd see them coming back from God knows where, sometimes him towing that boat of his, her sitting right beside him like she belonged there.

Clayton had taken on that moony look right after that boy-husband of Darlene's was killed. He'd come over on Sundays for dinner, same as he'd been doing since he first set foot in my house back when he was courting Berta Mae, and he'd be off somewhere in a world nobody else knew about. Have to say "pass the peas" three times before he'd catch on you were talking to him. Wasn't long before he stopped coming at all. I knew then there was something going on, something that would show in his face.

I said to Ruby, my beautician—I told her just enough to make her think it's everything so she'll tell me what she knows—Clayton's not himself. First, I had to sit through Ruby telling me what she thought, which I wouldn't give you five cents for. Finding Donald Ray dead like Clayton did would be enough to sober anybody up. Clayton didn't have any place to put what he was feeling. The family could mourn right out in the open, but he didn't have anywhere to go with his part in Donald Ray's death. Who was he, just a name on an accident report? Not much satisfaction in that.

Sometimes when Ruby got going, she didn't know when to stop. What about Darlene? I asked, interrupting her. That Ruby didn't miss a beat. Oh, she told me, that girl put on a regular show at the funeral, carrying on about shutting up the coffin, wearing white shoes and it not even Easter, let alone Memorial Day. Won't wear black, says Donald Ray liked her in bright colors. She was at the record shop not an hour after they put him in the ground. They say she's at Ramsey Lake almost every night, sitting right there on the road where he got killed.

Just when I thought I should stick my head in some magazine and let Ruby's voice blend in with the hum of the dryers, she said, "Stranger things than death have brought people together."

Ruby's sister clerks in the personnel office at the hosiery mill. She'd seen Darlene when she had first come in applying for a job, like she thought she was going to find some piece of Donald Ray there. Clayton came in and hung around like Darlene had something he needed to put himself to rest. And Darlene looked right back like she could see Donald Ray on him.

Ruby was right about death. Nothing like it for making you realize what you've lost or what you're missing and how little time you may have to get it. But the whole world didn't have to know.

There was Meg, she knew. She saw what felt like the whole of my life played out before her eyes. But her knowing something was like nobody knowing it but me. The two of us were together through everything; we were even together the afternoon before Meg died.

Side by side, we cleaned the house like we'd done for over thirty-five years. I had churned butter that morning and when it was time for Meg to go, I took it from the Kelvinator, turning the mold over onto a plate. "Meg, half this round's for you, we'll never eat it all before it takes on that stale icebox taste."

Meg nodded her thanks, shuffling to the silverware drawer, her left hip stiff with arthritis. She was moving the smooth edge of a dinner knife through the butter as easy as you please when the plate broke clean in half.

The air went dead except for the jangle of broken ceramic against the metal tabletop. "I've been meaning to throw that thing out," I said, breaking the awful silence. "It was cracked right down the middle. I don't know why I keep putting it back in the cabinet."

Meg laughed and I felt some of the tension go out of me. "You always did have a hard time letting go of things. All that junk in the china closet you make me dust each time I come. What any woman need with so many glass slippers?"

"You never can tell when a prince might come knocking at the door." Tiny beads of sweat had formed on the butter while we stood staring at the broken plate. I dabbed the surface with cheesecloth, moved the butter to a new dish, and wrapped the whole thing in waxed paper before I looked at Meg again. It was a sure sign of death we'd just seen—we were both superstitious enough to know it—and it had to be Meg's since she held the knife.

I pressed five dollars into her palm. I squeezed Meg's fingers closed and pulled her hand to my chest. All those years and never once had I expressed my affection for her. At the door Meg looked back at me. My second sense told me I should say some word of goodbye, some remembrance. I smiled at Meg, my eyes bright with tears.

Meg said, "You know that's the truth," and closed the door gently behind her.

Two days later, Joe drove me over to the colored church for Meg's funeral. I sat right in the front pew with Meg's family, the only white person in that whitewashed room, saying goodbye to my last living friend, the last one alive to know my story. My whole life, the whole of it happened to me all at once and the rest of it was nothing but a long line of consequences strung out through time and everybody I touched.

Part of me couldn't help but feel glad for Clayton, seeing him with this girl. Maybe he would get enough out of his time with Darlene to last him; my six months with Hank carried me until Joe died and I was finally free to live as I pleased.

But Clayton was too straightforward for that. His guilt made him pull away from Emogene. There that poor little thing was, left with the mess he'd made and Berta Mae shooting her full of poison bullets. That's when I saw I had to do something. Not for Berta Mae. Jesus himself could be married to her and she'd still be laid out on the bed with a wet rag on her head. It was Emogene that concerned me. The last thing a father thought about was his daughter needing him. My own mother had stepped in with Berta Mae, doing right by her when I couldn't. It was my turn to think for those that couldn't think for themselves. In saving Emogene maybe I could redeem something from the ruin spread out at my feet.

DARLENE

Darlene pulled over, checking the faded box number against the one scrawled across the top of the letter. She'd half-expected to hear from Berta Mae at some point. Somebody at that beauty shop they all went to had to know. She'd been waiting for something to help cut her loose. She knew it wouldn't be Clayton. He wasn't brave enough to leave Berta Mae or her. She turned the car off, wanting to think things through before she saw Clayton's mother-in-law.

More than a year now she'd been with him, longer even than Donald Ray. He didn't show any sign of leaving Berta Mae, not that she was sure she wanted him to. Still, she had watched the special days tick off this last year—Christmas, New Year's, her birthday—all perfect occasions for him to offer this up, and he never made one move for the lawyer's office.

She thought back to how it was in the beginning with him. She had needed to know she hadn't died too, that someone could bear to hear her speak about that. Clayton had been there for her when everyone else was ready to move on. He had listened and he had proved her alive, and, for a while, her past and present fit back together.

Donald Ray no longer haunted him. Clayton never said as much, but she knew. It had been months since a comment from him had knocked her off balance, since she had felt their strange bond of loss and death work its magic. She had lost her husband twice. She'd been lonely after he died but it was nothing next to the emptiness she now felt with Clayton.

What could Berta Mae's mother do to her? Offer her money? The life insurance had given her that. Threaten to ruin her good name? She'd been doing that for herself long before Clayton, ever since her brother had the bad sense to get himself killed right before her wedding. Tell Berta Mae? She had to know, even if she was choosing not to look at the truth. There was nothing left for the woman to take from her. Darlene started the car and headed down the dirt road that led to the Cutter house.

AURILLA

I sat rocking on the front porch when I heard Darlene coming in that loud car of hers. I'd watched her leave the hospital enough to know the throaty sound. That and red hair was all I really knew about this girl.

Darlene parked over by the pair of silver maples planted for the girls when they were born. I sat up straight and tall as she got out of the car and turned to face the house. Something about her felt familiar, but I couldn't name it. Maybe it was just her age and her coming here. She wasn't much older than me the first time I came. And Emma Cutter couldn't have been a day over fifty, standing by the door, sizing me up, but she had seemed so old to me. Now here I was, changed by her, changed by all the Cutters from that first Sunday on. Too old and too much like them to make a difference in my own life, I was starting in on the next generation. That's what Emma was doing that day; maybe everyone came to this.

I started to get up and greet Darlene, then caught myself. This was no social call we were having. Besides, at my age I don't have to fool with any of that politeness mess.

"Lemonade's here if you want it." I nodded at the wicker table beside me. If I was in the girl's place, I wouldn't be able to swallow a thing. I watched Darlene drink down a glassful, then another, before she said one word. Looking me over she was, thinking how I could be anybody's old grandma.

"So, why's it you writing me?" Darlene pulled her chair around so she faced me. Her eyes were dark, almost black, so unlike the rest of her I thought right off she was a beauty. Then I saw the freckles and the nose that turned up just a little too much, and the coarse hair that stood out from her head. It must have been her bearing and those eyes that got Clayton. She didn't need much else to carry her looks.

I let out a cackle. "You didn't think it would be Berta Mae, did you? Clayton must have told you something about her." The familiar tone I took with Darlene surprised me but it didn't seem to faze her.

She turned up her empty glass and tapped the bottom, breaking the ice cube that slid to her lips between her even white teeth. "Never mentions her. Except when he's trying to come up with some story about where he's been."

"Not very good at that, I imagine."

Darlene's laugh, abrupt and harsh, said the girl knew how to hide her emotions as well as me. "Most of them have to do with hunting and fishing, depending on the time of year. Bad part is he thinks he has to have something to show for his time when he gets home." She caught herself and cut her stream of talk, her face settling back into the hard look she came here with. I could see what she'd done to protect herself. She'd told no one about Clayton. She had the careful remove about her of someone living a secret. Was Darlene protecting Clayton too? Maybe Ruby had been right about Clayton having nowhere to put his feelings about Donald Ray.

"You didn't ask me here to find out what I know about your daughter, did you?"

"It's not my daughter who concerns me. If she had any hold on Clayton, he wouldn't be with you. It's my granddaughter I'm interested in. I want this running around stopped before she's old enough to figure it out for herself."

"Why should I do that?"

"No reason for you to." I poured myself a glass of lemonade, playing my own stalling game. I listened to the ice crack, watched the cubes float to the surface. "He told you he's going to leave his wife?" I leaned toward Darlene to see how she would answer. She shrugged and looked at the pink begonias in the planters along the balustrade. I sat back, satisfied. "That's all right, you don't have to say. If he'd said he was leaving, you'd be crowing about it. He's afraid, but you aren't, are you?"

Darlene's black eyes sparked. Here was somebody that enjoyed a challenge. "Can't say I know the meaning of the word."

"His child is holding him. There are some things in this world that carry more weight than love when it's hot and new."

I thought of Hank and that last time, him wanting me to leave with him. Berta Mae was still a baby and I couldn't do it, much as I loved him. And there I was, carrying his baby and not knowing. I pulled back from the twisted spiral of "if onlys" my mind knew how to travel to as easily as the words to the Lord's Prayer. At the end of that coil of imagined lives and outcomes was Malinah alive and grown and loved by both her parents, and me, more than the husk of my own making that Meg had warned me I'd become.

"You've got to bend, girl," I heard myself say as if Meg was speaking through me, trying one last time to reach me.

"You think it's love I have with Clayton?" Darlene threw her head back and laughed. She leaned toward me, close enough for me to see the tears behind the fire in her eyes and the bright relief of being able to speak her truth at last. "I don't love anybody but Donald Ray. You think that's crazy, loving a dead man?"

She looked like a person drowning. Drowning and holding fast to restless memories of happiness and pain that sucked the life right out of the here and now. This was what I had sensed about her when she first came up to the house. Loving the dead and gone was the sweetest love of all. Just like me, Darlene had to keep it all inside, except maybe for a little while with Clayton when he must have had his own Donald Ray talking to do. I loved Hank more because he was the only thing that never changed, never got old and sour.

I felt something in me soften. I hadn't been able to help myself. Maybe I could help this young woman so like me. "That's the only kind of love I know," I said, telling her the truth I'd never told anyone, knowing Darlene would take it the wrong way, thinking I meant Joe. The girl sat back in her chair, her eyes clouded over, seeing some picture of longtime marital love. There was more I could say, but nobody tells everything; there's never enough time. Something shifts, like now, the breeze lifting her hair, taking your attention, and the thread of telling is broken.

There was still Emogene to think of, and freeing her from any part in all this. "Filling time, that's all you're doing with Clayton." I cracked my palm against my knee. The sound brought Darlene out of her daydream, but for me the certainty of my gesture rang hollow. Maybe Darlene's way was better than mine: enduring, living off spite, waiting for time and death to make my changes for me. Darlene couldn't begin to imagine that kind of endless waiting—the kind that made you mean—not at her age, maybe never. She took what she wanted without thinking twice about the consequences for her or anybody else. "Just waiting for something better to come along," I went on, playing up to Darlene's impetuous nature. "Around here, it's not going to. The whole place knows what you're up to."

Darlene shook her head, as if she wanted to dismiss me but wasn't sure she should just yet. "Men don't gossip," she said, challenging me. Feet planted on the floor, she held her rocker still, waiting.

"Don't have to. The women around them do it so much they can't help but hear and they don't miss a word if it's something to do with sex. You're ruined all right."

"That's just here." She started rocking as if the thought of the rest of the world freed her.

We sat there awhile, listening to the squirrels run in the white oak, their half-chewed acorns dropping on the end of the porch. I didn't have a thing left to say, and I waited for the girl to know it.

Darlene wiped the sweat off the bottom of her glass on her skirt, set the glass on the table. She started down the stairs. "The world's a big place," she said, turning to face me. "You forget that?"

I hadn't forgotten, I just didn't believe it anymore. I had seen the whole world played out with the few people I had known; somewhere else I'd just see the same thing all over again.

The farthest I'd ever been away from home was that trip I took to the ocean with a church group not long after Joe died. The whole way there I thought about the water and how it would feel to stand in front of something so vast. I pictured the boardwalk all lit up and crowded with people, each one more glamorous than the next.

Turned out to be the first and last trip I needed to take. That boardwalk was nothing more than a county fair set up on sand instead of sawdust with people looking and acting just like the ones at home. And if I wanted to see something blue and boundless, I didn't need any ocean. All I had to do was go out in the yard and look straight up.

I watched Darlene's strong young back and the fine way she carried that flaming head of hair. It was so easy now to see the beauty of the young, the tragic beauty they can't see on themselves.

I had wanted her gone for Emogene, but now I needed her gone to free some part of me. Darlene's spirit was like the beautiful bird that had lived inside me and died long ago. I felt a lightness, like wings struggling to stir in my chest, then a sweet fluttering in my throat, urging me to speak. "Death can make you over if you let it. You better go find out how while you still want to know."

Listening to Darlene tear up the road, I closed my eyes and saw that blue car, unmistakable, moving fast down some fancy four-lane highway. I'd outlived them all: Louellen, Hank, Malinah, Mother, Mrs. Cutter, Joe. When my time came, I would know, just like I had with the rest of them. I dreamt of a river, of muddy water every time. Not a thing like that glorified creek they call a river that wound its way shallow and slug-like through Potter. No, the river of my dreams roared and carried on something terrible, all the mud from the bottom churned up until the water was as red as blood. I'd have my dream and it wouldn't be three weeks before somebody would drop dead or take sick.

The first time the dream came to me, for Hank, I didn't give it a second thought. Then, with Malinah, we'd studied about Moses in the bulrushes at church that Sunday and when I woke the next morning, the sound of water rushing and a baby crying still in my head, I put it off on the scriptures. But when Mother's time came, she'd been lying sick so long the dream stayed with me like a strip of gauze across my eyes, coloring everything I saw. I remembered the first dream and all that came after, and began to prepare myself for the loss.

I knew right off when it was Joe's turn, when the dream was for him. Not a day over sixty and his mind suddenly gone. The baiting I'd done all those years hung out there empty and pointless. He took to following me around the house and talking, two things he'd never done. And he was sweet, not like I remembered Hank, but the unthinking sweetness of a little child that comes from their ignorance of how the world works.

His interest in work dried up that fall, and we'd of lost everything if I hadn't had Meg's husband bring in some help. Joe never knew the difference. I'd come out of the washhouse to hang the clothes on the line and I'd find him asleep under the hickory tree, his head and knees pulled into his chest like a baby.

At night he took to putting his head on my chest for me to run my hands through his hair. It was awkward for me in the beginning to touch him with any kind of feeling. I told myself this wasn't the man I'd held myself apart from all these years. His hair was still black and thick. The smell of him released by my fingers, the rich dark smell I'd almost forgotten, the one you learn from lying down with a man year after year, brought memories back, stirring up the vanished pieces, things so far in the past they felt like someone else had lived them.

Oh, the moments that pearled up on the string of my life. Hank smoothing my hair after a windy drive into town, my hand touching his as we worked to settle the earth around a rhododendron shoot. Malinah sneezing when I tickled her nose with a dandelion, her tiny hands batting against mine as she tried to grab the flower. I saw Joe and me in the beginning, riding back from church with my mother, the three of us silent, my stomach tied in knots in anticipation. I felt the horsehair sofa in my mother's parlor chafe the backs of my legs through the thin cotton lawn dresses I favored that courting summer. I saw the light on Clear Creek broken by the ducks gliding downstream, and Joe laughing, unguarded.

I found myself wondering if this disclosed softness in him was what I had looked for so long ago when he was my hard secret. Those bitter, lonely years in between, what would they have been like if I had seen through him before all the bad passed between us? How would Berta Mae's life have been changed? Sometimes you need to work for love. I couldn't know it then. Like anybody young, I didn't want to know, but I knew now.

Maybe that was God's way of leaving me with some sweet and treasured memory out of all our years of emptiness. What else could you feel for an old man who cried over nothing—TV commercials, the six o'clock news—whose hand sought mine when dark came each day? It took a young boy's death and the longings of a redhaired girl to know that the humanity Joe had at last embraced was an overwhelming and freeing thing.

20

DARLENE

Darlene had a hard time letting off the accelerator, convincing herself to pull in at her parents' house. Her hands trembled on the steering wheel, the turn indicator.

She had put off facing her feelings about Clayton. Part of her had been afraid to think about being alone again when the fact was, she already was. She got more out of a trip by herself to Ramsey Lake. There the quiet and calm of being alone was so deep that every blade of grass and clot of dirt strained to get her meaning.

She stared at the front of her parents' house. She saw a parade of future years not much different from the one she had just lived, each one like the one before, until finally, it would be too late for her to make a change. She hadn't wanted Clayton so much as she wanted to know he'd give Berta Mae up for her. She needed to be first again in someone's life, to matter more than anything.

The realization splintered, then slipped away as suddenly as it had come, leaving her unable to pull it back together. In its place was the memory of the *Ice Capades*, her moment alone in the coliseum and the feeling of hopelessness she had run from.

The truth about Clayton was so uncomfortable she had not been able to call it up again even when she tried. She had gone on acting as if there was nothing for her but Clayton and their shrunken world when that wasn't true at all.

Something better, something wonderful was just around the corner, she felt it hovering, opening somewhere beyond this moment. "Death can make you over if you let it." The shift that had started when Aurilla first spoke these words accelerated, jolting the whole of Darlene's life forward. She was never meant to stay here. The smallness of Gold Ridge stood between her and her idea of what she would be somewhere else. Her love for Donald Ray had pulled her off course, and now his death had set her free again.

In her mind she saw the creek that snaked along the rocky slope of the lower pasture, then changed its mind and turned toward Clayton's land. Life was like that. It flowed along and you did the things you were meant to do. She had loved Donald Ray, and maybe for a while even Clayton, and now the time was right to go.

The more she let herself think about leaving the more she was sure. The idea of going had been traveling back and forth in her mind since she left Aurilla's. Maybe the old woman was right, maybe she should leave. She could do that.

She had practically every cent she'd made at the hosiery mill these past six months stashed in a shoebox in her closet along with the savings bonds she'd bought with the last of the insurance money. And she had the trailer.

Where else had she been besides here? Only the beach with Donald Ray. She put herself there, thought about the feelings that new place had brought out in her. She felt open, bigger somehow, knowing for herself what a wave cresting and rolling onto the beach felt like when it hit her in her middle, nearly knocking her down with its strength and then pulling the sand out from beneath her feet and her with it when it rolled back out to sea. Or how the stars and the sky and the ocean could all become one late at night on an empty beach. Recalling these pictures, something quickened somewhere inside her. She could have this, she could have more of this. In the glove compartment was a map of the Eastern Seaboard—even the name sounded exotic. That was more than enough direction to get her started.

Chrissie stuck her head out the front door, motioning for Darlene to come. "Supper's almost ready," she called to her from what felt like another world. Getting out of the car and walking in and sitting down to her mother's pot roast, her father's belches, and Chrissie's silly talk no longer seemed possible. She left her pocketbook on the passenger seat and went inside to pack.

Chrissie and Emogene were setting the dining room table. Bits of their private talk, a kind of code, drifted broken and unintelligible onto the porch. Darlene paused and leaned her head against the screen door, closing her eyes. Of all nights for Clayton's girl to be here.

She eased the door open, walked down the hall. Unmoored, tiny pieces of her had already started to float away. Her room felt different, unfamiliar and no longer hers. She took in the eyelet flounce on her white vanity skirt, the family of tiny blown-glass deer that had sat on her dresser since she was seven, seeing them with a detachment she could never have imagined. She pictured Chrissie living here. Beatles posters would cover the violet-sprigged wallpaper Darlene and Mama had picked out for her twelfth birthday; the cedar shavings in Chrissie's hamster's cage would overpower the lingering bouquet of her perfume and cosmetics. And then later, Chrissie grown and gone, her parents dead, the house empty and waiting for someone new to move in and erase them. She would never see this room again, not as her room where everything and everywhere she looked told some story about who she was. She fought against the wave of grief that rose in her, threatening to suffocate her from the inside out. *Pack*, she told herself. *Just pack.*

Her suitcases had only been to Myrtle Beach, and both times with Donald Ray. The side pockets still held grains of sand, bits of broken shell. She stopped to read the matchbooks from the restaurants where they'd eaten, the hotels where they'd stayed. Their names felt like proof that things could be different, not just in the past, but now.

She pulled out her underwear drawer, skipping over her plain panties and white bras. This was the start of something different and the right underwear had everything to do with attitude and how you came across. She packed her collection of perfume atomizers in the side pockets and wrapped Donald

Ray's pictures in with her good underwear. She dumped her jewelry box on the vanity and picked over the glittering pile. Only the real things were worth taking: the cross Donald Ray had given her for her birthday that first summer after they were married, her engagement ring, his class ring, and her grandmother's pearl earrings, the "something old" she'd worn on her wedding day.

She opened the door a crack and listened. The way Chrissie and Emogene both talked at once she knew her father hadn't come in from his chores yet. Beyond the girls' chatter she could hear Beulah preparing supper. She took off her flats, carrying them in one hand, and slipped down the hall to the stairs leading to her parents' room.

She turned the key Beulah never bothered to take out of the little cedar chest. Her hand dove beneath insurance papers and tax records, feeling for the mourning brooch that held a lock of her grandmother's hair. The urge to look at it was irresistible, to lay a piece of her own hair across the glass, pleasing herself with the sameness in color, but she dropped the brooch in the pocket of her skirt and tiptoed down the stairs.

Skimming over the summer clothes in her closet, she chose only the things she'd worn this year. "If you haven't worn it in a year, you won't wear it again," she remembered reading somewhere. She felt lightheaded, drunk with the power of deciding, of discarding her belongings. The aqua prom dress took up half the suitcase; money and bonds filled in the space around the atomizers. She collapsed on the bed, took stock. She had her makeup to sort through yet, and Donald Ray's records, not much else. And she couldn't forget her coat in the hall closet.

She opened her dusting powder, taking in the scent she'd worn with Donald Ray, with Clayton. She traced the red fluff over her arms, the white powder clinging to the tiny blond hairs, thinking, one more time for Donald Ray. The rest she'd send to Clayton. The stores in Simmons closed late, plenty of time to buy a new scent at one of those fancy department stores.

She opened the door a crack. "Chrissie, you and Emogene come here," she called.

"What?" Chrissie managed to get out in her loud voice before Darlene pulled her inside. "Where are you going?" Chrissie flopped on the bed, ran her hand over the prom gown's sequined bodice.

"Never mind about that. I got some things for you girls." Emogene stood by the door, one hand on the knob like she couldn't wait to leave. "Here, Emogene, this talcum powder is for you."

"But I like Tabu," Chrissie whined.

Darlene pinched Chrissie's arm, her hand flying to Chrissie's mouth to stop her squeal. "Take something else. Anything you girls see there on the vanity you can have." Darlene rummaged through her purse for paper, taking a deposit slip out of the back of her checkbook.

"Any sign of Daddy yet, Chrissie?" she asked, her hand flying across the paper.

Chrissie shook her head, picked through the pile of costume jewelry on the vanity. "Mama said he's going to be late tonight. He went to the livestock sale this afternoon."

"You're not eloping, are you, Darlene?" Emogene opened a bottle of foundation, running her little finger around the neck, testing it on her hand. Her fingers were long like Clayton's, the palm wide. She looked up, her eyes meeting Darlene's, and Darlene saw him so plain it made her pen tear right through the note she was leaving her parents. Darlene had missed how much like him Emogene was, the brown hair that went blond in the summer, the wide-set blue eyes that could bore through walls.

"Just with myself, sugar." Darlene took the blue scarf she wore over her hair when she and Clayton drove to the lake and draped it around Emogene's shoulders.

"Chrissie, you give this note to Mama before you sit down to eat, you hear?" Nothing calmed Pap down like eating. She was counting on food to take the fire out of the fit he was bound to throw when he found out she was gone.

"You're not eating?" Chrissie stuffed the note in her shorts pocket to free up her hands. "Mama's frying pork chops."

Darlene felt light, empty, ready to run. She opened the record case beside her bed, packed the 45s beneath her prom dress. "No, I'm leaving. You give me a hug right here so you can say with a straight face you didn't see me go." She pulled her sister's head close. The smells of sun and yard dirt were confused with the scent of her own makeup and perfumes.

Chrissie pulled away, smoothing her hair in the vanity mirror. "When are you coming back?"

Darlene let out a deep sigh. Why did it hurt so much? She wouldn't be back, this had to be the last time she said goodbye. Chrissie at twelve was still too young to grasp the finality of her leaving. "When you least expect it." She closed her suitcases, fastened the clasps.

As long as the suitcases had been open, leaving hadn't been her only option. Was she really doing this, leaving everyone and everything? Packing had been like necking. There was a fine line between rubbing willingly against a date and the point when the boy would take over, wedge himself between your legs. Now that those clasps had snapped shut there was no turning back.

Darlene rubbed her wet eyes with her fist, then patted Emogene on the arm. "You girls make me into a big romantic mystery, all right?"

Darlene moved through the cemetery; her eyes locked on the angel atop Donald Ray's gravestone. The marker stood out from all the others just the way Donald Ray had for her in a crowd of strangers.

"Usually people want angels for children," the stonecutter had said when she went to get Donald Ray's stone made.

"He was nineteen years old, that's all." Darlene held out Donald Ray's senior picture. "And I want this on it."

He let out a low whistle. "Now that's going to cost you something."

"Can you do it?"

"Oh yes, ma'am, but the glass has got to be ground just so to make it watertight. Come on in the back with me, I'll show you some samples."

"I want white marble, the kind that looks lit in the dark," she called after him.

Beulah touched Darlene's arm to hold her back. "I never heard tell of such a thing," she whispered, her eyes on the stonecutter, making sure he continued to move out of earshot. "You don't go to a graveyard to be reminded of how somebody looked when they were living. You're supposed to have your mind on higher things."

Darlene shook off her hand and started toward the showroom.

"What are his people going to say?" Beulah asked, worrying out loud.

"I don't want the angel staring at the sky," Darlene said, pointing to the upturned face on an angel statue they passed. "I want her wings closed, her head bent a little, like she's looking down on him."

"I don't know, Darlene," Beulah murmured, "that sounds so sad."

"Of course, she's sad," she'd snapped, making Beulah's chin pull back. "He's dead, isn't he?"

She had stopped thinking about his grave after she started going to the lake. Though she had never seen the stone in place, she liked to think the angel prayed for Donald Ray, kept him company. She needed to see for herself and make sure before she left.

She ran her hand over his stone, feeling the lingering warmth of the sun. She opened the cover on his picture, kissed her finger, and touched it to the glass. All the images of Donald Ray she once held in her mind had faded. When she thought of him now, she only saw photographs. She had a wedding album and a shoebox full of snapshots but looking at them didn't do her much good. One way. He only looked one way in each photograph and the frozen expressions were as bad as death.

The only picture that didn't leave her frustrated was the enlargement of a picture Donald Ray's brother, Ramon, had taken of her and Donald Ray when they were first dating. They are standing on the dirt road that runs by the Spencer house, she in front of him, his arms wrapped around her, her hands on his. She's wearing the skirt she lived in that summer—the full white one with the red train chugging along around the tail—and a white sleeveless blouse. Donald Ray's sleeves are rolled up, his shirttail is out; he never tucked in a shirt in warm weather. Their shadow stretches across the road, a solid shape with no light breaking between them. The toes of her left foot curl up—she's so happy she can't hold still—and behind them the road stretches up and around a hill.

She loved the picture so much she wanted it big, big enough to fall in, to get lost again in that warm day when she was sixteen years old, her head swimming with love. But in the enlargement their features were blurred, vague as the stand of trees across the open field behind them. Disappointed, Darlene had put it away.

It wasn't until after he died and she came across the picture again that she realized it worked better than all the others. Edges softened, expressions unsettled, this was how you had to see somebody to keep them perfect. If she stared at the picture long enough, she could give Donald Ray any look she liked, fill the empty eyes with whatever emotion she pleased.

The dark of the graveyard did the same thing with his senior picture. He was sad, she could see it in his eyes, sorry to see her go, but smiling so she wouldn't catch on and spoil her plans.

Darlene closed the cover slowly, the way you would the door after coming home from a date with a boy who's lingering on the other side, holding out in case you decide to open it and kiss him one more time.

The service station attendant inspected the gas line. "How come your husband sent you down here for the trailer?" He pushed his hat back with the edge of his blackened palm. "Seems to me you'd wait awhile. Hell, it ain't even Labor Day. Maybe you're just tired of the place. All that rain we had last spring made it a buggy year."

Darlene nodded; she'd forgotten his name again. She couldn't make out the navy letters that looped across his chest pocket. She'd looked straight at his shirt pocket and asked him by name to give her a hand disconnecting her hookups. There was another boy working at the filling station and one more visiting; she could have asked any one of them for help. Whoever she chose was bound to ask questions, but this one, she knew, had a habit of answering his own.

Planning on catching some bass today? He'd call out to the pumps where Clayton bent over a gas can he was filling for the boat. *I don't know about that,* he'd answer before Clayton could open his mouth. *So many bugs this summer the fish don't even bother going after bait.*

"I got no use for trailers myself," he said now, kicking at a tire, squatting to test one of the cinder blocks Clayton had wedged on either side of the wheel. "I'd feel like the thing was going to run away with me."

"That could happen mighty easy," she said, her voice private and low. She thought about how carried away she'd been with the whole idea. She was going to walk naked from one end to the other, Clayton watching her from the couch, the one seat where he could see her in every room, his eyes on her upturned breasts, her smooth backside. Most nights it had been her walking the floor, waiting and hoping he would come.

"I'll just be inside," she said, "making sure things are tied down. You let me know when you're ready to cut the electricity." She tapped the rose-colored lantern that covered the fluorescent coil in the kitchen ceiling. The trailer still insisted on smelling like someone else, even after all the perfume she had dropped on light bulbs. Her scent, slightly scorched, would linger, then give way to the smell of boiled cabbage and skin full of oils. Now that she would be living in the trailer people might think the smells belonged to her. Maybe that was the

problem; she and Clayton hadn't been around enough to make
their smell stick.

She opened the refrigerator door, banged the button next
to the temperature dial to make the light go on. Nothing but a
half-empty jar of mayonnaise, the molded heel of a loaf of light
bread, and a Pepsi—small, sad remains of their last weekend on
the lake. Who had bought the bread? Clayton? Her? The Pepsi
was his. Not even worth a trip to the dump. She could drop
these things in the trash at a rest area first time she stopped to
pee. She opened the Pepsi on a drawer handle and turned the
bottle up. The drink tasted warm, syrupy. Somewhere along the
way she'd have to get the refrigerator looked at. She deposited
the bread and mayonnaise in the grocery bag under the sink and
rolled the top of the bag closed.

She moved through the trailer. Nothing to pack, nothing to
discard, everything was built in or bolted down. She had never
left anything here of meaning to her, keeping it all in an overnight case in the trunk of her car instead. There was nothing
for Clayton to pick up, turn over in his hand, smell, or rub
across his face. When he complained, she said she was trying to
keep the romance alive, but maybe she was really just keeping
herself free. At any point she could have cut things off and not
had to ask him for a thing back. She would have missed her
paper lanterns, but she could buy more. It was the same with
the Melmac dishes with blue and green shafts of wheat across
the face that she had picked up at Rose's. They were common
as dirt; every five and dime store sold them.

She lifted the seersucker bedspread, checked under the bed.
Clayton's tackle box, now what was she supposed to do with
that? Leave it on the ground for him to find and have this boy
she'd brought along asking her questions he wouldn't, for once,
have any answers to himself? Leave a note pinned to a tree
saying where she hid it in the woods? That boy'd have the note
in his hand as soon as her taillights rounded the first turn and
that tackle box in his trunk by the time she hit the main road.

Clayton would just have to lose it, just like he was losing her and the trailer.

"You ready in there?" the boy called. "I'm all set to disconnect the last hookup."

"Go ahead," Darlene shouted. The room dropped into blackness. She moved toward the kitchen and the door as easy as if it were daylight. There was nothing to trip her up, no steps or turns to remember, the doors all in a straight line like the cars on a train.

The Pepsi was still in her hand. She wondered if she should offer some to Jerry, that was his name, same as half a dozen other boys his age she knew. "I've got a drink here if you want some."

He took the bottle. Even through the dark she could sense his eyes on her as he drank. He offered it back to her, disappointment all over him when she waved the bottle away. Their drinking after each other, she bet he could of made that into something by the time he got back to his buddies at the station.

"You're all set to go." He tossed the bottle into the weeds, wiped his mouth with the back of his hand. "Get the car started, and I'll pull the last of the cinder blocks. Go easy on the gas when I give the call. All the rain we've had has this ground as slick as glass."

Darlene watched him in her rearview mirror, listened above the hum of the engine, anxious to feel herself roll free. The engine strained toward the paved road.

"You're all right," Jerry called out. "Only thing you got to worry about is turning the wheel too sudden."

Being pregnant must be a lot like managing this trailer. She remembered her mother, heavy with Chrissie, moving her arms and legs around her swollen middle so the extra weight didn't pitch her off balance. Darlene had to get the hang of which way the trailer was moving, fall into a rhythm with her new appendage.

She shifted into low, gave the car a little gas, and eased onto the road, waving her thanks to Jerry in the rearview mirror. She guided the trailer around the first set of curves, foot steady on the gas. The gleam of the trailer in the side-view mirror caught her eye.

She marveled at her newfound self-containment, as complete as that of any animal with a shell. A big road, that was all she needed, one with four lanes and green signs hung overhead, big and kind as angels.

21

CLAYTON

"Emogene is spending too much time at the Cavenesses'." Berta Mae picked at the ham on the plate set out at Emogene's empty place. "I told her when she had to be home. I can't even call up there. How in the world do those people get by without a telephone?"

She wasn't looking for answers from me. This conversation she had with herself came from spending too much time alone. It was one of the few things I knew about her anymore. Her smell, her face when she was waking up, the feel of her skin: that was all gone now. The talk was going too, becoming part of the noise that went on all the time like the hum of the refrigerator or Emogene's chatter.

But whenever Emogene mentioned the Cavenesses, I listened, ears tuned to Darlene's name. I'd learned all kinds of things—the color of her bedspread, how many pairs of shoes she had, that her vanity was covered with perfume atomizers and pictures of Donald Ray. I used all this to make her more real. There was nothing of hers in the trailer. She kept everything closed up, putting it all back in her trunk each time she left. Just the thought of the things I kept there—a razor and shaving cream, cut-off pants, my tackle box, the coffee mug from my truck—made me uneasy.

"Here she comes." Berta Mae stood, stared out the window, hands on her hips.

"Looks like she's dragged something home with her." She met Emogene at the door. "Haven't you been told to be on time for supper? You can just eat it cold. I'm not heating up the kitchen twice tonight."

"I ate at the Cavenesses'." Emogene sat down, tore a piece

off her ham, and reached for a biscuit. Skinny as a rail and she ate night and day. "I wouldn't have stayed but Chrissie begged me to. It was awful. Her mother crying and her father yelling at her for letting it happen."

"Letting what happen?" Berta Mae pulled up her chair.

"Darlene's gone. Left a note and everything. Didn't say where she was going, just that she wasn't coming back."

My stomach turned over. She had time off coming, I told myself, and she'd been talking about fixing up the trailer. That was where she was. People born here stayed until they died. I didn't know of a soul who'd ever left.

But there was Darlene's other talk, the lights off, lying in bed, late-at-night talk about us starting over somewhere. Silent, I'd let her run on, carrying me off with her, watching it all happen in my head from a safe distance, never telling her yes or no.

"People just don't run off," Berta Mae said. "Where's an eighteen-year-old girl going by herself?"

"How do I know?" Emogene snapped. Lately everything Berta Mae said irritated her. "If she does come back, she'll be plenty mad, because her daddy's burning up her stuff, except for what I got in this bag and what Chrissie has in hers." She upended the bag on the table. "Don't tell, but she gave us things when she was packing to leave."

There in the jumble of makeup and jewelry was the blue scarf I'd seen around Darlene's neck. I struggled to regain my balance. Darlene could not have undone me more if she had walked through the kitchen door herself.

"You're not playing with that used makeup, Emogene," I heard Berta Mae say. "I don't know why you bothered bringing it home. That's a good way to get an infection."

"But I know Darlene. This isn't some stranger's stuff." Emogene opened the little tubes and pots, showing me the colors I'd seen on Darlene's face. She pulled a box of talcum powder from the pile, rubbing the fluffy red puff over herself. "Smell this." She put her arms in my face.

It was Darlene. I'd never thought of her smell as something

she paid money for, then put on like a dress or a skirt. This was the scent I worked so hard to get off each time I left her, scrubbing with Dial soap until my skin turned red. How much else of her was right here on the table, broken into little pieces that glittered and smelled pretty?

"Maybe she is gone," Berta Mae said. "They say she's wild. Her people haven't been able to do a thing with her since Donald Ray died. She must think being a widow gives her license."

I looked at Berta Mae, seeing her for the first time in months. She looked drained, almost sick. Had I done this to her, worn her to exhaustion with my lies and the looming possibility of shame? Maybe it was just the overhead fluorescents washing her out. There were no bare bulbs in the trailer. Darlene had hung rose-colored paper lanterns over every light until the air itself looked pink.

Why did every thought, no matter where it started, end with me thinking of Darlene? Pictures of her flashed in my mind. I saw her waiting for me in the parking lot at the mill that first day, sitting under the stars at the lake. Emogene, the makeup, this was just another lure, one of her tricks. I'd been holding back on her and she wasn't going to stand for it. She was at the trailer, her skin, her red hair glowing in all that soft light, waiting on me to act on this, her latest ultimatum.

The thought made my heart rock against my ribs. A familiar sick feeling of things being wrong and pushed too far rose in me and settled, twisting sharply in my gut. I had tried weaning myself from Darlene. I stayed away from the lake, avoided her at work, and still I found myself with her, and miserable. I couldn't live this way, not anymore. She made me crazy, and she would keep on as long as I let her.

I felt more reckless thinking of breaking off with Darlene than I ever had about being with her. I scrambled for a reason to get out of the house. Every alibi was exhausted but what did that matter if this was the last time? The room fell away as though I had already left.

"I've got to follow Cecil out to Badin," I heard myself say.

"He's having some trouble with his truck." I busied myself with the domestic motions of folding my paper and stacking dishes.

"You're going all that way and back tonight?" Berta Mae asked. "He can't find some room for you in his fine new A-frame?"

I bent over my place, brushing at biscuit crumbs to allow time to take this in. Berta Mae had done better than I did, giving me even more freedom than I needed. I met her eyes for what felt like the first time in months. I saw the fear, the anger that was always there, and something else, a flicker of understanding. "I'll see how I feel when I get there. If I'm not home by ten you can figure I'm staying."

Emogene tossed aside a case of eye shadow. "I look awful," she said. She stared into the hand mirror she'd propped against the napkin holder. "What's wrong with this stuff?"

She looked up at me, her face orange against her white neck, her wide blue eyes ringed with green. A million things I could never say ran through my head—you're beautiful, you don't need that stuff, I love you, I'll be here for you, don't let your mother turn you against me. I put my thumb under her chin, tilted her face to the light. "Maybe you got too much on," I said.

She batted my hand away. "What do you know?"

I didn't bother calling her on her sass. Maybe she already hated me. I'd earned that.

Berta Mae swept the makeup back into the bag in one motion. "You're too young, that's what's wrong. Now go wash your face. Besides, this makeup is not meant for you, it's for a redhead. Their coloring's not a thing like anyone else's."

Not a thing like, I repeated to myself.

I pulled away from the filling station in Potter, the tank on full. I'd gone out of my way to gas up, knowing there'd be nothing open between home and Badin Lake. The headlights swept across the school playground, lighting up a tangle of orange plastic play equipment. The swings were gone. Made of simple plumbing pipe, they had stood there for at least fifteen years that I knew of. Berta Mae was on those swings the first time I saw her.

I had watched her from this very filling station. No one around her could have been more than ten years old. To me she looked like a fairy queen among the dwarfs. The breeze lifted her yellow dress and sent her black hair flying as she moved back and forth, back and forth. She was unlike anything else in my life, I was sure of it.

"I tell you what," I had said to the station attendant, "that's the girl I'm going to marry."

"That a fact?" His smile broke narrow and yellow above the cigarette he held in his mouth. The grease from his cracked fingers stayed on the bills he counted back to me. "That ain't what the rest of the young bucks that hang around here have in mind. Won't do them much good, though. That's Joe Cutter's girl. Picks her up himself every day. Just to keep the likes of you boys away from her."

I didn't hear much of anything after I got the father's name. I stuffed my change in my pocket and wandered over to the phone booth, kicking a rusted bottle cap across the lot as I went. I flipped through the worn directory, half its pages missing, praying that the Cs would be there. I found a Joe Cutter listed just outside of town. Judging from the route number, I figured it to be about to Clear Creek.

For the attendant's benefit, I walked back to my car with the gait of a man headed nowhere in particular, though nothing could be further from the truth. I was going to see her house, the place where she would be when I thought about her that night.

Once I was past the town limits, I watched both sides of the road for some sign of the Cutter name. I was halfway to Siler City before I realized how far out of the way I had gone. I turned around, taking my foot off the accelerator as each mailbox came into view, hope rising, then falling away as the letters came clear. When I finally found it, the name was so faded I had to stop the car to be sure. I strained my eyes to see down the dirt side road that led back to the Cutter property. The road ended at a rambling white farmhouse not much different from the one I grew up in. My eyes began to sort out the color I saw around it, mounds of flowers mixed with green.

What little grass there was around my parents' house was scratched up regularly by my mother's chickens and my father's hunting dogs. Nobody ever took time to plant anything that couldn't be eaten or sold. Then I saw it plain as day. The Cutter girl in her yellow dress out planting flowers in front of my parents' house and me building a porch where we could sit and look at the beauty she had brought about.

Behind me the lights from the filling station died. The pictures held in my mind of that long-ago day disappeared, swallowed by blackness. The ideas I got in my head back then were so big. What had made me think such things about Berta Mae, that I could be saved by her?

Maybe all along I'd wanted somebody to do what Donald Ray's dying had finally done, to change me in ways I couldn't begin to imagine changing myself. The image of Berta Mae, a tender Berta Mae, arose, and I felt the stirrings of my old feelings for her. That longing belonged to the hopefulness, the dreams of being young. But what if I could feel those feelings now without the timidness and doubt that came with youth?

Maybe I'd come far enough away from the marriage that I could at last see it whole and for what it was. When we were first married and lying together, her sweet melting into me had been all the more precious because I knew how hard it was for her and that this part of her was for me alone. All the time between that moment and now, some of it terrible and impossible, had helped push us farther and farther apart, but hadn't it bound us too? We had become each other's family by default; that was the contradiction of longtime marriage. I thought of the moment tonight in the kitchen when our eyes met. The look held so much—anger, acceptance, allowances. I'd have to hope for forgiveness.

If Darlene left, she'd be going alone. I needed to end it, and

I needed to end it now. The realization flooded me with an unfamiliar sense of peace and resolve.

The station attendant pulled up beside me and rolled down his window. "We had real swings in my day," he said, pointing at the playground. "Now they got kids playing in plastic boxes." He shook his head, waving his hand in the rearview mirror as he drove off.

Not a day over twenty-five, he could have been on the playground that first time I saw Berta Mae. The boy, the swings, it all felt like a sign that my old life could change and still go on.

22

BERTA MAE

She sloshed her rag in the pail, watched the soapy water turn gray. Berta Mae scrubbed the stove for the second time tonight. Cleaning was her way of making things so she could think. The smooth surface of the range hood gleamed like a mirror. She moved closer, her face dissolving into a blur with holes for eyes. The orange hands of the stove clock jumped out at her. Way past ten; he wouldn't be back tonight.

The Big Bang. The words sprang into her mind. Sometimes the things Emogene learned at school frightened Berta Mae with how open and unsafe they made life seem. Stars and planets moving out through time, away from each other, then folding back up to explode and start all over again. Just look at her and Clayton. Her life had burst wide open when she met him, offering her an escape. She was going to love somebody and feel good about things, she had told herself the afternoon she took off across the road from the schoolhouse for the filling station.

All the years they had been together she had gotten along focusing on things outside the two of them. They would get along better when they let Clayton off third shift, when Emogene was bigger and not so much trouble, when they moved out from his parents' to a place of their own. These changes came and went and she and Clayton kept right on moving apart.

Since that Spencer boy's death, it had been harder to put their troubles off on everybody else. Days, then months passed, with Clayton withdrawing more and more until it felt like they were in two separate worlds. He had tolerated her before, but now he was either indifferent or gone. Even the anger and resentment—all so familiar—he didn't even show these. The running of the farm, the house, looking after Emogene, the everyday duties of their shared life continued, as regular and impossible to stop as breathing, carrying them along, allowing them to act as if nothing was happening.

Clayton had never known her, not the real Berta Mae who longed to love and be loved. Nobody did, not even Emogene, at least not anymore. She was a secret person no one could get near, even when she wanted them to. What had made her so undeserving?

She stood on tiptoe, removing the odd assortment of chipped cups and plates she had stored away in the cabinet above the stove. Her fingers reached to the very back, collided with the familiar webbing. She stretched upward, bringing Grandmother's berry bowl to her with both hands.

Years of dust had settled into the bowl's many openings, obscuring a white she remembered as being rich as that of fresh cream. Over and over, she soaped and scrubbed and rinsed until the bowl in her hands matched the one in her memory. Berta Mae touched the beads of water suspended in the openings, feeling herself soften as they disappeared one by one. The fragile bowl had held this feeling all this time. How she wished someone knew this was in her.

She willed herself to look at the kitchen table, at the bag holding Darlene's things. When Emogene took the lid off that dusting powder her world fell back in and exploded again. The opening of the powder was like the top of her head being ripped off. All the hunting, fishing, and boating trips of the last year marched past her. Right up the road was the reason her husband hadn't touched her in longer than she could remember.

The scent she recognized from Clayton had overwhelmed the kitchen. It was the one she had trained herself to ignore, to put off on imagination, until finally, she stopped noticing, making a coward's truce with the calamity of her marriage. She convinced herself he was staying to himself the way she did, making his absence into something she could understand, something that was all right. She shut out anything that didn't match, like her sleeping with Emogene in a fit of pride and him letting it go on. She told herself it was no different from having twin beds, and she kept thinking she would try to find some on sale. It was natural for people to be more interested in their rest as they got older.

Clayton never looked rested when he came back from his trips; used up was more like it. She put it off on his sleeping in a strange bed; he'd always been miserable away from his own things. The few times they'd gone to the beach they had come back early, the newness of it exhausting him.

But when the lid came off that powder and she recognized the heady assault of flowers and spice that clung to Clayton's towels and to the work clothes he left in the laundry room, she saw Darlene, lush and strong with youth, and she had to face the terrible truth. It had taken everything in her to act her usual self. Easier to provide him with an excuse to stay away from home than to watch him sit here, one ear cocked to the road, waiting, the way she'd seen him do so many times, not knowing what he was listening for, and being afraid to ask.

She wished now she had some of that nerve medicine Doc Martin tried to give her. "Help you walk right through the change of life without noticing a thing," he'd said, patting her arm like he was soothing a high-strung cat.

She'd thought *pregnant* each of the three times she missed before she went to see him. But then she remembered how things were between her and Clayton and she thought tumor. At night, lying in bed, running her palm over the hollow between her hipbones, she thought she felt it, round and hard; felt it move away from her fingers like a new baby's head. But the doctor said you bled even more with a fibroid, so it was just the change. Thirty-seven and it was happening to her already, and there Aurilla had gone on until she was fifty-eight.

Berta Mae emptied the pail, filled it with fresh water before starting in on the cabinets. Aurilla kept coming around in her head tonight, but that was understandable. The woman had had a hand in every embarrassing situation she'd known.

"Pregnant, are you?" Those were the first words out of Aurilla's mouth the day she and Clayton got back from the justice of the peace in Spartanburg. Aurilla had opened the front door that Sunday evening without so much as a hello. And she'd asked Berta Mae, right there in front of them all, just as they sat down to supper and everything got quiet. She never actually said pregnant, Aurilla was too clever for that. "You're looking hollow-eyed these days, Berta Mae."

There was nothing for her to do but sit there and turn red while Clayton said some silly thing about how she seemed to get her deep-set eyes from her father. Nothing to do but pray that Aurilla wouldn't tell him what hollow eyes were a sure sign of.

Not two days later she remembered going into a store in Potter and some clerk she'd known all her life stared right at her middle, never saying one word of congratulations or good luck. Everywhere, people drifted into twos and threes, their eyes cutting her way as they talked low, their mouths pulled into a straight line, barely moving. Clayton said she was imagining things. It went on for months before people paid her no more mind than anyone else and looked her in the face when she talked. Aurilla knew she wore herself out worrying over what other people thought. And knowing exactly what people would be thinking about Berta Mae after the elopement Aurilla had set her up to notice.

Had Aurilla done something like that again? The wife is always the last to know; she'd read that somewhere. So maybe Aurilla knew about Clayton and Darlene, along with everyone else, and had decided to keep her mouth shut.

Aurilla didn't love her. Not like Berta Mae loved Emogene, even though Berta Mae knew she did a bad job of showing it. How could she know how when she'd never felt a mother's love herself? Sometimes life felt like one long avalanche of hurt. The snarl of who had or had not loved whom enough threatened to overwhelm her. She would start with just one piece, with Clayton, and follow that thread past this trouble to a new place where the two of them could be different together.

When she married, she had believed it was forever. But what about when your husband didn't love you, when part of you hated him for hurting you? Was that supposed to be forever too? Everywhere she looked she saw their marriage. So big, like the ocean it went on and on, touching everything. It was the same for him; she knew that.

Tonight, for the first time in longer than she could remember, he'd looked her in the eyes. He told her a lie, but the difference was this time they both knew. The girl had gone too far, using their child to invade their home. Strong as blood, the old bond of marriage was still here despite all their trouble.

Berta Mae paused, surveyed her handiwork before turning out the light. Tomorrow Emogene would make one trip through here and the wax would be scuffed; by breakfast the aroma of fried bacon and toast would replace the simple antiseptic smell of bleach. Nothing lasted, not this spotless kitchen, not looks, not love—not even the pain it brought.

One of these Saturday nights they will all be eating at the Blue Mist Drive-In, just like they had every weekend before he started in with Darlene. They will be talking, him turned toward her, his arm resting on the seat while they wait for their order to cool down on the tray propped in his open window. She will remember every little thing—the chili on Clayton's cheese dog bleeding through the waxed paper, Emogene's french fries perfuming the car, the sweet smoke rising from the barbecue pit and curling around the building, the fountain's blue lights dancing over the parking lot.

She will remember because Darlene will pull up beside them in that fancy car of hers and Clayton will look once to see what all the racket is. He will look right through Darlene and keep on talking and Berta Mae will smile at him and remember this night and how worked up she was over nothing.

23

CLAYTON

The tombstones broke the darkness like strands of white Christmas lights. I felt as crazy as Darlene, standing in a graveyard in the middle of the night.

"I was with Donald Ray last night," she'd start, in a voice lazy as spent sex, just so I would know Donald Ray had something I was missing. That was all she had to say, I did the rest. I pictured her not at Ramsey Lake where I knew she went, but here, at the place she never came. Laid out on the grave, her lips close to the headstone, whispering, just the way she did when she was in bed with me. The picture made me want to pin her to the floor and love her hard until she screamed and joined the living. Sometimes I did, my face pressed close to hers, no way for her to pretend I was Donald Ray.

I turned to look at the south wall of the church and the magnolia trees, half-expecting to see Donald Ray sitting on the bench in front of the curtain of waxed green leaves. I walked down the gravel path until I found him beside his grandfather.

"I drove all the way to Badin to tell her it was over," I began under my breath, part of me feeling awkward talking out loud in a graveyard. What did it matter? For more than a year I'd carried on like a man ready to walk away from everything I knew. Back now from the edge of a cliff where I could never have imagined myself, I saw how little most things meant. "Nothing waiting for me. I walked all around that lot, beating the weeds back with a stick, looking for a note, anything that would say she thought of me. Gone as sudden as she came. Guess that makes me the fool."

I crouched down, took off my hat out of respect. I tapped the bill against the ground, rustling the fine blades of grass.

New and soft as down, they stood out against the tired crab-grass that covered the grandfather's grave.

I lifted the cover on what looked like a locket carved on the face of the headstone. Donald Ray stared back at me. The last time I saw him he was dead and evidence that he had ever been anything different sent a jolt through me. My eyes had adjusted well enough to the darkness that I could make out the blond hair and strong jaw, but that didn't tell me what I needed to know.

In the months after Donald Ray's death, the particulars of the boy's stilled face—the shape of his eyes, the distance be-tween his ear and chin, the width of his nose—had become as unforgettable as the lay of the fields that rolled away from my house. I saw him when I drifted toward dreams and when I made my way back again in the morning; as I strode from one end of my knitting machine to the other; at night in the black face of Ramsey Lake.

In some strange turn, all that Donald Ray lost had rushed in on me. *Look here and here*, Donald Ray seemed to say, as if he was showing me the reasons he had loved living and why I should too.

Just when I almost caught my breath, there was Darlene. Between the two of them I had turned into someone different, someone that almost dared to be alive with hope and an open heart.

I struck match after match, holding them to the picture until they burned my fingers and then, at last, I saw. Life never got the chance to mark Donald Ray. His openness held a promise as wide as the world.

If I had fallen under his sway, what must that poor girl feel? I sat back, my legs cramped from my long squat.

A resigned sorrow came over me. There wasn't a man alive that could compete with that, not for long. A string of untried young boys lay ahead of Darlene, each one thrown away when life started narrowing in on them.

I stood up, took one last look at the grave where I had

imagined Darlene so many nights. "They sure weren't talking about you when they said till death do us part," I said. "You got her for at least as long as she's breathing and able to say your name."

It was past midnight by the time I got back home. I killed the lights halfway up the drive and came to a stop by the well. I sat there, staring at the blacked-out house, needing to figure out what being back here meant.

All the time I had been with Darlene, she had taken up every bit of my mind. I couldn't remember the last time I heard the music of the creek or stopped to watch the slow lope of the cattle as they crossed the high pasture at twilight.

I cranked down the window. The keen smell of onion grass mixed with the green scent of fresh-cut grass. Berta Mae had left the sprinkler on the flowers Emogene was trying to grow. The summer tang of water evaporating filled the hot air. How long had it been since I'd been calm enough to draw breath deep and really smell?

I laid my head back on the seat and let the familiar scents carry me away and back through time. I saw myself as a boy tumbling down the hill that sloped to the creek, crafting a whistle from a bright blade of grass held taut between my thumbs. And driving the thresher for the first time, the stalks of wheat bowing down before the blades.

Off somewhere the breeze shifted, bringing the sweetness of new growth and the beginning of autumn decay. I drank the scent of the woods like water from the spring.

It was a relief somehow knowing that with Darlene gone some of my old evenness could return. I wouldn't have to worry about losing her anymore, or fill my head with ways to be with her, or feel responsible for her hurt. I had been desperate to give Darlene what she wanted, desperate to relieve her pain, as if helping her could make up for failing with Berta Mae.

Donald Ray had opened me to life again. Shut out by Berta Mae, I had stayed shut out, even knowing the softness that waited there inside her—I saw it when she slept. I had seen it again tonight, when I left for Badin.

I knew I loved my daughter and what that felt like. What could I find with Berta Mae if I tried?

The breeze picked up, stirred the bank of willows I had planted at the pasture fence. The tough yet supple branches swayed together with a clattering sound like the twilight chatter of birds, then parted to reveal the open sweep of the pasture, and beyond, the fields newly planted with fescue.

I got out of the truck, knowing I would smell grass or cow dung, depending on which way the wind was blowing, and that the thin crust of ground would give beneath my feet as I crossed the bare yard that led to home.

ACKNOWLEDGMENTS

Sometimes the road to publication is circuitous but rich and layered. The Ohio Arts Council, the Virginia Arts Commission, the Virginia Center for the Creative Arts, the Virginia Film Office, The American University Graduate Writing Seminars, Duke University Writer's Conference, the North Carolina Writers' Network, the Jenny McKean Moore Writers Workshop at George Washington University, the MFA program and Visiting Writers Series at American University, the Chautauqua Writers' Center Writer-in-Residence program, the Sewanee Writer's Conference, The Writer's Center, Bethesda, Maryland, and Fundacíon Valparaiso all supported me at different points during the writing of this novel and throughout my career, for which I am deeply grateful. I am indebted to all the talented teachers and astute readers and writers who read for me and offered invaluable counsel along the way: Shirley Cochrane, Elizabeth Cox, Kelly Cherry, Richard McCann, Richard Peabody, Lynne Sharon Schwartz, Edward Falco, Margo Livesey, Jill McCorkle, Terry McMillan, Harold Thompson, Deborah Krupenia, Michael Mastrofrancesco, Helen Hooper, Irene Owsley, Miki Reilly-Howe, and Kay Sloan.

Thanks to my late cousin, Dan Gallimore, whose vivid family memories helped my own coalesce, and to my son, Nicholas Bell, who, throughout his childhood, tolerated endless hours of my being 'off lemons' while I wrote. My enduring gratitude for my decades long writing fellowship with late writer Barbara Scheiber, who read not only this novel, but all of my work, through every single rewrite. She was there from the beginning, providing unflagging wisdom, insight, and encouragement.

Other kinds of vital and generous support came from Kimberly Witherspoon and Alexis Hurley at Inkwell Management, Robert Newlen, Stephen Ryan, Carrie Ann Williams, Kelly

O'Donnell, and my husband, Shinji Turner-Yamamoto. My sincere gratitude to Jaynie Royal and the entire Regal House Publishing team for welcoming me. Special thanks to Pam Van Dyk whose nuanced editing brought new life to these pages.

Stories excerpted from this book appeared in different form in the following journals and anthologies:

The Washington Review
The Washington College Review
The Village Rambler
Parting Gifts
Short Fiction by Women, Snake Nation Press
Walking the Edge: A Southern Gothic Anthology, Twisted Road Publications, 2016